The Girl with the Flaxen Hair

AMELIA GRACE

Lilly Pilly
PUBLISHING

Also by Amelia Grace/Julieann Wallace

Amelia Grace (print and ebook)
<u>Adult fiction</u>
The Colour of Broken
All the Colours Above
A Dream of Light
The Book Keeper

Julieann Wallace (print and ebook)
<u>Young Adult</u>
You Before Me

<u>Middle Grade Chapter Book</u> (print and ebook)
Captain Vertigo, and unfortunately... Fart Man
(a superhero with a cochlear implant)

For Children
<u>Picture Books</u> (print books)
Forever and a Day, Love Mama
Henry Bear
Darth
Who Said?
Lily's Lollies
THING
THINGY

Ménière's disease (print and ebook)
(donating profits to medical research)

Vanilla Swirl (children's print book)
Blueberry Swirl (children's print book)
Dear Ménière's - letters & art (#1 on Amazon)
Ménière's Woman
Daily Ménière's Journal
It Will Change Your Life - a cochlear implant journey

Amelia Grace is the pen name of Australian author, Julieann Wallace. Her best-selling adult novel, *The Colour of Broken* was longlisted to be made into a movie, twice and was #1 on Amazon in its category.

Julieann is also an artist and secondary arts teacher, empowering students to be change-makers to create a better world for themselves and for future generations.

When she's not writing, teaching or creating art, Julieann tries not to scare her cat, Claude Monet, or her mini sausage dog, Pablo Picasso, with her terrible cello playing. Her deaf cat, Jameela, is her #1 cello music fan.

Julieann lives in Brisbane with her husband. She is the mother of three amazing grown-up children and has a gorgeous grandson. She has a cochlear implant and is an Ambassador for Ménière's Australia.

www.julieannwallaceauthor.com

For Mum, with love xx.

"Our grief is as individual as our lives."

Dr. Elisabeth Kubler-Ross

The beginning.

Well, not the beginning of Jane Piccadilly's story.
But the beginning of the end.

Chapter 1

'You have dialled emergency Triple Zero. Your call is being connected.'

'Hello. Police, Fire or Ambulance?'

'Police.'

'Please hold the line while I put you through.'

'Thank you.'

'Police. How can I help you?'

'There's a person...'

'Is the person threatening you?'

'No.'

'Is the person trying to break in?'

'No. They are not br-bre—'

'Is the person conscious or breathing?'

'No.'

Chapter 2

Jane

Jane Piccadilly looked up at the three story, seven bedroom, Victorian Terrace house, the colour of a pale, sickly yellow. Or was it green? She scrunched her face and scratched her head.

Pale avocado perhaps?

Nevertheless, it was the colour of a sick heart. Jane's eye twitched and her body tremored at-the-ick.

Nevertheless, Jane needed a new home. It wasn't that she didn't like the last residence. It wasn't that rumours had spread in her street at her last residence.

And the residence before that.

And perhaps, the one before that...

Nor was it that Violet had clutched her fists and stomped

2

her foot when a neighbour accused her of being presumptuous and preposterous and pretentious, the police officer putting her in handcuffs and taking her to the police station after she had poked her tongue out at the neighbour. *A darn public nuisance* he had said. It wasn't her fault she reacted that way. It was her neighbour who had triggered a glitch in her personality.

The *violent* Violet glitch.

Jane Piccadilly tilted her head and sighed. She just needed a place for her and Poppy and Daisy and Rose and Flora and Violet and Zinnia.

A place where everyone had their own rooms. A place where they weren't in each other's pockets and heads and personalities and spreadsheets. A place where they could have their own… privacy.

A place they could call *home*.

And stay there for more than two months. Perhaps even, their forever home, like they were pooches and kitties looking up with sad eyes at the pet adoption centre.

Jane Piccadilly calculated the mortgage repayments. Mentally, of course. Her mother and father said that mathematics *must* be done mentally. And it made them proud of her when she did. No need for calculators they always said. Calculators were for nincompoops.

Jane looked up the street, and down the street. This suburb looked more affluent with their grand mansions and beautiful streetscapes, so the homeowners would be more likely to go to work each day, with no time for gossip. Unlike the previous three houses where people were nosy busybodies. Watching. Judging. Criticizing. And asking too many questions. Comparing their answers in their little exclusive gossip circles that Jane had not been invited to, like they hadn't grown out of the small-minded cliquey groups you find at school. All they had to do was ask her about what was going on. Simple. Instead of the cowardly twats that they were just assuming and twisting the truth.

Jane's eye twitched and her body tremored at-the-ick of her memories. She never understood the mean girl mentality. The exclusion, the backstabbing and the manipulation.

Jane Piccadilly recalculated the mortgage repayments again. Mentally of course. She certainly was no nincompoop! She tilted her head and sighed then pushed her lips together into a hard line. She didn't like this seven bedroom, three story Victorian Terrace house the colour of a sick heart. Its ugliness didn't fit into her world of exterior perception. Of architectural beauty. What would people think of her when they found out she lived in the terrace house at the end?

The sound of a car was behind her. She turned to see it slow until it was stationary. The engine turned off. It was a real estate agent with a family. The driver got out and straightened his perfectly black real estate suit, ran his hand through his perfectly parted hair, then opened the passengers' doors. And out they stepped like an orchestrated move with a clash of cymbals at the end. They each peered at the terrace house, smiling, a glaze of happiness forming over their eyes like it was the most beautiful house they had ever seen.

Jane's eye twitched and her body tremored. *Ick. Ick. Ick.*

Jane Piccadilly's eyes widened at the realization they were about to purchase the house. She stepped forward into the high, overgrown weeds at the rusty wrought iron gate and froze as her perfectly white shoe sunk into something soft. And smelly. She gripped the gate, her knuckles turning as white as her perfectly orthodontically straight white teeth as she spoke through her clenched jaw. 'This house is sold! It is OFF the market!' She had said it with a firmness that sounded like a school master.

Ick. Ick. Ick.

She watched as the family all grimaced and turned away. The youngest child dry retching at the wafting smell, while the real estate agent waved his hand in front of his nose.

Jane stared at them as they drove off, unable to move, not wanting to face the abominable situation of the shoe-in-the-poo.

Situations required solutions.

And with this situation, there was only one.

Jane Piccadilly closed her eyes and summoned her inner strength like she had learned at Girl Guides, then pulled her foot out of her new, favourite, comfy, fashionable white sneaker, leaving it stuck in the intestinal dog deposit.

The shoe stuck-in-the-poo.

And hurried off. The clomp of her remaining shoe hitting the pavement in a rhythm reminding her of the introduction to the *Dance of the Sugar Plum Fairy* by Tchaikovsky. Jane's eye twitched at the hideousness of people who never cleaned up after their fur babies. *Ick. Ick. Ick.* And *she* would NEVER do that!

This was their fault!

All their fault!

Now she had lost a perfectly white shoe to dog poop, AND bought a house that gave her the ick!

Chapter 3

'Have you commenced CPR?'

'No.'

'Start that now and continue until an ambulance arrives.'

'I can't. The body is in no condition for CPR.'

Chapter 4

Jane

Jane Piccadilly drove her vintage blue and white Kombi Van Deluxe onto the bumpy driveway of her recently acquired three story house the colour of a sickly heart. Well, it wasn't *her* Kombi van, it was Violet's flower power van. She wouldn't mind, would she?

Jane smiled. The Victorian terrace she had bought was the *only* terrace that had a driveway. Even though it led to a white brick wall. No garage.

'At least we *have* a driveway!' snickered Jane. Talking to yourself was a sign of high intelligence according to research. And Jane *was* highly intelligent. She smiled again. Her mother and father liked it when she out-performed others. They would be proud. She couldn't wait to call them.

She turned off the klak-klak engine and waited for the splatter and the bang and the sigh like punctuation marks, before she looked in the rear-view mirror. The van was filled to the hilt with boxes-of-books. She always packed the books first, and moved them into the house first whenever she would have to move. Nine hundred and ninety-nine of them!

No more and no less.

'Here we are, friends. Home at last… well, at another home again.'

If a new book did come Jane's way, she would have to donate an older book to a street library so that she still had nine hundred and ninety-nine books. Exactly. Afterall, a house wasn't a home without books. Without an escape from reality. Where she could ignore everything going on inside the house, outside the house, and in the world.

You know.

Everything.

Like *people*.

She grabbed the house key and pressed her lips together. Her stomach churned. She hoped this accidental house purchase was a good one. It was the only house she had bought without inspecting it. She exited the car and walked along the weedy beside the house path, and up four steps to the front verandah and door, thankful she wouldn't have to walk through the front gate where her white shoe-in-the-poo sat. Still. She inhaled deeply, and wished her mother and father could be here with her. But they couldn't. Not after the incident. A flash of orange stabbed at Jane Piccadilly's memory like a distant echo.

'One, two, three.' She pushed the key into the lock of the door the colour of blood, wondering when the colour police were going to knock and tell her the sick heart terrace paint and the red door didn't match.

She heard the slight click of unlocking, and pushed on the door. It didn't budge. So she pushed harder, then turned around and leaned her back against the door and pushed as hard as she could with a grunt like you would hear at the tennis, and WHOOSH! It flew open. And Jane tumbled down onto her back in the hallway with a thud. 'Aghh! Great start, Jane!' She scrunched up her nose then, at the great, terrible, stink that hung thickly in the house!

Jane closed her eyes and held her breath to control the anger that brewed inside. *Blue-faced-Jane* her sisters would call her, point and laugh at her. She didn't like surprises, and falling backwards was a surprise. She opened her eyes and looked up at the ceiling. Then tilted her head to the side and frowned, followed by a sigh. The aged, yellow ceiling harboured a crack. A CRACK!

A crack-in-the-ceiling!

Like the signature of an earthquake.

'Fabulous. Door. Ceiling. What else?' Jane was feeling positively glum as her heart sank.

Jane Piccadilly sat up. She wanted to kick herself for buying a house unseen, but she didn't like to inflict pain on herself, or anyone, or anything. She probably had hurt the door just by opening it. She rolled her eyes. She should have ventured inside the house to see what state it was in before she vowed to purchase it with her shoe-in-the-poo. But she and her sisters were desperate for a new house. They had to get away from the other one after the incident.

And that was Mistake-Number-One. There's always a mistake number one. And a mistake that would end all mistakes.

So-you-could-start-again.

And again…

Jane raised an eyebrow. She let out a breath. 'Thank goodness your sisters aren't here, Jane. Imagine the commotion!' Flora would have blamed the people who never cleaned up the poo-at-the-gate for us not inspecting the house. She would have said this was their fault! Daisy would be fuming at the sight of the crack-in-the-ceiling, demanding that it be fixed by the seller. But Violet, she would have positive words and encouragement, while Rose would have photographed the soul of the house, cracks and all, looking at the house through her lens giving the house character and love and a story. Zinnia, well she would have worried that we didn't have enough to fix the ceiling. Not enough money, or resources, or time. But Poppy. She would be happy. She would use her artist eye to come up with a creative solution.

Jane grimaced at the repulsive aroma that hung thickly inside the house. A combination of unpleasant dank and wet wood and rotting smells in pipes and old cheese. It was suffocating, and undeniably a marker of Mistake-Number-One. If she had inspected the house, she would have run from it. Far, far away.

Run, Jane, run! 'If only I could. But then that would be giving up. And Piccadilly girls do *not* give up!'

Mistakes.

Consequences.

Situations.

And this situation required a solution.

A solution-for-the-situation.

She stood, and stepped back outside into the fresh air, then re-entered the house, holding her nose like a four-year-old who had just a fatherly fart, and walked quickly along the hallway, her body shuddering at-the-ick from the tessellating, terracotta tiles that sounded like an alliteration as well as a tap dancing floor.

Browns and oranges and greys. Really?

She walked past a closed light oak door on the right, then another closed light oak door on the right, and on the left, a painted blue staircase with a strip of red, worn carpet, creeping up the treads like a snake. The staircase had a dark wooden balustrade, the paint worn down and grubby, with a thousand hand prints leaving the identity of people of the past. Straight ahead, and further down the hall was a light oak door.

She pushed it open to find a large area to the right with room for a long table. There was a gallery kitchen on the right, a large window showing the backyard, and a vestibule to the left.

Jane walked to the vestibule with a stink, and opened the door to left. It was a utilities room for laundry, with a separate toilet with the father-of-all-stinks. Jane shook her head, her face turning red, then blue as she held her breath. The separate downstairs loo was a positive for this unintentionally bought house-with-the-situations.

Jane returned to the vestibule area and rushed toward the door in front of her. She turned the knob and pushed it open, revealing a terribly overgrown backyard filled with the gloriousness of fresh air.

Jane inhaled deeply, her face returning to its natural colour, and lifted her arms toward the sky, looked up and yelled, 'Yes!'

She froze on the spot then, and moved her eyes from left to right and right to left. Had she disturbed the neighbours? She didn't want to disturb the neighbours. It would be terrible to disturb the neighbours. She couldn't disturb the neighbours if they wanted to live here. They wanted to remain under the radar, out of sight, and slide right into the impression of the street without a fuss. Like the quiet people did. The people who didn't speak. Or breathe.

Jane returned to the house and opened every window on the first floor, hoping for fresh air to resuscitate the old terrace house of possibilities. She latched back the door separating the kitchen and dining area from the hallway, to let the air tunnel through the first floor, then walked toward the first room from the front red door, unconsciously lifting her wrist to her nose to smell it. Like she was wearing perfume.

'What are you doing, Jane? You *know* you are not wearing perfume. Like never. You haven't been—' Jane Piccadilly's eyes widened and she sucked in a sharp breath. Red Door? The perfume? Was that when the subconscious takes over?

Had *she* been brainwashed by advertising?

No. Not Jane. The Piccadilly's could *never* be brainwashed. They were too smart for that nonsense in marketing aimed at making profits.

She opened the door to a large bedroom with light purple walls, a high ceiling, wide wooden floor boards and a bay sash window, which when she opened, seemingly allowed the room to inhale deeply like it had been holding its breath forever. Jane spun on her heel and tilted her head to the right. 'Poppy would love this room!'

Jane Piccadilly held up her phone and photographed the room, exited room #1, and walked down the hall to the next room on the right. Baby blue walls, high ceiling and one large window, which she opened. It was like a nothing room.

The room-of-the-between.

Room #2. Photos taken.

Jane stood at the bottom of the blue painted stairs with an old carpet with imprinted memories of a thousand footsteps. She looked up, and up. Two more stories of up. And Jane took the first steps of the creaky risers, each singing their own moan of struggles and desperate calls for help.

The second story housed four bedrooms. Hers would be the biggest front bedroom with a bay sash window looking out over the street, and a little verandah.

Violet, Daisy and Flora would have the others.

Rooms #3, #4, #5 and #6. Windows open. Photos taken.

Up the next staircase to the third floor. Two rooms. #7 and #8. Rose would have the room with the street view, while Zinnia would have the back room. Windows open. Photos taken.

And a sigh of relief.

'There. Decided.'

Jane Piccadilly walked back to the steps, her hand gliding over the banister rail, catching on chipped-off paint and dust. It would *never* pass her mother's overt dust test! She mentally noted the renovations she would have to do, not only to the bedrooms, but the other rooms in the Victorian terrace.

Every room.

Every freaking room of the terrace she didn't-inspect-mistake.

Jane walked down the steps, noting the worn and holey carpet runner. From this view, it slithered down the staircase like a liquid cat. And then she stalled. Her left shoe heel caught in the carpet threads.

'Aaaaaaah!' Down Jane Piccadilly went. Her body bumping on each of the step treads. Jane landed on the second floor hall with her plain white dress up around her waist, her plain white undies showing. As she tried to smooth down her dress in a panic, there was a squeak of a mouse.

A mouse-in-the-house.

Jane screamed again and the mouse scurried away.

Jane picked herself up off the floor and smoothed down her dress. Her eye twitched and her body tremored at-the-ick of her undies being exposed. *Good girls never show their knickers!* her mother always said. And Jane *was* a good girl.

Jane walked double time to the next staircase and, holding on, descended like an intoxicated clumsy koala, her knees buckling as she slid backwards to the floor. She stood, chin raised high, and re-assembled herself after feeling like a Picasso painting, after the mouse-in-the-house fiasco, and her horror at showing her undies. 'Great work, Piccadilly. At least no one was here to see it. Wait… nobody ever sees me anyway.'

She turned to revisit the kitchen and gasped in horror at the huntsman spider, larger than her hand. It climbed down the wall and along the floor towards her. She froze on the spot before her adrenaline sent her flying toward the front door.

'Run, Jane, run!' she said, like the taunts at school. She put her hand on the door knob to open it, and crack, it fell off in her hand.

Jane Piccadilly put her back against the hallway wall and slid down to a sitting position and mouthed "help". She bowed her head, her shoulders curling over her chest. If she was a bad girl, she would have said a swear word. But her mother and father had told her that good girls don't swear. And Jane *was* a good girl. A defeated, failed and beaten, good girl.

Run, Jane, run.

But no. Jane wasn't a quitter her father would say. Jane will rise up and win! She *was* a Piccadilly. There are no problems for the Piccadilly family, just challenges to be overcome!

So, Jane Piccadilly picked her ego up off the dusty floor, pulled out a piece of paper and pencil from her pocket, a proper sketching pencil of course, and sketched a floor plan of the house. She started a spreadsheet of what needed to be resolved, redone, renewed, restored, redesigned and refreshed in the house.

She allocated rooms to her sisters, according to their idiosyncrasies. There would be conversations and arguments for certain, but Jane was the peacekeeper of the family.

The middle-of-seven-girls. Daughter number four.

The one who was the least seen, but saw the most. The one who would speak but nobody heard. The one who could slip out of a family gathering and no one would notice. The one who could pretend to be dead, sitting on the chair, and nobody noticed.

The middle, invisible child.

Neglected.

Ignored.

Overlooked.

But then, Jane Piccadilly discovered, there were absolute advantages to being the unseen child. Like when an incident happens that nobody saw because they were too busy looking at the others.

Jane grinned. What if *she* was the one to cause the incident, like a carefully orchestrated plan, standing back to watch the fallout of blame and squabbles and screaming and fights and stamping feet and pulling of hair.

Seven sisters.

Jane-in-the-middle.

Depleted of energy in her newly acquired mistake-house, after the stress from the fall, her white undies showing, the mouse and the tumble and the spider, plus the spreadsheet and allocation of rooms, Jane decided the books would have to wait until the renovators came and corrected the house that was a mistake.

And then she would move in.

As simple as that.

Chapter 5

Phone silence.

'Please remain at the scene until police arrive.'

'You mean, right next to the body?'

'Yes.'

'Can I... can I... keep watch over the body from my window?'

Chapter 6

Jane

Jane Piccadilly drove Violet's vintage blue and white Kombi Van Deluxe onto the bumpy driveway of her seven bedroom, three story, Victorian terrace house four weeks later, still the colour of a sickly heart.

The Victorian terrace, still with the red door like red lipstick that stuck to a wine glass. To the collar of the married man.

Jane raised an eyebrow and blotted out the memory of *once upon a time*.

She was home at last after procuring and organising and supervising the work people after choosing design elements for the new kitchen, bathrooms and laundry. Every wall and ceiling in the house was scrubbed and painted. White. The oak floorboards were sanded and waxed, windows sanded and painted white, and the staircases given a makeover. White with oak timber risers and a dark timber handrail.

Jane turned off the klak-klak engine and waited for the splatter and the bang and sigh to finish before she looked in the rear view mirror. The van was filled to the hilt with boxes of books. Today was the day she could move the books into the house, first, before the sun went down. Nine hundred and ninety-nine of them!

'Here we are, friends. Home. At. Last.'

But first, a celebration was in order. Her mistake terrace house was now an un-mistake.

Jane climbed out of the Kombi Van, lifted her little looooooong chocolate and tan long-haired dachshund out of his basket and placed him on the ground.

The dog-with-the-short-legs.

Then grabbed the house key, and reached over to the variegated Pothos plant and bouquet of white flowers. 'Come on, Oliver Twist. Welcome to our new house!'

Jane walked along the weedy path to the front door, the sound of mini dachshund tippy-tappy toes behind her, wondering whether her white shoe-in-the-poo was still at the front wrought iron gate in amongst the long weeds. She lifted her chin and sniffed the air. No canine poop smell. Then she looked down at her feet.

In front of the red door was an envelope.

An envelope-at-the-door.

No address. No name. Just plain white.

Jane Piccadilly frowned and picked it up before the miniature shredder dog could grab it. She flipped it over so she could make a judgment about it. There was nothing to judge.

She shoved it into her pocket and unlocked the red front door and it opened, quietly and smoothly. She smiled. The colour would have to wait for a change with the rest of the exterior of the house.

'Here we go,' Jane said to Oliver Twist, and they stepped into their newly renovated three story, seven bedroom, Victorian terrace house together, and headed straight to the renovated kitchen out the back.

She placed her variegated Pothos onto the windowsill in the gallery kitchen and laid the bouquet of flowers on the island bench. Then, with Oliver Twist behind her, she opened all the windows of the ground floor rooms, the breeze of the new day stretching and whispering and dancing throughout the house, carrying scents of coloured blooms and whispers of home.

Jane got to work in the library at once, placing her nine hundred and ninety-nine books on the floor. Later, when the book shelves were in place, she would arrange them by colour. To be finished by sun down.

That was the books-in-the-new-house rule.

A knock at the door heralded the brand new furniture delivery for the library sitting room, dining table and chairs, and her own bedroom furniture. Jane and Poppy and Daisy and Rose and Flora and Violet and Zinnia had all agreed that they would have their furniture delivered on different days, like the days of the week, so that there would be no confusion about what furniture pieces went where.

They hadn't viewed their rooms yet. It was better that way. There would be less didactic, exaggerated conversations that signalled the virtues of their rights and needs and wants.

Less verbosities heralded in the personality glitches that were annoying and preposterous.

Less work for Jane the peacemaker. For the invisible middle child, able to manipulate and shape her sisters into what she wanted them to do.

Jane Piccadilly wondered why they called it a peacemaker?

For the peacemaker was far from peace as they installed the peace, which was stolen from them like perfection and anxiety steals peace.

Blessed are the peacemakers.

Jane knew she had to be strategic. Like playing a game of chess. So that's why she moved her belongings into the terrace house first.

After the recycled dining table and eight coloured cloth chairs and library furniture were in place, Jane Piccadilly ran up one flight of stairs to her room, little Oliver Twist riding up the steps on his Oliver-Twist-dog-elevator behind her.

Room #3.

It was perfect.

Complete.

Exactly like the number three.

The walls had been painted white as per the detailed instructions on the renovators' and interior designers' spreadsheet. She added white sheer curtains to add a visual element of textural depth and dimension to transform the white bedroom space. A white double bed. White bed linen. White pillows. A white floor rug on the timber floor.

White.

White.

White.

Plain white.

Plain Jane.

Once, Jane's eye would twitch and her body tremor at-the-ick at the words she once hated. *Plain Jane.* Dear Alice's little girl, Jane. She's so plain!

But, she discovered, being plain Jane was far from plain. She could be unassuming. Unnoticed. Unsuspected. She could change things to suit herself without anyone thinking it would be her.

Plain Jane.

Plain. Just Jane.

The wallflower.

The blender-inner-er.

Jane stood back and admired her room. Plain and perfect. Like the white canvases that lined her wall. Untouched. A mysteriousness swirling around them. Just white. Just Jane.

'What do you think, Oliver?'

She walked over to her white shelf, and ran her index finger over the Barbie doll she had placed there. In the exact same position on the bedroom shelf in every house. The fashion doll that originally was a Christmas gift that lit up her face when she was eight, Santa *finally* giving her something she wanted, be it from her aunty, swiftly pushed aside by her mother. And the very next day, returned to the shop in exchange for money. Because fashion dolls were *not* for smart girls. And Jane Piccadilly *was* a smart girl.

Jane grinned back in the memory. Her mother didn't notice her sneak away from her squabbling six sisters. The squabble that she had started. Her mother didn't notice as she went back to the shop and reclaimed her very own Barbie doll. In a white dress. Her first doll ever. Not this exact fashion doll sitting on the shelf now. Oliver had claimed the original one and buried it like it was dead. Never to be seen again.

Jane smiled. This *was* the Barbie doll that wore a floral dress with many flowers. Like Jane's sisters' names. A hat and white shoes, a floral bouquet and tea set. Plus, the "special" white bunny that winked at her.

All she needed were different coloured wigs for the ultimate play.

Beside the fashion doll sat her colourful bouquet of flowers made of Lego. There were seven flowers like the seven sisters. Made by her. 'It's a dust collector,' her mother would have said, not seeing the value and joy of the creativity involved. The lowering of anxiety and stress. The patience required. The mindful escape.

Like… from *everyone*.

Oliver Twist trotted up the white dog ramp and onto the white bed cutting into her thoughts. Jane smiled and twirled on the spot with her arms out wide.

'It's lovely, Oliver, isn't it! Our new bedroom in our new house with the nice neighbours. Our new start. And here is your bed right here.' Jane pointed to the white velvet covered regal dog bed, then went and opened the white French doors that lead to the quaint verandah with white outdoor furniture.

She returned downstairs to the library sitting room, the mini dachshund taking the Oliver-Twist-dog-elevator so as to not injure his back. He was well trained in using his dog-elevator, having used one in the house before this one, and the one before that, and the one before that, and… the one before that.

Little Oliver Twist, the operator-of-the-dog-elevator.

'Book time, Oliver. See if you can find your special dog-lick-a-book.' And Jane got to work on her new library, admiring the colour co-ordination and special ornaments she added. As she placed the last book on the shelf and stood back to admire her new library and study, there was a knock on the door. Oliver Twist barked and Jane frowned. Deliveries had finished for today. On her spreadsheet, there were no more people who would arrive in her new space.

The knock sounded again.

And Oliver barked again.

Jane Piccadilly walked to the front door, admiring the arched stained glass transom that surrounded it, and the light falling through the colours, and the white of the timber door creating a heavenly presence.

The knock sounded once more, and Oliver's loud bark added to the ensemble of noise like a clash of cymbals. Jane's eye twitched and her body tremored at the impatience of the uninvited visitor. She took a deep breath and opened the door.

A man stood there.

An-uninvited-man.

Messy hair. Unshaven. Old clothes and a black backpack slung over one shoulder.

A man-with-a-stink.

He gave her a smile and looked down at the barking Oliver then back at Jane. 'Thank fuck.'

Jane's hearing dulled at the sound of his profanity. Self-preservation. Self-protection. And a way of coping with PTSD.

'I've been waiting for fucking six months for some bloody one to open this fuckin' door.'

Jane Piccadilly narrowed her left eye and frowned at the obnoxious foul-mouthed man.

Run, Jane, run!

'What?' Jane scrunched her eyes tightly, turned her head to the side and held up her hand at the man. 'And before you answer, kindly be considerate and don't use such a potty mouth!'

'The red door house, right? A place of rest and a meal for travellers. Wobbily Wallaby Way?' He reached into his pocket and pulled out a piece of paper and held it up in front of Jane, who scanned the text with her extraordinarily fast reading ability beyond anyone her father had ever met. He said she was extremely adept at skimming, scanning and chunking identifying key information with her superior memory, focus, brain performance, logic, and problem-solving abilities. There was a sketch of the house as well. Undeniably this one.

'And do you have a little … *more* … to offer? I promise not to step on your guard dog.'

Jane Piccadilly's eyes widened and her body tremored at-the-ick before her eye could twitch.

Oliver Twist gave the side-eye.

'Most. Certainly. Not!' Jane said with a firmness that made the man recoil and shudder. And with that, she carefully closed the red door that was like lipstick on a wine glass and lipstick on the collar of a married man. Red like the blood that coloured her fingertips after a blow to her head. And now, the red door that was like an invitation to travellers wanting rest, a meal, and a little… *more*. The red door that had feelings.

The red door with a story-to-tell.

And that was Mistake-Number-Two—not researching the previous owners of the house.

Jane Piccadilly wiped the perspiration off her brow. Mistakes. Every time she made a mistake it caused her pain. A loss. A struggle. Now she would have to sort out the red door and strangers situation.

Jane sighed and walked down the hallway of her new house, through the dining room and to the back window of the gorgeous, newly renovated gallery kitchen. White shaker cupboards, white Caesar stone bench tops on either side of the island bench in the middle of the narrow kitchen, the white Caesar stone bench top and VJ panelling and shaker doors the colour of a deep, cool blue with a green undertone like a forest blue. Stunning.

Oliver Twist barked. Jane found him standing by the back door to the yard. 'Good boy,' she said, and opened the door.

Oliver trotted out into the weedy overgrown backyard for a toilet stop. And disappeared.

Jane put her hands on her hips. At least she had already created a landscaping to do list on her spreadsheet.

A pigeon cooed and Jane stepped out onto the dirty back

landing and looked up. And there on the roof of her house were a gazillion pigeons and nests, with messy sticks and long grass sticking out of her roof.

Jane Piccadilly turned at the sound of a loud, deep, bellowing and grunting sound. A pig?

'Ollie. Come!' Her voice was in fast forward.

As Oliver Twist appeared from the long grass with a snake-skin-in-his-mouth, a flutter of wings sounded from above… and the wet warm plop-of-bird-poo landed on her head.

On her *cherished,* curly, flaxen-coloured-hair.

Her hair-as-fair-as-flax.

The only Piccadilly daughter with an untarnished beauty, indestructibility and innocence.

Until she wasn't.

Jane's hand froze mid-air. She wanted to swear like the man who knocked on her front door. But she didn't. Her mother and father would somehow find out and tell her how antisocial and offensive she was. *Profane* Jane. Like that time before the situation that really put her in a pickle.

'Oh, shhi … poo!' She'd almost said it. And it would have been the truth if she had said the word she wanted to say, but didn't.

And of course, that was Mistake-Number-Three—not watching the behaviour of animals around the house. She should have seen that first. With an exterior inspection. Well, she would have, had she not stepped-in-dog-poo and run off like a one-legged nutcracker with a prosthetic leg that made no noise.

Things always happened in threes, according to Mrs. Alice Jane Piccadilly the 3rd, her mother. 'Third time's a charm,' she would say, matching with her belief in *omne trium perfectum*—a trio of Latin words conveying a simple philosophy: "everything that comes in threes is perfect", or "every set of three is complete".

Like Jane. She was a triplet. Every set of three is complete.

Until she wasn't a triplet.

Bad things happen in threes as well, Jane Piccadilly had noted. Triaphilia was the name given to it. Not that Jane believed in superstitions. She believed that the three situation came out of people's intuitive view of the world, not an analytical one. And besides, the brain loves to find patterns, and groups of three is easy for the brain to grasp.

The power of three. Three really is the magic number. The persuasive effect of three. Use four and people become suspicious. It's overdone.

And so it came to be that Jane would never admit to Mistake-Number-Four, for her mother's sake.

Jane Piccadilly sighed. Tomorrow was another moving day. Not for her. It was Poppy who had bedroom number one and Violet who had bedroom number two upstairs with her. The order of her sisters moving in must be in sequential birth order.

That-was-another-rule.

Jane looked down at her feet, frowning. At least she wasn't standing in dog poo like the day she made the mistake of buying the house. Or pig poo—that would be worse!

Do snakes poo?

It was then that Jane spied a small, red half-sphere type of jewellery on the landing. It looked like it had been snapped off. Part of a whole. Like that day her childhood ring jewel snapped off in the violent struggle that left her finger broken. Jane picked up the red half-sphere. Maybe the previous owners would want it back. She made a mental note to wash it and leave it in the drawer of miscellaneous things, aka, the junk in the drawer.

'Come on, Oliver Twist.' Jane and Oliver returned to the house after Jane had wrestled the snake skin off the little looooong dog, the bird poop dribbling down her forehead while she looked over her shoulder every few moments to check that a pig in the backyard wasn't charging at them.

Flora should have been here. She was the farmhand. She was used to this type of wild thing.

'Good night, Oliver,' Jane said, as she climbed into bed after a long shower and thorough head cleansing that deleted some brain cells as well, then leaned over to turn off the bedside lamp. And there sat the envelope.

The envelope-at-the-door.

Unopened. Jane Piccadilly picked it up, turned it over and slid her finger under the back fold of paper, and opened it.

A handwritten note.

You really shouldn't have bought this house.

Jane's eye twitched and her body tremored at-the-ick. A negativity in the form of written words had entered her house. And now her mind. An uninvited negativity. Overstepping her boundary.

The-words-in-the-letter.

Her hand shook as she pushed the words-in-the-letter back into the envelope, and slipped it into the drawer of emptiness beside her bed, where it could enter the void and be consumed like in garbage in a disposal unit.

Jane Piccadilly turned off the white beside lamp and lay back on the bed, her eyes focussed on the ceiling. She placed her left arm out beside her in a straight angle, and positioned her right arm above her head at an acute angle, one leg straight, the other outward from the hip and bent at the knee at a right angle. Her father said that mathematics was beauty. Visual pleasure absorbed from abstractness, purity, simplicity, and orderliness. Mathematics is an art form he had said. Like the large Leonardo da Vinci's *Vitruvian Man* drawing he had framed on his study wall.

Her mother, the scientist, delighted in da Vinci the scientist and his applied scientific method to observe the world.

Jane blinked. How could she be the offspring of a mathematics professor and scientist? She held her breath and pretended-to-be-dead. Staring. Like she did when she was young. That way, she had discovered, she could believe that nothing bad was ever going to come her way. Again.

Jane Piccadilly released her breath. All she needed was the chalk outline like the scene of a crime.

Would anyone notice if she was dead-in-the-bed?

And that was a day, and a night.

Chapter 7

Jane

Jane Piccadilly was a list maker. And she left a list for Poppy. And Violet. It was how Jane and her sisters rolled to get things done, with all of them in and out of the house at all times of the day with their jobs and social lives, never having time to sit together and have conversations. So, they left lists and notes for each other.

And lists had rules.

Well, one rule.

Whatever is on the list, you MUST complete.

No excuses.

Unless you're dead!

Jane reread Poppy's and Violet's lists on the white hand-made paper written in baby blue and purple ink. She folded them and placed them on the long wooden dining table in front of the blue coloured chair and lavender coloured chair respectively.

She sat, frozen for a moment, on her white coloured dining chair, staring, adding a new pretend-I'm-dead-position.

Would anyone notice if she was dead-in-the-chair?

She reanimated herself and said to Oliver. 'I have to go now, Oliver. You're in charge of the house. Poppy will be here in the morning, and Violet will come in the afternoon.'

Oliver Twist gave a little jump. Jane stood and lobbed him a treat, then turned on her heel and walked out the front door and jumped into Violet's Kombi van and drove off, her hair-as-fair-as-flax blowing in the breeze.

Poppy Piccadilly dismounted her pastel blue cruiser bicycle with a basket-on-the-front, removed her black bicycle helmet, and smoothed down her shoulder length wavy, grey-streaked hair. She was the oldest of the Piccadilly sisters. She walked up the four concrete steps to the verandah to the red front door and inserted the key, immediately hearing Oliver Twist's bark.

'Jane, Jane, quiet Jane… and her LOUD dog!' she muttered under her breath. Jane was the quiet one Poppy had agreed with her sisters one day. So it made sense that she had a loud dog.

She opened the door to see little Oliver giving her the side-eye.

The side-eye-of-judgement.

'I know… it's lovely to see you too little loud dog. Sssshhhh. Quiet!' Poppy said, holding her finger to her lips. Oliver wagged his tail in a frenzy the moment he recognised her.

Oliver Twist sat and didn't bark.

'Good boy, Twisty. Good boy!'

Poppy pulled out the house map to double check that she still had the same room she had chosen when she talked to Jane via text.

'Yep,' she said to herself, popping the "p". 'Downstairs, first on the right, next to the library. Yippee!' she said to herself, half-truth, half-sarcasm. Jane always put her next to the library in the houses they inhabited. Just because she was a librarian at the local library didn't mean she had to be beside the library room in every house.

Jane, Jane, bossy Jane.

Jane-stuck-in-a-rut.

Poppy looked up at the staircase in front of her that led to the second floor. At least she didn't have to go up-and-down stairs every day.

'Yep,' she said again, popping the "p". 'No steps. Happy daaays.'

Poppy opened the door to her bedroom. Timber floor. White walls. White shutters. En suite. She scanned the room to see which wall she would use to paint on.

'Yep,' she said, popping the "p". 'The wall straight ahead would be perfect.' Jane hated it when she painted on the walls. But it was like her little bit of revenge as well as her statement about how much she hated white walls. Artists make statements. And Poppy *was* an artist-with-a-statement.

Poppy exited her room and walked down the hallway towards the kitchen, her eyes lighting up at the renovated delight. She eyed the white note on the table with the blue handwriting, but then went directly to the kitchen to admire its design, colours, textures. She was the artist of the family after all. She ran her fingers along the cool bench tops, the sound of her court shoes creating a relaxed pace of clacking on the floorboards.

Oliver stood at the door to the backyard and barked once.

Poppy let him out into the yard of chaos. Of long weeds. Of mystery. Her librarian mind said, *There could be a dead body buried out the back and no-one-would-ever-know. Genre: crime fiction.*

Poppy changed her thoughts at once to, *that back yard will look superb once-it-is-landscaped. I wonder if Flora or Zinnia will work with it? Or perhaps, Jane will outsource the job?*

Poppy left the back door open for Oliver Twist, and went to her list on the table. She wondered why Jane didn't call her to discuss it, but then she remembered that she would most probably forget everything she had to do. She was visually dominant and remembered things better if she saw it written down. She decided that lists were good, after all. Especially for Jane. Nobody listened when Jane-the-middle-child spoke. At least her notes were words-inked-onto-paper, not words that floated off with the breeze to the unheard words dump.

Poppy opened up the Jane note. The note of perfect handwriting.

It was a list.

Dear Poppy,

Welcome to our new house.

1. Set up your bedroom. The front room on the ground/1st floor. It has a perfect spot for you to keep your bicycle at night.

2. Put away the groceries when they arrive. I've ordered you a special treat to eat once you have done that.

3. Feed Oliver some lunch and check his water.

4. I need your feedback on an exterior colour for

the house, and a new front door colour. If you go out the
back, there may be a pig in the yard, and a snake.
    5.   Violet will arrive at 12pm.

From Jane

'Bedroom. Groceries. Feed Oliver. Exterior house colours. Violet 12pm. Got it.' Poppy looked at her watch. The removalist truck was arriving in 10 minutes.

She walked to the back door and called Oliver inside. Snakes. Possible pig. Oliver trotted in with his head held high, a bone-in-his-mouth, and dropped it into his collection of dog-things-box. Poppy shut the back door. It was safer that way. Flora would deal with the snake and the pig. And maybe Daisy, who worked with bones.

Poppy smiled.

A knock-at-the-front-door.

Oliver barked loudly like every savage guard dog does. Like every good boi. And Poppy quick-stepped to the front door and opened it.

A man stood there. Tall and burly. A fine looking removalist if she had ever seen one. And she had seen many removalists in her lifetime.

He looked at his piece of paper. 'Popcky... PPPocky... Popppp-py Picca-picca-dilly?'

Poppy blinked at the stuttering of her name. Everybody did it. All of her life. It was as if her name was a tongue twister. 'Yep,' she said, popping the "p". 'I am she.'

'Delivery for you Miss...' he said and cleared his throat.

'Thank you. The first room on your right. And everybody does it, you know.'

'What?' he said, and raised an eyebrow at her.

Poppy frowned. 'Stumbles over my name. You know, like Peter Piper picked a peck of pickled peppers.'

'Oh that. Sorry.'

'Forgiven.'

Poppy propped the front door open, picked up Oliver and placed him in the library and closed the door. It was safer that way. For Oliver. He didn't like being the guard dog that got stepped on.

Poppy stood in the middle of her bedroom and orchestrated where her brand new bedroom furniture and other items should go. Not that she had much. Just a queen size bed, pillow, bedside tables, lamps, a wing chair, an art easel, clothing, shoes. A desk. And an artificial poppy flower and a jar of poppy seeds from her mother. A reminder of the day of her birth on the 11th of November at 11am. She didn't cry for a minute. But at 11:01am, she let out a cry that shook the walls of the delivery room.

Sixty minutes. And the removalists were all done. Except the unpacking of clothing boxes. That would be done later in time.

The groceries arrived. Packed away.

Oliver fed, and watered, and toileted.

Poppy dressed for work for the afternoon, and before she left on her bicycle, she scribbled on her blue note paper, supplied by Jane, folded it and pushed it into the empty-note-jar sitting on the dining table for Jane. In front of white coloured dining chair.

Plain chair. Plain Jane.

Outside, she stepped back to look at the exterior of the house to consider new paint colours that would pack a punch of look-at-me in the street. Jane liked that. Her invisible becoming visible. Like an extension of Jane-with-no-personality. Plain Jane.

Then Poppy pedalled away to her second home. The local library.

Violet Piccadilly arrived at 12:30pm, her vintage blue and white Kombi Van Deluxe spluttering to a stop. Her client's hair colour took longer than she had anticipated. Before she entered the new residence, Violet turned around in front of the red door, ran her fingers through her blonde pixie cut with a side part, sucked in her cheeks and arranged her lips in her signature duck lips and took a selfie. She opened her Instagram and posted it, excited about how many likes and comments she would get. She would check it later for her mood stabiliser. Or... destabiliser. Violet's eye twitched and her body tremored at-the-ick.

She inserted her key into the door and set off the alarm. Barking Oliver. Then opened the door to a wiener dog and the side-eye-of-judgment. Or fear. Violet smiled at him, showing her extra white teeth. She didn't like little dogs, but this one was kind of cute.

'Show me the house, Ollie Wollie,' Violet said in a cute little voice for the cute little dog. When Oliver recognised her, he wagged his tail. Then she proceeded to follow him to the kitchen. The favourite part of the house for any dog. Then the dog treat drawer. Treat given.

Violet chugged down some plain Jane milk from the fridge, straight from the container, smiled, and put it back, then walked to the dining table and opened up her note. Purple ink on white hand-made paper.

Dear Violet,

Welcome to our new home.

1.   Set up your bedroom. The middle bedroom on

the 2nd floor.

2.   The kitchen appliances, cookware, glassware, dinnerware, cutlery and utensils will arrive at 3pm. Please choose where they will go in our new kitchen.

3.   I will feed Oliver when I get home. Don't listen to him when he tells you he is hungry. Ignore the cute puppy dog eyes as well.

4.   Can you grab a large vase and buy some fresh flowers to put on the table in the hallway of the 1st floor. Thanks.

5.   I need your feedback on an exterior colour for the house, and a new front door colour. If you go out the back, there may be a pig in the yard, and a snake.

6.   I'll be home at 5pm.

From Jane

'Oops,' said Violet. 'I broke Rule-Number-Three. At least there's no evidence, hey Hotdog!'

A-knock-at-the-door.

Violet pushed barking Ollie Wollie into the library sitting room and shut the door.

'Delivery!' a man called.

'Alright, alright,' Violet said, and opened the door.

The man's eyes widened at the sight of her. 'We have a furniture delivery for Violet.' And his eyes settled on her lips.

Violet pressed her red lipstick lips together, and brushed her fingers through her short, blonde wavy hair. *It does it every time,* Violet thought. *Men.*

'Great. Up the stairs and the bedroom opposite the staircase.'

Violet ascended the steps to her new abode. In the middle. Shouldn't this be Jane's bedroom? The middle child. The middle room on the middle floor. That made more sense for Janie. The quiet, bossy one.

She opened the door to reveal her room, the smell like dry cleaning and new carpet mixed together. Except there was no carpet, just a rug. The timber floor shined, and the walls were white, except for the "violet watercolour large roses and purple leaves" wall paper, as she had requested of the interior designer. There was a white en suite and a large window opposite the door.

The removalists entered with her brand new bedroom furniture and she instructed them to where each piece should go. And then they left, after Violet scribbled her name on the job order, as well as her Instagram handle. She smiled.

Violet followed the last removalist to the front door. Just to be safe. There's nothing worse than a lingering removalist. Like the last time. But Violet had dealt with that situation with her knee and had the satisfaction of seeing his eyes water.

Violet let Ollie Wollie out of library jail and he followed her upstairs to her room on the dog-elevator. Violet set about unpacking her designer clothes and shoes and handbags for the wardrobes, and toiletries for the en suite. She made her bed with the white bed sheets and white duvet cover with cascading violet coloured wisteria flowers.

Violet. Her name. Like the colour. One of the seven colours that Isaac Newton labelled when dividing the spectrum of visible light in 1672.

Violet. Like the flower. Sweet violets loved for their perfumed flowers.

Violet. The colour of her hands when she was born.

At 3pm the delivery of kitchen appliances, cookware, glassware, dinnerware, cutlery and utensils arrived. Jane was always precise like that. With time. With instructions. With bossiness like she was in charge of everyone.

Like she *was* everyone.

Violet guided the delivery to the kitchen, where the parcels were placed on the benches. And then she placed them in their spots. She put the new dinnerware, glassware, cutlery and utensils into the dishwasher and turned it on. Like they always did when they moved into a new residence. The sisters-in-the-new-house-girls. Over and over again. Violet loved opening the boxes for the kitchen. It was like birthdays and Christmases wrapped up into one.

Violet jumped into her Kombi Van to buy #4 on her list from Jane. Some flowers for the hall table outside her room. She returned empty handed. Apparently flowers were in high demand today. She glanced up the road to another terrace house voluminous with flowers blooming in the front garden.

Violet smiled and sneaked into Poppy's room and grabbed a pair of her art scissors. *The* art scissors. The shiniest and sharpest ones that nobody could touch, then walked casually up to the garden, looked this way and that, then snipped off a bounty of flowers, inconspicuously dropping them into a large paper bag, and walked quickly back to the new house-of-the-seven-sisters.

She set them in the new white vase and plonked them onto the hall table as requested. Then she left a lavender note on the dining table for Jane. At the white chair. The plain white chair. Plain Jane. Then left promptly for the evening hour at the hair salon.

The front door opened at 5pm on the dot to Oliver Twist barking.

Jane Piccadilly stepped inside to the guard dog with the wagging tail. No side eye. 'Home at last. Did you have a busy day?'

Oliver gave a little jump, then ran off and returned with his lead.

'Walkies?' Jane said. 'Give me fifteen minutes and I'll be ready.'

Jane checked the kitchen for the appliances, then opened Poppy's and Violet's room and peeked inside to see how their bedrooms looked with the furniture added.

Perfection-given-by-direction.

Then she proceeded to her own room and changed into her activewear. Black Flashdance pants, because who wants to see lumps and bumps on thighs and unshaven legs, and an oversized pink Tee.

Jane put on her pink and black and white sports shoes. They matched her activewear perfectly. She grabbed her pink dachshund cap and flipped her pony tail of flaxen-coloured-hair through the strap-back, then walked past the flowers on the hall table and smiled, pleased that Violet had managed to purchase a lovely bouquet for their second floor.

She skipped down the steps, secured Oliver's harness, clicked on the lead and headed out the front door for their very first neighbourhood walk.

A neighbourhood-that-was-new.

A neighbourhood that had people who had never seen her or her six sisters before.

A neighbourhood that was a new start. Fresh, like crisp apples on an apple tree.

Jane led Oliver along the path beside the house, avoiding the wrought iron gate with her white shoe-in-the-poo. Her eye twitched and her body tremored at-the-ick of the memory, and also at the state of the overgrown and chaotic front yard. This mess would never do for Jane Piccadilly. That wasn't her brand. That wasn't her style. Her mother always told her the outside was a reflection of the inside. And people would judge. People would label her as messy and uncared for. They would call her insane Jane. And avoid her.

Jane's eye twitched at-the-ick of the thought of insane Jane, then she turned right at the end of her driveway and walked along the sidewalk, passing others walking their large dogs.

'Hi, I'm Jane, and this is Oliver Twist,' she said to all. Talking to people with dogs was the only time people seemed to hear her voice.

Nice to meet you.

Lovely to meet you.

Hello.

Good evening.

Welcome to our street.

Cute sausage dog was the normal conversation, followed by "What-do-you-do?".

Jane huffled and puffled inside. Why was it always about *what-do-you-do*? As if any job was more important-than-another, or as if your job lifted you higher-in-status in the street, or made you more trustworthy-or-likable. Why couldn't they ask Jane what her passion was, or what her favourite thing to do was, or… how many bodies were there, and did she remember it?

And then there was the response when she told them which terrace house she had moved into, in *this* street… "You moved into *that* house!"

'Yes,' Jane replied. 'It has a fabulous layout for my sisters and I, and we're going to repaint the exterior and landscape the yard. It will fit *perfectly* with the other terraces in *our* street.'

The thirty minute walk turned into an hour walk by the time that Jane and Oliver Twist had greeted people. With a smile. Her mother said to always put a smile on her face. She would be likable Jane then.

On the return walk home she studied the terrace house gardens, to make sure that her design would blend in. Jane frowned at the flowers of one garden, where a patch of blooms were missing, the stalks of the flowers cut with scissors that ripped into the stems, instead of floral shears that left a clean, less painful cut for the plant. Plants had feelings after all. She wondered for a moment whether the flowers had been stolen by some lowlife. An inconsiderate human.

Jane Piccadilly and Oliver stopped in front of their new terrace house. In front of the wrought iron gate. In front of the once offensive smell that caused her to buy the house in anger. There, standing at the red door like red lipstick was a woman with a backpack. Knocking loudly. Causing a disturbance in her brain. Her sound-processing disorder. Misophonia her doctor had called it.

She tried to shrug off the feeling of annoyance and anger. Just like that time with the pen clicking when she was ten. When she found herself in the principal's office. It wasn't her fault that she'd snapped Jessica's pen in half and shoved it into her arm, making her bleed. If Jessica had stopped clicking the pen when she asked her, the situation would never have happened.

Jane's eye twitched and her body tremored at-the-ick.

Jane Piccadilly took a deep breath and swallowed the annoyance that was bubbling inside her, and walked to *her* driveway, along the weedy path and to the front door.

The-red-front-door.

'May I help you?' Jane said with a voice of calm. A practised skill. For survival.

'Thank goodness. I thought you hadn't returned from the holiday abroad yet.'

Jane raised an eyebrow. 'That was ah… that was the previous owner. I'm the new owner—'

'With the red door. Thank you for continuing that legacy. I'm Lucy.'

Jane closed her eyes and scratched her forehead. 'Wha—'

'Of travellers welcome to rest and to have a meal. I haven't eaten in three days. THREE DAYS!'

Jane picked Oliver Twist up off the ground for safety. A sausage dog was not the dog to look at when you were hungry.

'Lucy… I—' Jane wanted to tell her to go away and that she wasn't giving her food away to strangers, but she remembered that time sitting on a park bench, in her favourite sitting-dead-pose, after the horrible-terrible-incident, and how she felt when a stranger had given her some food. Jane's heart softened. '— Come back in an hour and I will have something for you to eat.'

Jane noted that she would talk to Poppy at once about changing the colour of the front door. Sooner rather than later. She didn't know how much longer she could put up with strangers knocking on her front door wanting rest and a meal. And perhaps… something *more*.

Uninvited.

Unwelcome.

Unannounced.

And Jane noted that she needed to start researching the history of the house. *That* house, as the neighbours had called it.

Jane entered through her front door, the colour of blood. Well, not like the dark coloured blood she had seen at the situation. This was more the colour of the blood of a living person. She put Oliver down and he trotted through to the kitchen and waited by his bowl for dinner, and spun around in one complete circle when he saw his food coming.

The little-vertigo-dog.

Jane made herself a super sandwich for dinner, and three for Lucy, and left it outside the front door with her name on it.

Beside the new envelope at the front door.

The envelope-at-the-door.

She hesitated before she picked it up, and then whooshed it into her pocket, then locked the front door and went to her adored library for some reading before bed. There, she sat reading her book under the light from her phone, lighting her face and her flaxen-coloured-hair, making it look golden, like she was Goldilocks. But also making the house look like nobody was home, so that no one would knock on the front door so she felt like stabbing them with a broken pen.

Or a knife.

It was safer that way. For them. Maybe she should install a pleasant sounding doorbell, so the aggressive knuckle knocking on the door wouldn't make her blood boil.

At 9pm on the dot, Jane Piccadilly and Oliver Twist went upstairs to bed. Because 9pm was bedtime.

Every night.

'Good night, Oliver,' Jane said, as she climbed into bed, then leaned over to turn off the bedside lamp. And there sat the envelope from the front door.

The envelope-at-the-door.

Unopened.

Jane Piccadilly picked it up, turned it over and slid her finger under the back fold and opened it.

A-messy-handwritten-note.

You have something that belongs to me.

Jane's eye twitched and her body tremored at-the-ick. Her hand shook as she pushed the words-in-the-letter back into the envelope, and slipped it into the drawer of emptiness beside her bed, where it could enter the void and self-combust, ashes to ashes, dust to dust. Jane Piccadilly hoped her mother wouldn't find that dust.

Tomorrow was another moving day, she thought, refraining from reverting to her safe space of checking out of reality, and pretending to be dead-in-the-bed. *It was Daisy who had bedroom number four and Flora who had bedroom number five, upstairs with her and Violet.*

Jane Piccadilly turned off the light.

And that was a day, and a night.

Chapter 8

Jane

Jane Piccadilly wrote a list for Daisy. And for Flora. She folded the white notes and left them on the table in front of the dark yellow dining chair, and the orange one. She said to Oliver. 'I have to go now, Oliver Twist. You're in charge of the house. Daisy will be here in the morning, and Flora will come in the afternoon.'

Oliver gave a little jump. Jane lobbed him a treat, then turned on her heel and walked out the front door.

Daisy closed the door of her yellow 1964 Holden EH Ute and looked across the street. The three story terrace house with the red door. There it was. She crossed the road and walked up the driveway and bounced up the steps of the Victorian Terrace house and inserted the key to the front door. Oliver Twist barked, a couple of times, or four. Perhaps ten. Daisy opened the door and he gave her the side-eye-of-judgement.

'Oli, Oli, Oli… OI, OI, OI!' she said, and petted the little loooooong dog, who now wagged his tail in recognition of her.

She looked about the entry and hall. The renovations were amazing. Was this the same place that Jane had bought? The ugliest house on the street?

She walked through to the kitchen, Oliver passing her and standing in front of a drawer with his right paw held up. Daisy raised an eyebrow, then walked to Oliver's draw, opened it and gave him a treat. 'Crikey Charlie, Oli. Is food all you ever think about?'

She about turned, admiring the Hamptons style kitchen, looked over to the dining table with multi-coloured chairs, and saw two notes. She walked over to the table and picked up the note with her name on it in front of the yellow coloured chair. 'Bloody oath. Jane and her notes and her colours!'

Dear Daisy,

Welcome to our new home.

1. *Your bedroom furniture and clothing etc is arriving at 9:00am. Set up your bedroom. The third room on the 2nd floor.*
2. *Feed Oliver some lunch and check his water.*
3. *I need your advice on landscaping front and back. If you go out the back, there may be a pig in the yard, and a snake.*

5.   *Flora will arrive at 12pm.*

From Jane

Daisy smiled. A bloody pig-in-the-backyard! Delightful! Nothing like a mud loving squealing pig who can't sweat so all the toxins stay in its body in our backyard. Flora will love it!

Daisy reached for a green apple in the fruit bowl in the centre of the table, but stopped and brought her hands to her nose and took a whiff. Did her hands smell like death this morning after the leaking-coffin-incident yesterday? She had washed her hands two hundred and fifty times in foul smelling COVID hand sanitiser, and twenty times in Tahitian Lime & Grapefruit hand sanitiser. She took a longer whiff. Who on earth could smell the entire repertoire of the fragrance top notes of grapefruit, lime, orange, blackcurrant, the middle notes of jasmine, freesia, muguet, rose damas and the base notes of orris root, cedarwood, and tea? All she could smell was the lemon and lime. Crikey Charlie!

She narrowed her eyes as she assessed whether death was sufficiently removed from her hands, then grabbed a red apple, turned and made her way up the first flight of steps to her bedroom and swung open the oak door. And there it was. Her bedroom styled as she had asked. White walls (Jane's insistence) with a feature wall of yellow wallpaper with white daisies. She opened the sash windows, checked out her en suite and wardrobe, then went downstairs to open the door to the furniture arrival, and instructed the removalists on which bedroom was hers. And then Daisy got to work making her bedroom homely and loved like a real dag.

Daisy placed her framed daisy flower art on her study desk. Now her room was complete. She traced her fingers over the petals her mum had painted. Her mother the scientist could paint well. Daisy reached over and picked up the Daisy chain hair piece and placed it on her head. They were the daisies her mother had grabbed in the throes of the pain of labour when she unexpectedly gave birth in the flower field. Daisy smiled. If her mother had grabbed a seeding dandelion she could have wished the birth to be quicker and less painful. And then she would've be called Dandelion.

At 11am Daisy wandered out into the backyard and watched Oliver disappear into the long grass. She put her hands on her hips. 'Well that is devo! The back yard's a bit iffy. I bet it makes Jane want to chuck a tanty. And what would I, a true blue carpenter know about landscaping?' And then she saw a little glint of light in through the bush. She brushed her brown fringe to the side, and the glint was gone.

Was it a pig-with-a-glint?

Oli returned to the house, a bone-in-his-mouth. He promptly added to his collection of dog-things-box.

Daisy left a yellow note in the glass jar in front of Jane's dining chair. At the white chair. Plain white chair. Plain Jane. Then she gave a lopsided-grin as an idea came to her mind. She raced out the door to the butcher up the road and bought a gift for Jane and placed it into the fridge. Wrapped in white paper. Plain white paper. Then left the house at 11:30am to return to work with death. Or wood. Or both.

Flora parked her classic, retro, pastel green 1991 Nissan Figaro on the street, under the leafy, picturesque Jacaranda tree. This was the spot for her car. Insta worthy. Her spot. She removed her long white Audrey Hepburn style gloves, the right one with a red splot, like blood, her white rectangular retro sunglasses and smoothed her auburn pony tail and brushed her fingers through her extra short fringe. She checked her phone to see if the baby scans had been uploaded yet. Nothing.

She exited her car and looked over at the home of the gnomes. The Piccadilly girls were the gnomes. The seven of them living together like seven gnomes or the seven dwarfs. She looked over the chaotic garden to see if Jane had put the seven freaky ugly gnomes out yet. Flora rolled her eyes. 'Thank. Bloody. Goodness,' she said under her breath, then walked to the red door, inserted the key that set off the dog doorbell and opened the door to a sausage dog giving her the side-eye.

'Olivier!' Flora said to Oliver Twist in her best French accent. And suddenly Olivier recognised her and wagged his tail.

Flora and Olivier walked about the house together after Flora had found his blue bandana with colourful retro roller skates on it, and put it on him. Olivier took her to the treat drawer, naturally, and was rewarded for his cleverness.

Flora saw the note on the table in front of the orange dining chair. She raised her left eyebrow and looked up to the ceiling while she closed her right eye as a silent disapproving response at the colour orange assigned to her. Again.

She opened the note.

'Yadda, yadda, yadda. Blah. Blah. Blah,' she mumbled under her breath.

Dear Flora,

Welcome to our new home.

*1.	Your bedroom furniture and clothing etc is arriving at 2:30am. Set up your bedroom. The bedroom directly ahead of the stairs on the 2nd floor.*

2.   *I need your feedback on an exterior colour for the house, and a new front door colour. If you go out the back, there may be a pig in the yard, and a snake. Can you check for them, please.*

3.   *I will feed Oliver when I get home. Don't listen to him when he tells you he is hungry. Ignore the cute puppy dog eyes as well.*

4.   *I'll be home at 5pm.*

From Jane

Flora's eyes widened. A-snake-and-a-pig! Here? Near the city? A snake is a possibility, but a pig in suburbia? Come on! And… just because she was a farm hand didn't mean that she would be happy handling either of those. Flora rubbed her forehead with her fingers.

Jane says. Flora does.

It's what she expected. *Always.*

Bossy plain Jane. The middle child who could only be seen via a written note.

She made haste back out to her car and grabbed her backpack of work clothes, then went to her room to inspect it. All white walls except for the large print watercolour floral wallpaper in pinks and oranges and green leaves. Perfect. She walked to the window and opened it up to the view of the back yard. And the neighbours' back yards on either side, plus the top floor of the house behind. If she could see into their room, could they see inside hers?

'Hmmm,' Flora said to Olivier, and changed into her long khaki pants and checkered long-sleeved button-up shirt. She exited her room and opened the bedroom door next to hers. 'Daisy,' she huffed after seeing the daisy wall paper. 'Again!'

She opened the next bedroom door. Violet flowers. 'Violet. Again.' And the final door of the front bedroom. White. 'Plain Jane. Again.' Why couldn't she have new-bedroom-neighbours? Why was she always stuck with these sisters? Flora about turned and descended the steps, and walked through to the dining, kitchen and back door.

Olivier Twist stood there, facing the door. Wagging his tail.

Flora opened it up and out flew the little looong dog and disappeared into the long grass.

She pulled on her bright orange gumboots, then stepped into the backyard of extra long grass and weeds and stilled to listen. She looked about to see if she had disturbed any animals. She had not.

Not even the gazillion pigeons that sat and cooed on the top of the roof with messy sticks and long grass stuck in nests.

Flora cupped her hands around her mouth. Mission pig begin. 'Sooie!' She used her normal voice. The backyard remained still, like it was hiding.

Like Jane-in-the-closet.

Locked Jane-in-the-closet.

Covering her ears to stop the man's loud voice from seeping through the closet's timber grains, adding another story to its once I was a tree.

'Soooooooie!' Flora used her louder farm voice. No movement in the backyard. Not even a grunt.

'Here piggy-piggy!' Flora called in a singsong voice. Nothing.

Not-even-a-squeal.

Flora rolled her eyes and took a deep breath, then let out a terribly loud pig noise. It wasn't a right proper English "oink" as if the pig lived in the Queen's palace grounds, nor a "piggy-pig-pig-squeal" but a raucous, irritating grunting sound that rattled her bones.

No pig.

Just the neighbours, with peering eyes and a chorus of "Shut up!".

'Sorry,' she called. 'Just calling the dog,' she lied. She didn't want to tell them a pig could possibly be inhabiting the backyard of a suburban home. An illegal pig.

'Yadda, yadda, yadda. Blah. Blah. Blah,' she mumbled under her breath. 'Olivier. Come!' she called, and the mini dachshund's tail elevated in the air above the long grass like the collector pole at the back of a dodgem car as he navigated his way back to Flora.

No snake. No pig. One dog.

She breathed a sigh of relief.

And one bone.

Flora shrugged one shoulder and tried not to do the ICK.

Flora checked her analogue watch. She detested smart watches. Tracking you. Listening to you. Predicting you. 1pm. An idea had presented itself to her when the pig did not. She grabbed Olivier's harness, her purse, then left the house and walked along to the corner store. She returned 45 minutes later and placed the freshly cut meat in the fridge. Next to the white paper wrapped food on the shelf. Flora wrote on the white paper in black. Yes black. The colour Jane hated the most.

'Dear Jane, for you.'

With time to spare, Flora wandered about the house checking for the Jane style in the library sitting room. She called it a study. Nine hundred and ninety-nine books arranged by colour. One day she'll add book number one thousand to the shelf in the place of the wrong colour. 'Whoops!' Flora verbalised, then walked out the front door and onto the footpath, noting she must visit a bookstore.

Flora looked to her left. A man sat on a seat staring out across the road.

A man-on-the-seat.

He had dark hair and a manicured beard, a dark blue business suit, sunglasses and a large bag. A carpet bag of a beautiful design and colour. A classic and elegant design with a nod to the Victorian era. Floral teal with leather handles. She stood beside where he was sitting, but didn't look at him.

'A lovely afternoon,' he said.

'Indeed,' replied Flora, then looked at the sign near the seat. Bus stop. Was it new? Had it just been put there? She was sure it wasn't there when she parked her car earlier. And Jane would never have bought a house with a bus stop perched in front of it.

'Which bus are you catching?' he said.

'None. I'm looking at the house from the perspective of the road.'

'Ah. The new owner.'

'Well… technically not. I'm an occupant.'

'An occupant with a name?'

'Flora.'

'Lovely. Do you like flowers?'

Flora pushed her lips into a hard line. That question was always catapulted at her. 'Yes,' she said through clenched teeth trying to stop a tirade of verbalised words from leaving her mind. 'And your name is?' she said, returning to the demure of a calm person.

'Luciano.'

'Luciano like Pavarotti. Do you sing?' A subtle retaliation.

The man in the dark blue business suit chuckled. 'I wish. Are you off to work?'

'Not yet,' Flora said, feeling a little nauseous.

'A truck is coming,' Luciano said.

Flora frowned then looked up and down the street. She couldn't hear the sound of a truck, nor see it. And then there it was.

'Gotta go. That's my delivery truck. Nice to meet you.'

'Likewise.'

Flora leaped over the fence shedding its skin, the colour of a sickly heart, and into the long grass, then stood on the small verandah and watched the truck reverse up the driveway. On confirmation that the delivery was indeed hers, she opened the front red door like red lipstick, and led Olivier to the library sitting room and closed him in so he didn't get underfoot.

After the delivery was complete, she released Olivier from the library and they went to her new room. Flora set about unpacking her clothes and shoes for the wardrobes, and toiletries for the en suite. She made her bed with the white bed sheets and a white duvet cover to allow the wall paper with the water colour pastel pinks, yellows, and oranges of the flowers enjoy their own beauty without competing with anything. It was the only way to make it work without clashing and clanging and clacking in a noisy colour conflicting way. Poppy the artist would be proud.

Then she opened the pink hat box. The diamonds sparkled. It was a crown. The crown of Flora from the 1984 ballet titled *The Awakening of Flora*.

Flora. A Roman goddess of flowers and spring. A symbol for nature and flowers. People thought her mother loved nature so much that she gave her that name. They didn't know she was born on the floor of the house, her mother floored by her early arrival.

Flora-born-on-the-floor.

According to the lore, Flora was initially a Greek nymph called Chloris. One day when Chloris was roaming in a field, Zephyrus, the God of the West Wind, saw her and fell in love with her. He then kidnapped the nymph and married her. As proof of his love, Zephyrus gave his new bride the power to rule the flowers, plants, trees and orchards. And Chloris became Flora, the Goddess of the Flowers.

Flora placed the crown on her head and went to the mirror. It was beautiful. She removed it then placed in on the floral wig stand on her dresser.

Flora looked at her watch. 4:30pm. She opened her phone to check to see if the baby scans had been uploaded yet. Her face softened and she smiled. It was there. She had to get back to the farm. It was time to celebrate her baby news.

She quickly wrote a note to Jane, then stopped by the long wooden dining table and pushed the orange paper into the jar of notes on the dining table. At the white chair. Plain white chair. Plain Jane. And then she was off to the farm, unable to keep the smile from her face.

The front door opened at 5pm on the dot to Oliver Twist barking.

Jane Piccadilly stepped inside to the guard dog with the wagging tail, who couldn't contain himself, jumping up at her, his butt wiggling uncontrollably. 'Home at last. Did you have a busy day?'

Oliver gave another little jump, ran off and returned with his lead.

'Walkies?' Jane said. 'Give me fifteen minutes and I'll be ready.'

Jane walked through to the kitchen and went to the fridge and opened it up.

And froze.

There, sitting on a perfectly clean shelf allocated to fruit, TO THE FRUIT, were two parcels of food wrapped in white butchers paper that she had not approved of. AND, one had black writing on it! She held her breath and counted to ten. But not long enough to make her face turn blue like when she was a child. Then she reached over and pulled them out. She placed them both on the island bench side-by-side in perfect alignment, and tapped her foot, wondering which to open first.

The one with the black writing! *Dear Jane, for you.* She had to get rid of it.

Jane unwrapped the white butchers paper, the pink colour of bacon presenting itself, mocking her. And another note. *I found little cute piggie wiggie!* Jane's eye twitched and her body tremored at-the-ick. She hesitated before she opened the other parcel of food. But then opened it in a swift action to get it over and done with. Bacon. Again. And a note. *Is this the pig you were looking for?*

Both of Jane's eyes twitched accompanied by a body tremor. ICK. ICK. ICK. A poor innocent pig had been KILLED to become a lump of bacon for the consumption of humans.

Jane Piccadilly once watched *Babe* the movie when she was eight. And on that same day, she promised never to eat bacon, or ham, or pork.

'An abomination has occurred in this house, Oliver!' she said, then twitched, aware of the irony that she had bought a sausage dog. She cleared the image of a pork sausage from her mind before it made her head pound, and replaced it with an image of her homemade vegan pumpkin sausage rolls.

Jane Piccadilly suited Oliver up in his harness and lead, grabbed the bacon sacrifices and ran out the front door and down the road to a restaurant industrial bin, and ceremoniously dropped them in there. Then she ran back to the house with Oliver Twist.

'Consider that your walkies for today,' Jane said to Oliver.

And then there was a knock on the front door. Jane Piccadilly half closed one eye and rolled the other. She made her way to the front door and opened it before another knock would push her angry buttons.

A skin-and-bones-man stood there, his face gaunt, his hair unwashed. Swaying on the spot. He looked around then pulled a wad of money from his pocket and held it out to Jane, and looked around again. 'I need it. Real bad,' he said.

Jane Piccadilly's nose twitched at his smell. 'Food?'

'If you want to call it *food*, then okay.' His eyes were bloodshot and glassy.

'I have some vegan sausages—'

'What the fuck!—'

Jan lowered her head and shut down her hearing. Violent, aggressive words. She went to that place inside of herself that was safe. To protect herself from collateral mental damage. If she stood still enough, she would become invisible. PTSD her psychologist had called it.

'—Give me the heroin, you bitch!'

Jane tried to swallow but couldn't. She thought back to Hudson. How did she defuse him when he was in a rage? She hated the ticking time bomb that was inside of him.

The skin and bones man was sweating now, his fist clenched.

Jane Piccadilly put her weight onto her other foot so she became visible, and took a deep breath, punctuated with shudders. But still, the breath was deep enough to elicit a calmness inside her. She looked beyond the man to see if he was alone. Then satisfied he was, she said in a low tone that was completely void of aggression, like she had been taught, 'I can see you really need the drugs. I'm sorry. Those owners have left.'

The skin and bones man pushed the money back into his pocket and wiped the sweat from his face. He looked like he was about to cry. He was exhausted.

'I'd like to call a cab for you to take you to a safe place. Help for you.'

He ran his hand through his greasy hair and nodded. Once.

And that was enough for Jane. She pulled her phone from her pocket and organised a lift for him, and stayed out the front of the house with him until the taxi arrived, gave an address to the driver and closed the door for the skin and bones man.

Jane mentally patted herself on the back as she watched the taxi drive away. Her de-escalating tools had worked. But she was still as scared as a person buried alive, unable to breath.

When Jane Piccadilly returned to the front door, her bones shaking, there was an envelope-at-the-front-door.

After hesitating, she picked it up.

Jane went to bed that night, feeling out of sorts.

One, she hated it when her sisters made fun of her. Like she was an outsider. An outlier of the family. Like she was an only child.

Two, she had to get that red door repainted as soon as possible. What was this, a drug dealer house? Jane grunted. She should have done a house history search before she opened her bloody mouth and bought the house with her white shoe stuck-in-the-poo.

And three. Another letter!!!

'Good night, Oliver,' Jane said, as she climbed into bed after a long shower and a mind cleansing, washing away the orange blasts and dripping blood and deafening noise. She leaned over to turn off the bedside lamp. And there sat the envelope.

The envelope-at-the-door.

Unopened. Jane Piccadilly picked it up, turned it over and slid her finger under the back fold and opened it.

A-messy-handwritten-note.

It's red like the front door. I want it back.

Jane's eye twitched and her body tremored at-the-ick. Her hand shook as she pushed the words in the letter back into the envelope, and slipped it into the drawer of emptiness beside her bed, where it could enter the void and float like a wish that was captured on a breeze, landing on the ground unheard. Jane smiled. Mind visualisation was the best.

Jane Piccadilly wiggled down between the sheets at 9pm exactly and closed her eyes. Because that is what you did when you went to bed to sleep. *You can't sleep with your eyes open,* her mother would say, not able to see the tears streaming down her face, not being able to see her pretending-to-be-dead.

Would her mother love her more then. If she was dead?

Jane Piccadilly's eyes flew open at the sound of loud grunting. The pig was alive! Jane smiled and closed her eyes, her heart feeling lighter. She created a new dead-in-the-bed pose worthy of fine praise from mathematicians and artists alike, and fell into a peaceful sleep.

And that was a day, and a night.

Chapter 9

Jane

Jane Piccadilly wrote a list for Rose. And a note for Zinnia. She folded them and placed them in front of the pink dining chair and the green dining chair at the long dining table.

She lifted Oliver into her arms. 'I have to go now, Oliver. You're in charge of the house. Rose will be here in the morning, and Zinnie will come in the afternoon.'

Oliver licked Jane's chin. A kiss. Or a taste. She didn't know which. She put him down, lobbed him a treat, then turned on her heel and walked out the front door.

Rose swung her leg off her pastel pink moped parked on the

driveway and peered up at the seven bedroom three story Victorian terrace house.

She wondered which bedroom would be hers.

She needed the most spacious one to develop her photographs. She reached inside her brown leather satchel and pulled out her Canon EOS R3 camera, aimed it at the house and snapped-multiple-photographs.

She zoomed in to the red front door.

Click.

Squatted down and captured the weeds in the foreground, focussed, with the house blurring in the background.

Click. Click. Click.

Then vice versa. She about turned and photographed the road and houses opposite. The bus stop. Then she walked to the front door and opened it to the bossy little dachshund with the terrible case of the side-eye-of-judgement.

'Hello Dash! May I come in to your new house?'

Oliver Twist barked and wagged his tail when he recognised who it was. Rose looked up and about at the newly renovated house. She smiled then lifted her camera to mark the journey. First impressions count.

She continued taking images of lines and angles and furniture all the way to the dining and kitchen area. Then proceeded to capture the moment in time there. She spotted her note from Jane on the table, zoomed in and photographed it. Then placed her camera on the long wooden dining table after photographing the signature wood grain texture of it, and picked up the note and unfolded it.

Dear Rose,

Welcome to our new home.

1.   *Your bedroom furniture and clothing etc is arriving at 9:30am. Set up your bedroom. The front room on the 3rd floor.*
2.   *Feed Oliver some lunch at 11:30 am and check his water.*
3.   *I would like you to photograph the renovated house interior.*
4.   *I need your feedback on an exterior colour for the house, and a new front door colour. If you go out the back, there may be a pig in the yard, and a snake.*
5.   *Zinnia will arrive at 12pm.*

From Jane

The third floor? All those steps? When was Jane going to buy a house-with-an-elevator? The furniture people will not be impressed!

Rose looked down at the hound. 'Come on, Dash. Let's check out our room.'

Rose stopped before the first set of steps and looked up and sighed. She moved her camera to her eye and photographed the stairs, the height, the horizontal and vertical lines and perspectives, then took her first step towards her new bedroom.

When she reached the top of the second floor, she turned and filmed little Dash travelling up towards her as the operator-of-the-dog-elevator. She smiled at him. He was like Alfred Pennyworth, Batman's butler. He always answered the door and new everyone and everything that went on in the house.

Rose continued photographing her way to the third floor, and walked to her room, one of two on that level.

She pushed open the oak wooden door, wishing it had been painted white like the walls. But alas, it did provide a nice photographic contrast and would look brilliant as a black and white shot. Opposite her was a large window and to her right the feature wall of pink roses with greenery. As she had asked for. She walked to the furthest corner and took it all in. She pictured where her film developing equipment would go and where she would hang the photographs.

Satisfactory.

Rose walked around her room photographing, then aimed her camera outside her window and clicked. Across the street. Up the street and down the street.

The man-sitting-at-the-bus-stop.

Then she photographed the truck as it pulled into the driveway, stopping millimetres from her moped. A heart-stop moment.

Rose descended the steps, challenging herself to get to the door before the removalists, and opened it as a fist was raised to knock on the door. She hated the sound of door knocking. Misophonia apparently. It ran in the family.

Rose smiled. 'Good morning,' she said, out of breath.

The woman nodded then looked up the steps. 'You're on the top floor aren't you?'

'Sorry,' Rose said, and winced.

'It's what we do,' she said, then turned and whistled at her co-workers and pointed to the top floor.

And then it began. Dash was in library jail. Furniture travelled up the steps in the hands of the professionals, and Rose instructed them where to put her furniture in her room, photographing as they did so. Before they left, she photographed them together with her in front of the truck.

Then Rose released Dash from the library sitting room and went to her room to organise her bedding, clothing, en suite and dark room. The room was perfect for her needs.

Rose photographed the walkway outside her room, including the ceiling, and Zinnia's empty room before she made her way downstairs, noting that her and Zinnia should have a little tea-and-coffee-set-up outside their rooms so they didn't need to go all the way downstairs to the kitchen get a caffeine hit.

When she got to the kitchen and dining room, she let Dash out the back for a wee walk. And took a multitude of photographs while looking around for the snake or the pig. She was surprised by a glint of light at one point, that disappeared when she looked for it again. She hoped she had caught it with her camera.

Dash entered the house then with a very large bone-between-his-jaws. It reminded her of the Great Dane they once owned. Not the Great Dane carrying a bone in its mouth, but the size of the bones of the Great Dane. Rose lifted her camera to her eye and photographed the little mini Dash with the ginormous bone, and again as he dropped it into his collection of dog-things-box.

A 11:30am she fed the little looooong dog, had a cup of tea that Jane bought for her, the orange one of course, the Turmeric Ginger Ninja, then returned to her room to collect her photography bag and to write a note.

She descended two flights of stairs and went back to the long wooden dining table, and left the orange note in the glass jar. The Jar-of-Jane-Notes. At the white chair. And left for her next photography session.

The bus doors opened with a whoosh, and Zinnia stepped onto the footpath near the seven bedroom three story Victorian terrace house. She let out a sigh. This was the ugliest house Jane had ever purchased. Had she thought this through? And was this the last time they would be moving? Maybe Violet needed anger therapy.

It was always her fault that they had to move.

Violent Violet.

She clutched the handle of her heavy crocodile leather science bag that Jane-the-animal-lover hated so much it made her face go red with anger, and walked past the bus stop seat, along the pathway, up the driveway and to the front red door of the house. She wiggled the key into the lock and Oliver barked before giving her the side-eye.

'Hello, you Silly Sausage!' Zinnia said to Oliver Twist, who wagged his tail once he recognised her. She placed her science bag to the left of the entryway, then walked straight ahead to the kitchen and dining room area.

'This looks lovely, Silly Sausage. What do you think?'

Oliver Twist stood in front of the treats drawer and wagged his tail. He lifted his paw.

Treat given.

Dog's mission accomplished.

Zinnia walked over to the long wooden dining table. A note sat there in front of the pastel green dining chair addressed to her in green ink. She picked it up and opened it.

Dear Zinnia,

Welcome to our new home.

1.   Your bedroom furniture and clothing etc is arriving at 2:30pm. Set up your bedroom. The bedroom at the back on the 3rd floor.

2.   Can you please identify any weeds in the yard, and any plants that are poisonous for our Oliver Twist.

4. I need your feedback on an exterior colour for the house, and a new front door colour. If you go out the back, there may be a pig in the yard, and a snake.

3.   I will feed Oliver when I get home. Don't listen to him when he tells you he is hungry. Ignore the cute puppy dog eyes as well.

4.   I'll be home at 5pm.

From Jane

Zinnia pocketed the note, about turned and walked out of the kitchen area and back to the front door. She picked up her science bag and started the long ascent to the third floor. She couldn't believe Jane had allocated this room to her! Not with all the heavy science equipment and the academic necessities she brought home at times. And lysergic acid diethylamide. To give her intensified thoughts, emotions and sensory perception. To escape things that annoyed her.

You know.

Like people.

Like JANE.

How could she?

She reached the top floor, out of breath, then kicked open the oak door. The room was all white, except for the green wallpaper with pale pink and yellow zinnia flowers. The same wallpaper she had chosen for all of their houses. She had a window looking out of the side of the house toward the city, and one looking out the back, a wardrobe and an en suite.

She placed her heavy crocodile leather science bag in the en suite, then stepped out and made a mental map of where her bed and desk would be. Then her study equipment. She returned to the ground floor and went outside into the overgrown, untidy, unbalanced backyard with the silly sausage dog and photographed and identified plants and weeds and poisonous plants for dogs on her phone app. And marked them. Zinnia shook her head. Jane could have done this. It's. Not. That. Hard.

Oliver lugged over some bones, one by one, and deposited them in the house. Zinnia shook her head in disgust, then walked through the long weeds to the front yard and photographed and identified the plants there. And marked them. Zinnia raised her eyebrows. The dog should have been dead by now, living in this jungle of poisonous dog plants.

And then the truck arrived. And the loud moans and groans as her bedroom furniture went up, up and up.

And then they left.

Zinnia organised her bedding, her desk, her clothes and her en suite, wrote a note on the green paper Jane had selected for her, then down the stairs she went. Down two flights of stairs. She had to return to university for her botany experiment. She walked to the long wooden dining table and placed the green note into the glass jar. On the dining table for Jane. At the white chair. The plain white chair.

Plain Jane.

And left.

Chapter 10

Jane

Oliver Twist barked and bounced and wagged his tail as he greeted Jane Piccadilly at the door at 5pm. She was flustered. Like the wind causing havoc today.

She ran her fingers through her mid length, curly flaxen-coloured-hair, parted in the middle, because that is symmetrical of course, and then through her fringe that balanced the facial bilateral symmetry, *which lends to physical attractiveness and important social consequences,* her mother had said.

Jane stilled. If that was so, why was she still invisible to people?

'Home at last, Oliver. Did you have a busy day?' Oliver barked with a little jump, like doing a wheelie on a bicycle. 'That's good.'

Jane walked through to the kitchen and turned on the jug. She found her white tea pot, cup and saucer, then poured the hot water through the strainer in the teapot—white jasmine loose leaf scented white tea. She carried her teapot and cup to the dining table and sat on the white chair. She peered at the glass communications note jar.

It had six different coloured notes in it now.

She smiled. Her system worked well. A particular coloured dining chair and the matching coloured note paper was allocated to everyone, in accordance with their namesake. It stopped confusion and was instantly recognisable as to who the person was, like, so she could avoid the notes in the jar from certain sisters that she did not want to deal with.

Yet.

Jane turned her Alice in Wonderland teapot three times, clockwise, then poured the tea into her white Alice in Wonderful teacup and took a sip. She smiled.

A new teapot for new stories told in the new house.

She put her teacup down and reached into the jar and took out a note.

The blue note.

Poppy's.

Dearest Jane,

Thank you for the bedroom on the ground floor. It's perfect! I am all set and need nothing more.

Regarding the exterior house colour, I think a dark blue door (intelligence, power, and stability) and the house colour white.

Kindly,
Poppy

Jane Piccadilly raised her eyebrows then lifted the lid of her MacBook and opened up Safari. She typed in white houses with dark blue front doors. She perused the images. That colour combination was a definite possibility.

She reached into the jar and pulled out the lavender note, and opened it.

Violet's.

> *Dear Jane,*
>
> *I hope you are happy with the placement of the kitchen ware. Do not change any of the positions of what I have organised!*
>
> *A mustard front door colour is the only way to go, with a light grey colour for the house. Google it and you will find that it is the loveliest.*
>
> *Viole__nt__*

Jane Piccadilly frowned. Twice. Firstly at Violet's signature of Violent, and that at the colour choice. All she could think of was hot dogs with a squiggly line of mustard on top of the Frankfurt. She opened another tab in Safari and typed in light grey houses with mustard front doors. She perused the images. Jane's eye twitched and her body tremored at-the-ick. There would be no mustard coloured door and grey exterior paint like it had lost any inkling of personality. A grey person. Like a wallflower.

Like her.

She reached into the jar and pulled out the yellow note, and opened it.

Daisy's.

Dear Jane,

In the dead tree room, I've stashed landscaping sketches for you like a dag. The state of the yard is defo annoying me. We must do something about it soon so the sisters don't carry on like pork chops.

I didn't encounter the nope rope or Babe. Maybe they did the bolt.

For the money-pit, a black door with a white house.

I can contact a landie to do the work in the yard who's not a bludger and won't blow your dough. Pronto.

From Daisy

P.S. There was a durry by the front door. Don't go berko. I got rid of it.

Jane Piccadilly nodded her head. She totally agreed with Daisy's reaction to the yard. She searched white houses with black front doors and perused the images. Smart and clean. That colour combination was a definite possibility.

She reached into the jar of notes and pulled out the orange note, and opened it.

Flora's.

Jane,

How could I possibly find a snake or pig in that mess of a back yard?

I left you something in the fridge though.

Exterior house colours? Maybe a white door with a beige house colour, or a white door and white house colour? I don't know. The other girls will have a better idea than me.

Sincerely,
Flora

Jane Piccadilly's eye twitched at the memory of the something-in-the-fridge, then she searched for beige and white houses with white front doors. She studied the images. It was a perfectly fine colour combination. Flora needed to have more confidence.

She reached into the jar of notes and pulled out the pink note, and opened it.

Rose's.

Dear Jane,

I hate the stairs but I love my bedroom size. It's perfect for the dark room.

I have photographed the interior renovations, and organised the photographs so each space has the before and after. I will email the digital copies to you once I am happy with them. I have also photographed the exterior of the house and the front and back yard. No snake and no pig.

Oh… I have emailed a picture of the ceiling outside my room. There's something odd.

For the abode, I know a dark grey door - balance and neutrality – would be perfect, with a light grey or white exterior colour.

Warm regards,
Rose

Jane Piccadilly searched for grey and white houses with grey front doors. She studied the images. Either was a perfectly find colour combination. And besides, Rose does have the photographer's eye.

She reached into the jar of notes and pulled out the last note. Green.

Zinnia's. She opened it.

Dear Jane,

You know I don't like to complain, but, my bedroom and Rose's on the top floor is ridiculous. We are the ones who bring equipment home from work! Please reconsider a reallocation of bedrooms.

I have sprayed bright green paint on the weeds that are poisonous to the silly sausage. They are mostly in the front yard.

For the house, white, with a light sage green front door. I'm pretty sure we have that sage colour left over from the 2nd and 3rd house we were in.

Zinnia

Jane Piccadilly tilted her head to the side. She hadn't expected Zinnia to be so hostile in her note. She searched for white houses with light sage front doors. It was another lovely combination. So many great ideas for house colours. What would she do?

Jane went to the library sitting room, aka, the-dead-tree-room, and found her sketch book. She sketched their seven bedroom three story Victorian terrace house seven times, then went to Poppy's room and borrowed her pencils and coloured each of the houses with the requested colours of her sisters.

She looked over each of the colour specs. White was the most popular house colour, so that was decided. But the door? Jane Piccadilly sighed. A resolution for the situation would come. She was sure it would.

But now, Oliver Twist needed to be walked.

'Walkies!' Jane called. While Oliver Twist ran off and to gather his harness and lead, Jane went to her room and changed into her activewear, grabbing her pink dachshund cap that would control her hair in the wildest of windiest westerly winds.

On her quick walk, Jane kept her head low. The wind always wound her up as she tried to escape from it. And Jane Piccadilly knows what happens when you wind something up too tight. Like Violet. Today was not a people day.

Her phone buzzed as she stepped up her walking speed. She looked at the screen then answered it. 'Hi, Dad.' Her shoulders relaxed.

'Hello, my girl. How is Alice?'

'Jane, Dad. Call me Jane, remember.'

'Alice Piccadilly the 4th. Alice *Jane* Piccadilly. You sound down today. Is it windy at your new house?'

'Yes. I wouldn't be out here, but Oliver needs his walk.'

'And the walk will be good for you too, my dear.'

'How's Mum?'

'The usual. Happy. Bossy. Her life is an event of eternal sunshine… oh… except that day, remember?'

Jane held her breath. Like her sisters had. That day when three became one. Seven became one. When nine became three. Her throat tightened and she swallowed. Hard.

'Everyday, Dad.' Jane narrowed her eyes. Why did he have to remind her about that day? She bathed in the ugliness and fallout of guilt every day, trying to stop herself from drowning… like…

'Hey, Dad. Gotta go. Thanks for the call. I'll call back tonight.'

'Always happy to chat to my girl. Keep well. Hooroo.'

'Bye, Dad.'

Jane and Oliver were at the top of cardiac hill, Jane huffing and puffing and Oliver lying on the footpath, tongue hanging out. They had taken the route in the opposite direction to her usual walk direction with the little sausage dog. Her heart thumped harder than usual. After a moment's rest, they about turned and started the descent home, Jane taking in the landscaping of houses and terraces in the long street, and front door colours. As she continued to walk, an idea came to mind for the front door colour. She smiled and looked down, pleased with herself. She would have it done as a surprise for the others.

As she came closer to her Victorian terrace, the wind blew the tall tree at the side of the house, and she had a clear view of the roof line of the seven bedroom three story Victorian terrace house for the first time. She gasped. There was a window in the brickwork of what she thought was simply the roof cavity of trusses above Rose and Zinnia's rooms.

Jane Piccadilly raised an eyebrow. Mistake-Number-One. Not doing an inspection before purchasing.

After entering the house and feeding Oliver Twist, she beelined to the top floor. Rose did mention something odd about the ceiling up here. She lifted her head and scoured the ceiling.

What did Rose see?

Jane shook her head. It looked fine. She knocked on Zinnia's room. It was one of their house rules—*never enter someone's room without knocking first*—when there was no response, she entered.

The ceiling looked fine.

Jane knocked on Rose's room. No response. She entered, noting the ceiling was good, then about turned to leave.

That's when she saw what Rose saw.

The sag in the ceiling. Outside the rooms. Like the ceiling was going to cave in. It was like a person dumped with the worries and struggles and sadness from other people.

An empath.

Jane grabbed a tripod from Rose's room and lifted it up to the sag. It needed something to prop it up. She couldn't have a roof that was going to collapse.

At least it wasn't on Flora's level. She would think the sky was falling and all hell was going to break loose in their lives.

Jane connected the tripod to the sag, and pushed it a little higher. And that's when she closed her eyes.

And that's when the top of the tripod when through the ceiling with a pop.

Jane held still and opened one eye. Then another. There appeared to be a reinforced structure above where the sag was. She put the tripod back into Rose's room and closed the door, then ran down the two stories to the broom closet, grabbed a broom and returned to the third floor. She held the broom head up to the now open sag and pushed through it again, making the hole bigger.

It seemed to be a roof access point. To the inner roof.

But it was more than that. When she opened the access more—*she refused to call it a manhole when women were most capable of climbing into the roof cavity*—there was a ladder that unfolded, like steps with hand railings on either side, inviting her up into the attic.

Jane stiffened when images of what-could-be-up-there flashed through her mind. She retracted the ladder. She would send Violet up into the roof. If she challenged her to do it, she would. She was the one who always needed to win. The one who erased failure from her vocabulary.

Jane cleaned the floor of debris and looked up. She had ruined the ceiling. Absolutely ruined the ceiling. She went into

Rose's room and grabbed a piece of paper and wrote three notes.

A sorry to Rose.

A sorry to Zinnia.

And a note to herself to motivate Violet, and to get the house renovators back in to repair the damage. Why didn't they mention the ceiling and the attic when they were here?

Jane Piccadilly sat in the white wing chair in the library sitting room. She pulled out her phone and opened speed dial. Her father answered the call after three rings.

'Hi Dad.'

'Hello, my girl. How is Alice?' Frank said.

'Jane, Dad. Call me Jane, remember.'

'Alice Piccadilly the 4th. Alice *Jane* Piccadilly. What's up?'

'Not a lot really. Just winding down for the night. I was thinking about Poppy,' said Jane on her video call.

Alice Jane Piccadilly the 3rd opened her "hambag" and took out a ham sandwich. The corner of Jane's lips turned up. They had all fondly termed her handbag, the "hambag", when they were young. It was two-year-old Flora who thought the word for a handbag was "hambag", and when their mum took a slice of ham out of her bag it reinforced it.

Alice took a bite of her ham sandwich and stared straight ahead, as if she wasn't even present in the conversation.

'Dear Poppy. Your eldest sister. You were her favourite, you know.'

Jane looked down and smiled. It felt nice to be someone's favourite. She was always the rejected one. The-forgotten-child. In the middle of the middle with Another level of middle. A triplet.

'I don't think I'm still her favourite now. Grown-up relationships change all the time?'

'They can change, Jane. But those childhood memories

always come back.

'I hope so.' Jane smiled at her father, who smiled back. 'Good night, Dad. Love you. Good night to you too, Mum.'

'Good night, Jane. We love you too.'

Jane disconnected the call, then went upstairs to bed.

And that was a day, and a night.

Chapter 11

❀

Monday
Poppy

Poppy finished her flat white coffee. Her contraband coffee. In her bedroom. Jane was a tea tragic. But Poppy needed her morning coffee like she needed air to breathe.

She would have a second one at work as soon as she arrived. It would transform her creative introvert self into an extrovert who looked like she could handle anything. *Lie.* That's why she liked working in the library. She worked amongst the lies. The words inked onto paper that weren't true. That people believed. But they smelled so amazing. Lies and books. Addictive. So good that when new boxes of books came in, she would open the box, grab a book and run outside to the reading garden to inhale the giddying aroma of the addictive book perfume, ignoring the fact that she was inhaling several hundred volatile compounds of adhesives, paper treated with chemicals and petrochemicals in the ink. No wonder she would re-enter the library as high as a kite.

The-high-librarian.

Everyone thought she was just extra happy. She wondered if people could see the inked words reflected in her eyes like movies. She shut down the reflections in case the movie of her own life leeched out with sadness and tragedy and regrets and dark secrets.

Poppy turned to her childhood bookshelf she had set up as a library when she was ten. Her homemade novels, typed out and stitched together and added to her bookshelf. She couldn't bear to throw it out. It was filled with her hopes and dreams. She had been sucked into the world of book imagination when she visited the biggest library on earth with her mother, feeling the living words between pages, and chasing the colours of artists' illustrations.

Something in her brain changed that day.

She turned away from her childhood bookshelf. 'Twisty!' she called. 'Are you ready for work today as Schnitzel Von Krumm?'

Oliver Twist gave a bark. Poppy dressed him in his costume for today. A Minion. Oliver looked up at her with the disgusted look of a dachshund. She was waiting for his side-eye-of-judgement.

She picked him up and placed him in the front basket of her pastel blue cruiser bicycle, her work satchel in the back basket, then left the house. She stopped on the footpath and repositioned Twisty.

'It's a beautiful day!' It was a man's voice. He was waiting on the seat for the bus. A carpet bag beside him.

'Indeed it is,' Poppy said, moving closer to the man. It was polite to do that. She wondered why he hadn't said anything about Twisty dressed as a Minion. His costumes were always a conversation starter. 'Off to work today?' she asked.

'Always with Mondayitis. You?'

'Always. But never Mondayitis.'

'What do you do?'

'I'm a Librarian.'

'Nice. A quiet place.'

Poppy smiled. 'Only physically. They mind of readers are crazy-busy-noisy!'

The man with the carpet bag, the beautiful floral teal Victorian carpet bag, tilted his head, but didn't look at her. 'True. Do you write?'

'It's my dream to be an author. To tell the stories that aren't true—opposite to what we are taught as children, "Don't tell stories!" Mother would say, even though I wanted to tell her the truth.' Poppy pressed her lips together and shook her head. Plain Jane, the-girl-with-the-flaxen-hair, wasn't the sweet sister and daughter her mother and father thought she was.

Suppression.

Mother had suppressed her. 'Jane says fiction books are lies and authors are professional liars!'

'But what about you? Would you dare to write a book? It takes bravery you know!'

'Oh. I am writing my own book. Don't tell anyone though.'

Oliver barked and the man smiled.

'I know, Twisty. Time to go.' Poppy looked back at the man. 'Have a wonderful day!'

'You tooooo…'

'Poppy.'

'You too, Poppy.' The man smiled.

Poppy popped her prickly, pink, piggy-brain-bucket on her head. Others would call it a bicycle helmet. It was decorated with black cable tie spikes to deter attacking magpies, even though it wasn't the right season. She just liked the look of it.

Twisty was on lookout in the front.

The-mini-lookout-Minion.

As she picked up the pace on her bicycle, she collected car beeps and smiles. That's what Twisty did. He was the perfectly-ignorant-doggo-happiness-loop. How could a sausage dog in a Minion suit not make you smile?

Poppy arrived at the library, dismounted her bicycle, looked up and smiled at the most wonderful place in the world where words had power to change people. She adored the heritage listed building that was her second home. Away from her sisters.

Away from Jane.

She swiped her employee card, pushed the door open, closed her eyes and inhaled deeply.

Books. Titles. Pages.

Paragraphs. Sentences. Words.

Punctuation. Quotation marks. Lies. Secrets. Death.

Happily never after.

Happily ever after.

Imaginary worlds. A portal for the imagination. The gentle swoosh of a turning page.

The rip of paper...

She stored her bike inside at the lockers and lifted Twisty-the-Minion-dog out of the basket and placed him on the floor. And then he was gone.

'Schnitzel!' echoed through the library, and laughter. He was pure joy in the shape of a sausage.

Poppy grabbed her second coffee for the day and headed to the staff room, hoping her extrovert self was here this morning poking out from her ambiversion. She took a deep breath as she stepped through the doorway of the staffroom then said,

'Morning!' The letters assembled themselves in the correct order today. Some days they didn't. Some days it was a combination of words that came out in an entirely new word. She was definitely author material.

'Schnitzel looks fabulous, Poppy!' Leonie said. 'I still can't believe you won the case for reading dogs in public libraries. I mean, kids come here just to see Schnitzel Von Krumm, and they read to him!'

'Well,' Poppy said, 'he has to earn his keep. And it's a good way to hide his villainous toy shredding side of ripping the stuffing out of every-dog-proof-toy I buy for him, removing the squeaker like he is doing heart surgery and then acting all innocent and cute.' Poppy took a sip of her coffee, hoping she hadn't said too much. Her extrovert side had a habit of saying too much, and she worried about boring others.

Poppy moved her eyes to the stack of returned books. She needed to focus on things and experiences, not people, or her anxiety would be back.

Poppy looked up at the job roster for today. She raised an eyebrow as a delicious warmth flowed through her. She was on returned books duty. *Again.* Others hated the task, but Poppy relished it. More than she should.

Returned book duty felt like the times when she would find missing punctuation in a novel, when a complete feeling of joy would overcome her. Plus, she had the bonus of a room to herself, and the books, and two collection bins—one for the bits and pieces found in the pages, and the other for books beyond repair.

Poppy collected the large box of returned books from the book drop, replaced it with an empty one, and carried the full box to the returns room. She set up her work space. Sat on the cushioned chair and donned her rubber gloves.

First, she made a very tall book stack, only because she

liked challenging herself to how high she could stack the books before they toppled over. Twenty-three-books-tall-today. For now. She pulled out her phone and took a picture of the book stack, and then a selfie with them. They were like family and friends after all.

She grabbed the top novel and started to perform the librarian's book life or book death ritual.

> 1. The book smelling. Keeping the book a ruler's length from your face, inhale through your nose. If it smells weird, discard it. Note the title of the book for replacing. Check. ✔
> 2. The page flick. Riffle through the pages and check for damage, and for artefacts left in the books by readers…

Poppy smiled and held the book ready to riffle. She was a professional riffler, her technique perfected when she was little, making flip-books where the art moved along the page, like a movie. Like her mind. Snapshots of life.

Until the snapshots stopped on that day.

A newspaper article fell out.

Poppy picked it up. It was the article about Twisty, aka, Schnitzel Von Krumm, and how the library had won the right to use him as a reading dog to encourage children to read in the library. And grown-ups as well, Poppy wanted to add.

She smiled at the memory of one day when a four-year-old boy lined up his cars next to Schnitzel Von Krumm and read a picture book to him and his cars. Schnitzel sat perfectly and attentively, and couldn't tell that the little boy had made up the words. It was the act of copying reading that mattered at that stage in the boy's reading journey. The boy patted Schnitzel with a proud smile on his face. And that's what counted.

And the kids were encouraged to use the library Polaroid camera to photograph Schnitzel in the act of being read to, and add the picture to the "Schnitzel Von Krumm Wall of Fame".

Poppy gave a crooked smile. She hadn't yet told the library what Schnitzel's real name was. His library pseudonym name was perfect for the home of books. Twisty even responded to Schnitzel Von Krumm like he did with his given name.

Book life to that novel. Check. ✔

Poppy popped the book onto the trolley for quarantining for twenty-four hours before re-shelving.

Health and safety rules.

She reached for the next book and repeated the process.

Book stink. Unsalvageable. Book death. Check. ✔

And she continued.

And she collected a feather, a pressed flower, a five dollar note, a photo of a happy couple, a recipe for chocolate cake, a pornographic image, and Bronte's life list:

1. *Meet a man.*
2. *Buy a house.*
3. *Have a baby.*
4. *Make a home.*
5. *Repeat step 3 as required.*

Poppy laughed then frowned. The list needed rewriting. She grabbed a scrap of paper and wrote:

1. Meet a kind man who makes me laugh but not so much that I pee myself.

2. Buy a house that comes with its own cleaner and chef.

2.5. Create something that everybody needs and makes a lot of passive income so I can progress onto number three. Use cheap components so that people have to keep buying the so-called creation so the passive income doesn't end.

3. Have a baby who is well-behaved and toilet trained from birth who knows how to order groceries online.

4. Make the said house into a home that is filled with clean toilets and floors and clean washing and kids who play outside from sun-up to sun-down so they don't mess up the house.

4.5 And I suppose, add a large sprinkle of love, acceptance, happiness and forgiveness into the home, even if you have to steal the sprinkles from the tooth fairy.

5. Repeat step 3 as required.

6. Offload the kids before the age of 20 so you can spend more time with number 1 on the list.

Poppy read her list out loud. Because that's what writers do with their writing. She bobbed her head up and down like a ridiculous car bobblehead. Like the replica one of Jane she had made. Only, she didn't have a car to put it in, so she put it in different places in the house for plain Jane who didn't have any fun. The time she Blu Tacked it to the ceiling was the best. She wondered how long Jane would take to find it.

Six weeks!

As Poppy continued on her librarian's "book life or book

death ritual", she put aside the new novels that had ripped pages, or pages that had been defaced.

Or new novels that couldn't be repaired.

Or new novels that were exactly in the size of 6" x 9".

Or new novels that only had the crème coloured pages.

She carefully removed five pages from each of those novels after using her extraordinarily fast reading ability, beyond anyone her father had ever met, and after studying the story line notes on her phone. And pocketed the pages.

She was a rifler as well as a riffler.

She preferred to call herself a collector-of-sentences-and-paragraphs. Some would call her a page thief, but a word detective was more apt.

She was, after all, looking-for-something-specific.

Poppy stood and stretched after her duty was done, then stepped into the world of imagination. Of fiction and non-fiction. Of quiet people with busy minds. Of an entire wall dedicated to adding your own art, your mind-print, onto the library wall. And the superbly kid friendly inviting space instigated by her. Of Schnitzel Von Krumm delighting and drawing in visitors with his Minion costume.

He was becoming famous. Instafamous.

At the end of the day, Poppy and the Minion Sausage Dog called Schnitzel Von Krumm, who was really Oliver Twist, who she called Twisty, rode home, collecting beeps-and-smiles once more. Poppy stopped outside the three story, seven bedroom, Victorian Terrace house. Scaffolding was up. The painters were there.

She wondered what colour plain Jane was going to choose after asking for opinions?

Poppy entered the house, removed Twisty's outfit, put her bicycle under the steps, then went to the kitchen.

And there was a note. On white paper. From Jane.

Hi Poppy,

I hope your day was great.
The house painters will be here for three days.
We are back to our usual routine now that we have all settled in.
1.   Feed Oliver Twist his dinner. He doesn't need a walk after working Mondays.
2.   Make your own dinner and clean up.

Thanks, Jane

Poppy folded the note and placed it in her pocket of pages and words, then went to the kitchen to prepare dinner. She looked about the spick and span kitchen. She didn't want to mess it up. Food delivery it was.

'Dinner, Twisty!' Poppy called after she had placed his Dachshund food into his white bowl. 'Who's a good boi!' she said.

She released Twisty out into the backyard for a toilet stop, then rolled her eyes when he returned with a bone-in-his-mouth, and dropped it into his collection of dog-things-box. She closed the back door and went to her bedroom and turned on the light.

She pulled out the pieces-of-paper from her pocket and placed them on her study desk. She picked up the note from Jane and put it into her Box-of-Jane-Notes.

Like a-box-of-history.

A plain box for plain Jane. She wondered if her sisters did the same?

Then she lined up her rifled pages from novels, and read them carefully.

She turned to the wall behind her bed. To the three hundred and fifty-two pages of ripped out pages of bestselling novels placed on her wall.

She *was* writing her own novel.

Matching the pieces of stories written by other authors to create her own story. It was complicated and challenging. But Poppy loved the myriad of possibilities it offered. And she loved the task of keeping her plot going through the words of others. It was going to be a masterpiece. A bestseller.

Poppy carefully placed the new pages of her book on the wall. Then grabbed her work bag and pulled out the brown paper bag. Inside it was today's treasure-trove-of-book-inserts. She added today's haul to her collection—a bookmark, a feather, a black and white photo of a romantic couple, some kid's artwork, Bronte's life plan, and a leaf. People leaving traces of themselves behind. But not the pornographic picture. She had flushed it down the toilet at the library while she dry retched. Apt.

Poppy found her blue note paper and grabbed a pencil. Her blue note paper supplied by Jane. Why couldn't she choose her own blue coloured paper?

> *Dearest Jane,*
>
> *I had a good day today. I think I like this house. It feels like a new beginning and a place that will be our forever home.*
>
> *I met a lovely man at the bus stop this morning. Although he didn't look at or comment about Twisty's Minion costume. You know what Dad always said, don't trust a man who doesn't love dogs.*
>
> *Kindly,*
> *Poppy*

Poppy folded her note and took it to the long wooden dining table and put in the Jar-of-Jane-Notes jar in front of Jane's dining chair.

The-plain-white-chair.

Then returned to her room, picked up her pencil and started to sketch on her art wall. This is one of the things she loved about moving into a new house. She could start her wall art all over again.

She didn't have a particular plan in mind for this wall art. Except that it was free-form and free-flowing and reactive to the day.

And today was a good day. So her artwork was uplifting.

This time.

Chapter 12

Monday night
Jane

Jane Piccadilly stood on her bedroom verandah and looked down to see if Poppy had turned off her light at 9pm. She had. She gave a nod of approval, then returned to her bed and snuggled under the cover. Oliver Twist snored in his own bed.

Jane's mind was mulling over Violet and all the times they had to move. Was she angry about something? Or was it just her temperament?

She pulled out her phone and hit speed dial. Her father answered the video call after three rings.

'Hi Dad.'

'Hello, my girl. How is Alice?' Frank said.

'Jane, Dad. Call me Jane, remember.'

'Alice Piccadilly the 4th. Alice *Jane* Piccadilly. What's up?'

'Violet is what's up. I need you to tell me about when she was young,' said Jane on her video call. Maybe her mother and father could pinpoint flaws in Violet's personality, even as a youngster.

Jane watched as her father wiped a hand over his face on the video call. 'The Violet,' he said, 'her hands stayed purple for a long time after her birth. Your mother thought the colour and name were perfect for her.'

'Oh goodness, yes,' Jane's mother interjected for once. 'The doctors thought she had something wrong with her heart. But no, I think she was just born angry! She would have violent tantrums demanding that she was right, and she deserved what she was asking for. She would even stomp her feet. But I knew there was more beneath that tumultuous personality. She calmed when she was plaiting the horse's mane, or brushing the dog, or playing hairdresser with my hair—which was quite relaxing I might add. I bought her one doll—you know I detest dolls, Jane, but I bought her one just so she could be creative with their hair. And then there was the doll with the different wigs she could change. That was a big hit!'

Jane smiled. 'I remember that doll! So she has always had that violent streak?'

Frank rubbed his chin and took a deep breath while Jane's mother lifted her "hambag" onto her lap and pulled out a ham sandwich and took a bite, staring straight ahead. 'I'm afraid so.'

'Papa, would you call her dangerous to others?'

'Absolutely not! The Piccadilly's would never hurt another person. That is outrageous!'

Jane nodded. 'I agree.' But she wasn't so sure about Violet.

Jane's mother finished her ham sandwich.

'Thanks for the chat, Mum and Dad.' Jane smiled at her

parents, who smiled back. 'Good night, Dad. Good night, Mum. Love you.'

'Good night, Jane. Love you too, my girl.'

Jane disconnected the call, and leaned over to turn off her light. She rolled onto her side and positioned her arms and legs in a pretend-dead-in-bed pose, emptying her mind until she was asleep.

And that was a day, and a night.

Chapter 13

❀

Tuesday
Violet

'S hhi!' Violet's false eyelash was stuck to her forehead. She wanted to swear properly. She really did. And if she didn't live in the house with prim and proper Jane, she would. She removed the eyelash and looked down at the dog. 'Ollie Wollie, no more jumping at me! Sit!' She leaned toward the mirror and positioned her eyelash, successfully. She stood tall and battered her eyes, looking this way and that.

Perfect. Failure-was-never-a-choice.

She pulled out the bright red lipstick, removed the cap and wound out the colour, and leaned toward the mirror. Oliver Twist jumped at her again, sending a line of lipstick up her right cheek making her look like the Joker. Violet wanted to swear properly again, but Jane's room was beside hers and she didn't want to incur the wrath of Jane for swearing, or have to donate money to the swear jar.

The-*bloody*-swear-jar.

Again.

Like a thousand times.

Two dollars each time.

So Violent closed her eyes instead, and counted to ten, waiting for her anger to dissipate. Then she turned on her heel and whooshed Oliver Twist out of her en suite and shut the door.

She emerged twenty minutes later, her blonde, long-fringed pixie hair cut hair-sprayed into position, her makeup flawless. She rummaged through her closet for Tuesday's black shirt and black skinny jeans, her work uniform, spied her purple shoes and got dressed. She grabbed her designer purple handbag, and left her room, closing the door behind her.

A Jane rule.

Then skipped down the steps to the ground floor.

Her favourite client, the vintage Ness, was coming in today. And that meant it was guaranteed to be a good day.

Violet exited the house, dodging the scaffolding posts. She made her way to her vintage blue and white Kombi Van Deluxe, but turned her head to the noise from the right. A man was sitting at the bus stop, his drink bottle rolling down the footpath.

Violet ran to pick it up, and returned it to the man.

He held out his hand but didn't look at her. 'Thank you so much!'

'You're welcome.'

'Is that… Magnolia Grandiflora?' he said with an Italian accent.

Violet beamed. 'Yes. My favourite perfume,' she said, lifted her wrist to her nose and inhaled the sweet floral notes.

'It's stunning on you,' he said and gave a slight smile.

Violet frowned. Was this a pick up line? 'Off to work?' she asked to change the direction of the conversation.

'Yes, but with the Tuesday trudge.'

'The Tuesday trudge?'

'You know… dragging my feet.'

Violet laughed. 'Love your carpet bag and glasses by the way!'

'Thank youuuuu—'

'Violet, and no, not my favourite flower, nor colour.'

'You get asked that a lot?'

'Alwaysssss—'

'Luciano, and no, my favourite food is not pizza.'

Violet giggled. 'Have a great day, Luciano!'

'Likewise, Violeto.'

Violet smiled then turned and looked up at the seven bedroom, three story, Victorian terrace house. The front facade was now white.

A white-house-with-a-red-front-door.

Violet squinted and pulled out her purple sunglasses.

She clambered into her Kombi Van and turned on the klak-klak engine, turned on her good-vibes music list, popped some gum in her mouth, then drove with a smile singing along to the music. At each red light she blew a bubble, and popped it.

She parked her Kombi Van at the back of the salon, turned off the klak-klak engine and waited for the splatter and the bang and the sigh to end, then grabbed her handbag and entered the shop via the back door.

'Haaallllooooo!' she called. It echoed back to her from her fellow hair artisans. Violet placed her handbag into her locker, donned her black apron, and walked through to the front desk.

'Oh, thank you,' she said as she picked up her doppio— double shot of espresso coffee—inhaling the intense aroma, then took a sip.

Coffee = Contraband in the house.

Jane, Jane, tea sipping, Jane.

Jane = Bossy.

Violet looked over her day map, twice—three clients and housekeeping. Two nice clients, one not, and housekeeping. Violet bobbed her head. Once. Then skulled the remainder of her coffee. 'Woooo!' she said, smacking her lips. 'Bring it on!'

The doorbell ding-dinged. Client number one. Plus two angry children in tow. Violet smiled through her gritted teeth. 'Lovely to see you, Gabbi!' Violet lead her to a chair in front of the mirror, where Gabbi took a seat. 'How are you?' Violet asked, wanting to ask why she brought along her two outrageously wild, disobedient, loud kids, who would run feral around the salon, swing on chairs and rip pages in magazines.

Violet's eye twitched and her body tremored at-the-ick.

'Great,' she said to Violet, then 'STOP JUMPING ON THE SOFA!' at her kids. 'Sorry, Violet. I couldn't get a sitter for them.'

Violet smiled politely and nodded her head, knowing exactly why she couldn't get a sitter for her divine offspring. 'What are we doing today?'

'I'd love a loooong hair wash with that magical head massage you do.'

The boy screamed. Some cut-off hair on the floor had touched him. 'THAT HAIR THAT WAS ONCE ALIVE AND GROWING AND NOW IT'S BEEN MURDERED!'

Violet kept a smile on her face, her lips pressed so hard together she thought she would never open her mouth again. But then she did. 'I'm sorry, Gabbi. We have no water today. But I can still cut your hair—the usual?' Lie.

'MUMMMM. HE POKED HIS TONGUE OUT AT ME!'

Violet's eyes widened and her eyebrows-shot-up.

Gabbi pulled a picture out of her pocket. It was a celebrity. 'I'd like that hairstyle today!'

Violet took the picture from Gabbi as another scream bounced off-the-walls, followed by Gabbi screeching out, 'STOP IT. WAIT TILL YOUR FATHER FINDS OUT HOW YOU HAVE BEHAVED!'

Violet rolled her eyes. She hated it when mothers offloaded behaviour control to the father. Mothers are perfectly capable of behaviour control too. She looked more closely at the thumb size picture. *Oh, that hair style,* she thought, *the hairstyle that she doesn't know how to cut.* 'It's a great hair style, Gabbi. It will look amazing on you.' And fifty million other people, she wanted to add.

The apprentice hair stylist stopped beside them with a smock and placed it on Gabbi.

'I'll be right back,' said Violet. She walked with haste to the back room and opened YouTube on her phone and found the Jellyfish Cut tutorial.

She sighed. It was more complicated than she liked, and the kids were fighting again.

Violet returned to the floor and sidled up to Carly. 'I need a favour. I can't do a haircut with those screaming kids. Can you please give Gabbi the Jellyfish Cut? I will take the kids outside.'

'The Jellyfish Cut? Seriously?'

Violet nodded. 'I know, right.'

'And you'll take the kids out?' Carly beamed her a smile.

Violet nodded again. 'You can thank me later.'

'It's a deal!'

Violet returned to her client. 'Gabbi, I'm going to take your kids for an ice-cream so you can have some peace and quiet for a bit. You know you deserve it. Carly will create your hairstyle and you can enjoy the—'

'Oh. Will you?' Gabbi let out a breath of relief. 'You don't know how much those kids push my buttons! Can I get a coffee with Irish whiskey?'

Violet laughed. Then she realised Gabbi was serious. 'Unfortunately we don't have a license to serve alcohol.' She turned to the kids and called, 'Who wants an ice-cream?' And with that, Violet was out the door with two in tow.

She returned an hour later and the kids sat on the sofa with exemplary behaviour.

Gabbi, all finished with her new doo, walked over to Violet with a new confidence in her step.

'Wow! You look fabulous!' Violet said, wanting to add, if not a little ridiculous.

'Thanks, I love it,' said Gabbi then pointed to her troublesome two. 'How did you get them to behave?'

'Bribery.' Violet raised her eyebrows. 'Arthur. Yetzel. Come!' *Just like training furpets,* Violet thought. 'I love how well you have waited on the sofa. Here's your treat, like we agreed.' She handed them each a lolly.

Gabbi's mouth dropped open. Violet wanted to say, Behaviour Modification 101, reward the behaviour you want. 'Thanks, Gabbi. See you next time. Have a wonderful day! Bye kids!'

Violet kept smiling and waving at them until they were all out the door. Then she relaxed her smile and released a breath like she had been holding it since she was eleven. She turned and grabbed the broom and swept the floor, removing all traces of Gabbi and the mess her kids left behind. She was the one who needed the Irish whiskey coffee! How did her own mother handle seven kids?

Daughters.

Moody, excitable, disagreeable, sweet-ish daughters.

The lovely daughters of Alice Jane Piccadilly the 3rd.

The doorbell dinged. Client number two. For Violet. 'Glooooooria. Hello!' Violet's eyes wandered over Gloria's hair. Had she washed it in the last two weeks? Violet indicated to her where to sit and placed a cape on her. Violet reluctantly touched a few strands of hair. She hadn't washed it recently. Thoughts of grease and exploding teenage pimples and oily skin aimed arrows at her with echoes of eeeeewwww! 'What would you like today?'

'Just a trim please.'

'Sure. How much off?'

'Oh… you know, just half a centimetre.'

Violet smiled. But not with her eyes. She was sure she could cut just half a centimetre of hair off without too much damage. 'Let's go over to the basin for a shampoo.' Violet settled her in for a shampoo. 'Back soon,' she said, then went out the back of the shop.

She sidled up to Amy, the apprentice. 'I'll pay you $50 to wash Gloria's hair.'

'Deal,' Amy said and left at once.

Violet closed her eyes. She was sure she was allergic to washing hair, or the water, or the shampoo, or the conditioner.

Or the… hairdressing.

Violet returned to the back of the salon and opened her phone and googled "Basic Hair Trim Tutorial", picked up her scissors and practised cutting off some hair on Amy's human hair mannequin head. Just half a centimetre.

When she re-emerged in the salon, Gloria was sitting in the chair in front of the mirror, Amy drying her hair with a towel.

'Thanks, Amy.' Violet combed through Gloria's hair like she knew what she was doing. 'Chin to chest,' she said, and combed again, ready to cut the middle section first. She placed the hair between her fingers, visually measured half a centimetre and snip!

'Ow!' Violet said, pulled a tissue out of her pocket and wrapped it around her finger.

Blood.

'Amy!' Violet called. 'Would you mind combing through Gloria's hair while I get a band-aid.'

Violet went out the back of the salon to her locker. She opened it up and placed the red stained tissue with the rest. Ten of them. Red ink on tissue.

A prop.

She placed a new tissue with a red stain on it into her pocket then found a large band-aid for her finger, trying to remember which finger she'd pretended to cut.

The index finger. That was it. Wasn't it? And stuck it on.

She returned to Amy and Gloria. 'All good.' She held up her band-aid finger. 'Too sore to continue though. Gloria, do you mind if Amy does your trim? She knows what she's doing—hairdressing school student-of-the-week and all.'

Gloria smiled. 'Sure.'

Violet watched on as Amy worked. And finished. Happy client. Violet looked at her watch. An hour for washing and sweeping, lunch, and then her favourite client would be here. Ness. Vintage Ness.

Violet pottered around the salon. She was sure she was allergic to scissors too. And really, she tried so hard not to gag when there was a hair in her coffee. Just thinking about it gave her the ick.

At noon she left the salon and went to the park to eat. Whilst in the middle of a mouthful of her salad sandwich, her phone pinged. She wiped her hand, pulled out her phone and opened it up. It was a group text from Jane.

Hi everyone. We have an attic. Fully enclosed with walls and windows and a timber floor. Perfect for Mum and

*Dad. Does anyone disagree with them living in the attic?
It will be self-contained with their own kitchen and en
suite. Let me know soon.*

Violet rolled her eyes. Mum and Dad always ended up at their residence. Wasn't it time that the parents lived independently? And Jane? It would be good to get rid of Jane. Bossy Jane. Maybe Jane could move out of the house and move in with the parents. That would solve the problem.

Violet texted back: *All good with me.*

What else could she do? Nobody liked to incur the wrath of Jane. Scary Jane. It wasn't worth the angst.

Fifteen minutes after Violet was back at the salon, the door dinged.

'Ness. Hello!' Violet walked over to the ninety-two-year-old and offered her elbow. Ness put her arm through Violet's and they walked side by side to the salon chair like they were best friends. Like grandmother and granddaughter even.

'You look fabulous, Ness!' said Violet.

'Thank you, dear.'

'What would you like today?'

'The usual, please. And a cup of tea.' Ness gave Violet a wink. Their secret code.

'Your wish is my command.' Violet bent at her waist with a roll of her hand like a servant. She made Ness a cup of "wink tea" in Ness' personal teacup and saucer, and returned. She placed it in front of her on the bench, the smell of bourbon drifting and smiling around them, and started to brush Ness' hair.

Sirens. In the distance. Came closer. They looked out the shop front and counted seven ambulances. In a hurry.

Ness put her hand to her forehead and closed her eyes. Violet wondered if she was going to cark it.

Right-here-in-the-salon-chair.

It had happened once. On her day off. 'Are you okay, Ness?'

'Yes dear. The ambulances reminded me of the time… about twenty something years ago… when seven ambulances flew past my house. A terrible tragedy it was… that poor family.'

Violet stilled for a moment. 'What happened?'

'They lost six daughters.'

Violet frowned and shook her head slowly.

'Yes. That poor family.'

Nausea rose in Violet. 'Excuse me,' she said, and raced out the back door and leaned over, breathing through pursed lips. She closed her eyes and saw flashing red and blue lights. She shook her head, and when the nausea abated, she returned to Ness.

'So sorry, Ness.' Violet reached for the brush and picked up where she left off.

Ness closed her eyes, enjoying each stroke of the brush caressing her scalp. It was all she came for, plus a hair wash and head massage, a blow dry, and a social visit. 'Your last name is spelled the same way as theirs, you know.'

Violet's heart cracked. 'Long lost relatives perhaps. Or not even related. Just a name in common. Did anyone survive the plunge into the lake?'

'It was a dam. The mother and father, and a girl survived. She was eight.'

'Unimaginable pain,' Violet said.

'Yes. Did I say how it happened?' Ness said.

'No,' Violet said, her heart thumping, her hands shaking. She could feel a rage brewing inside her. 'What happened?' Violent said.

Ness frowned. 'Oh gosh,' she said. 'It's there in my head. I'll remember it at some time or another.' Ness took a long sip of her "wink tea". 'Let me just enjoy this moment with my hair.'

Violet's shoulders dropped with relief. She didn't like the unbearable painful stories spoken in the salon. Like gossip. The truth changed because that person wasn't there on that day, or night, or moment.

'Can you paint my nails today, Violet? I've got a dinner date at the nursing home tonight. I must remember to put my teeth in this time though!' Ness laughed.

'What a sight that must have been, Ness!' Violet laughed. 'Amy will wash your hair and while she is drying it, I'll do your nails. What colour?'

'The colour of you, dear!'

'Are you sure you want that colour?' Violet said with a grimace. The colour of violent was not a nice colour.

'Yes. Violet will match my dress perfectly!'

Violet walked Ness over to the wash basin and Amy took over. She walked out the back of the salon and poured a glass of water, lifted it to her lips and drank, her hands shaking.

She walked out the back door. Sunshine would help. It always did. Violet leaned against the paint-washed brick wall, closed her eyes and lifted her face to the sun.

Like recharging.

Fading the memory of flashing red and blue lights. And the silver blanket wrapped around her. Her mama's screams… all imagined. She had a vivid hyper-imagination.

Violet opened her eyes and returned to the salon. Ness was sitting back in the chair.

Violet grabbed the nail manicure set and the violet coloured nail polish. She pushed a small chair toward Ness, and sat opposite her and started to create a violet dream on her nails.

'You look just like her,' Ness said.

'Who?' Violet's head snapped up. She hoped Ness didn't catch the quick roll of her eyes.

'The mother.'

Violet stopped painting Ness' nails. 'I get that all the time. It's called the butcher-on-the-bus-phenomenon. You know, a nagging sense of familiarity. I may look a little like someone, but not exactly.'

'That must be it, dear,' Ness said.

Violet bobbed her head and continued nail painting while Amy blow dried her hair and styled it.

'You know, Ness, I also get told I look like Marilyn Munroe.'

'And so did Annie, or was it Alice?' Ness said, frowning.

Violet let out a silent sigh. *Distraction.* 'Hands up, Ness. How do your nails look?'

'Marvellous, dear, marvellous. He's ninety-nine and mostly blind you know, so he won't be able to see them.' Ness laughed and her face lit up like an angel.

'So… you're saying, we could do a punk rock hair style for you and he would still say you looked beautiful?'

Ness roared out laughing. 'Absolutely,' she said. 'Let's do it next time!'

'Sounds like a plan,' Violet said, helped her up from the chair and walked her outside to her driver. 'See you next week,' Violet said.

Violet stood on the sidewalk, waving to Ness as they left. Violet noted that she would have to redirect conversations better. She hated being mistaken for somebody else. Especially connected to that tragedy twenty-four years ago. She had heard about it before, but blocked the details out. She hated how she absorbed all the emotions from tragedies of other people.

She returned to the salon. Her afternoon was busy.

Towels washed. ✔
Equipment sterilised. ✔
Combs and brushes de-haired and disinfected. ✔
Bins cleaned. ✔
Mirrors cleaned. ✔
Chairs and benches wiped with disinfectant. ✔
Wash basins cleaned. ✔
Floor mopped before leaving. ✔
Not a single strand of hair cut. ✔

Every day had a beginning and an ending.

And today, Violet liked that the day was ending.

She grabbed her handbag from her locker and walked to her van. She started the klak-klak engine, turned on her good-vibes music list, popped some gum in her mouth, then drove without a smile. At each red light she let out a loud breath. She hated it when people offloaded negative words and emotions and memories onto her.

She parked her Kombi Van in the driveway of the terrace. Turned off the klak-klak engine and waited for the splatter and the bang and the sigh, then grabbed her handbag and walked to the front door.

The-front-red-door.

With painter's tape of squares on it.

Way-too-many-squares.

But nevertheless, home felt good today. Even though it was still slightly unfamiliar. She unlocked the front door to the four-legged welcoming committee giving her the side-eye-of-judgement.

'Ollie Wollie! You wouldn't believe my day! Jane will not be happy.' Oliver Twist recognised her now, and Violet squatted down closer to Oliver Twist. 'Who's a good hot dog? Let's have dinner before Jane arrives. Let's get organised.'

Violet retreated to her room after dinner, and picked up her lavender coloured note paper and wrote to Jane.

She reread her note, discovering she had written Viole*n*t instead of Violet. She crossed out the "n". She hated it when she absent-mindedly wrote Violent instead of Violet. Was that what they called a Freudian slip?

Violet folded the lavender note and took it downstairs to the long wooden dining table and shoved it into the Jar-of-Jane-Notes, then returned to her room.

9pm was lights out.

Just like a boarding school.

Bloody Jane!

Chapter 14

Tuesday night
Jane

Jane Piccadilly opened her bedroom door so it was slightly ajar. The hallway of the second story was dark, and there was no light shining from underneath Violet's door. She gave a nod of approval, then returned to her bed and snuggled under the cover, Oliver Twist buried himself under his blanket in his own bed.

Jane closed her eyes and tried to sleep. But fields of daisies kept clouding her mind, not matter how hard she tried to think of other things.

She pulled out of phone and hit speed dial. Her father answered the video call after three rings.

'Hi Dad,' Jane said. 'Hi, Mum.'

'Hello, my girl. How is Alice?' Frank said.

'Jane, Dad. Call me Jane, remember.'

'Alice Piccadilly the 4th. Alice *Jane* Piccadilly. What's up?'

'I had a funny dream about Daisy—she was wearing a dress!' said Jane.

Frank laughed while her mother lifted her "hambag" onto her lap, opened it and pulled out a ham sandwich. Disengagement complete.

'Dear Daisy James, the boy I never had. That would NEVER happen!'

'I know Papa. Dreams are so weird like that!' Jane focused on the screen. Her parents had seemingly ran out of things to say, and just sat there looking at her. Blinking. Swaying a little.

'So, I'd better get some shut eye now. Bye Mum. Bye Dad. It's so lovely to chat with you both. Love you.'

'Love you too, dear,' her father said.

Jane turned off her phone and placed it on her bedside table. She dangled her right foot off the side of the bed for a new pretend-dead-in-bed pose. But then lifted it up quickly and put her foot back under the covers—monsters-under-the-bed and all...

Jane Piccadilly closed her eyes. *Death play* her psychologist had called her death poses. And reassured her it was quite normal under her circumstances.

Jane counted up to seventy snores performed by the talented Oliver Twist, and fell asleep.

And that was a day, and a night.

Chapter 15

Wednesday
Daisy

Daisy looked out the window. The doors of the sky had opened. Pissing down. Like yesterday. She reached her arms high and stretched, then ran her fingers through her long brown hair and pushed her fringe to the side. It was a hair plait sort of day. That's what hair plaits were for. Rainy bloody days. Maybe she should chuck a sickie.

She closed her eyes and wished she had an indoor job. Like in an office. But then she stopped that barrel rolling thought. She liked it where she was. The people were quiet, even though they had a thousand stories to tell. And they never complained. Not. Bloody. Ever.

Daisy descended the stairs and went to the kitchen.

Oliver Twist gave her the side-eye-of-judgement.

'Good morning, Hot Diggity Dog. Oli, Oli, Oli … Oi. Oi. Oi!' When Oliver recognised her, she was rewarded with a rapturous tail wag and short bark hello. Daisy set her yellow teacup on the bench and brewed her Wakeup tea. A green tea with ginger and peppermint notes. A sprightly sip! She popped in two slices of bread into the toaster, and set out a bread and butter plate, knife, butter, Peanut Butter, and Vegemite, ready for the flurry of activity.

After the flurry, she sat at her yellow chair at the timber table and looked at her toast with half Peanut Butter, and half butter and Vegemite. Spread geometrically. Because geometry exposes the beauty and harmony in our environment, her dad said. And on her toast it was like a collision of triangular beauty and colour on a square. Daisy smiled.

The rain poured harder. Daisy looked out the window wishing she could stay at home. Like she did when she was a full-time carpenter. But now, she was the carpenter, machinery driver and landscaper. There was always something to be done. Rain, hail or shine.

The grandfather clock chimed. Seven times with a discordant bong in the middle. Like seven sisters. With Jane as the middle child. Daisy's heart rate picked up. She was late. She folded her toast in half, marrying the Vegemite and Peanut Butter together and ate in haste, washing the unique flavour down with her Wakeup tea. It sure packed a punch.

She raced upstairs and donned her black cotton cargo work pants and black long-sleeved shirt and pink and black beanie.

She grabbed her yellow umbrella, backpack and deep yellow steel capped boots, raced out the front door and put her sports shoes on.

She looked up at the sky and shook her head. The rain was

unrelenting. She straightened up, shouldered her backpack and popped open her umbrella and made a dash for her yellow Holden EH 1964 Ute.

But she didn't get there.

A dark blue umbrella flew past. She looked to her right and saw a gentleman sitting at the bus stop in a fluster. The umbrella was way down the street, and still moving. Unretrievable. So Daisy walked over to the man and stood next to him, her umbrella creating a safe haven for him, like she was stopping asteroids from bombing him, only allowing the stardust from the Ancient of Days to touch him.

'Crikey Charlie this rain!' she said.

'I'll say.'

'You'll say what?'

The man shook his head. 'Never mind.'

'What's that drongo doing up there?' said Daisy.

The man turned his head to the right.

'The other right,' said Daisy.

He turned his head to the left. 'I'm not sure. It hard to see!'

'Erg. What a boofhead!'

'What happened? I'm Luciano, and you're…'

'Daisy.'

'Like the cow?'

'Like the flower... the drongo, he's… ugh! Not worth mentioning. Some things can never be unseen.'

'Traumatised?'

'Defo. Hey, I can give you a lift to work if you like,' Daisy said.

'Yeah, nah. I'm good. The bus should be here soon.'

'Righto,' said Daisy and she stood there still. Her in her dark carpenter clothes with yellow work boots and a yellow umbrella, and Luciano in his wet dark blue business suit and a floral teal carpet bag.

After a moment of silence Luciano said, 'You don't have to wait with me, Daisy.'

'I know. I'm just hoping I get into your good books so when you die you'll leave me that carpet bag, and the contents.'

'What if it's filled with incontinence pads for the elderly?'

'I'll need them one day.'

'What if it's filled with the bones of my beloved dog?'

'I always wanted to be a palaeontologist.'

'You'd like to work with bones?'

'Yeah.'

Luciano stood. 'Bus is coming.'

Daisy looked up the street. There was definitely no bus coming, sight wise or hearing wise. And then there it was, looming, getting larger as it came closer and stopped with a squeak of brakes. The door whooshed open and Luciano stepped inside.

It left, and Daisy stood standing. In the rain. Waiting for him to say thanks for keeping the rain off him. She thought maybe the letters would puff out of the exhaust of the bus, and arrange themselves into a word. But it would most probably be "rack off!"

Daisy took a deep breath, then walked to her Ute, got in and drove to work. The local cemetery. The dead part of town. Where the quiet people lived. She was a caretaker. A groundskeeper.

She entered her work shed and checked the list of jobs for today. It was busy.

Two funerals. Two graves. Previously dug in preparation. Thank goodness. And one fresh grave to dig. She also had to place the tents and chairs for outdoor memorial services. With this weather, it was a black umbrella day when the cemetery would be adorned in a sea of gloom. Black clothes. Black umbrellas. Black suits and dresses and shoes and handbags. Black.

The opposite of Jane. Plain Jane.

Daisy threw on her midnight blue rain jacket and rain pants, grabbed two portable water pumps and put them into the trailer attached to the garden tractor, and drove to the grave sites. The covers were up but there was still water in the four foot graves. So she threw the suction hoses in to pump out the water. An hour and a half before the graveside service time she would put out the green synthetic grass around the grave and chairs and an umbrella supply. They were always prepared on time. Even in weather like this.

Daisy and Edward stood in the distance behind some trees and waited for the services to finish. Then they grabbed their shovels and walked to the first grave and started to shovel dirt on top of the coffin. They always did this until all the mourners were gone. It meant more to them then, instead of the heartless mini-digger pushing the earth over their dearly beloved.

Daisy looked around while she shovelled. 'I wish they'd rack off now, Eddy. My back is done with this water laden dirt.' When she looked back into the grave, the coffin was floating. FLOATING!

The coffin-that-was-floating.

Like it was a boat floating on an ocean of tears.

'Crap. Just what we need. A bloody floating coffin to make the mourners scream and faint. You might have to go and tell them a furphy to get them to move on or we'll be here 'til Chrissy.'

Edward loped off then slowed with his head bowed, his hands together in front of his chest, like a mortician, and the mourners left at once. When he returned, Daisy went and grabbed the mini digger to speed up the dirt-in-the-hole, while it rained harder again.

And the coffin kept floating.

To the top.

Bobbing up and down with each shovel of dirt like it was dancing to the song of human cries.

Daisy pushed the coffin to the bottom of the grave with the bucket of the mini-digger, and left the weight of it there. The depth placement of coffins was specific according to council guidelines. Daisy climbed out of the mini-digger and shovelled dirt with Edward. It was slower but it got the job done. And then they had to repeat it all over again after the second funeral.

'Poor bloody ratbags,' Daisy said as she looked at the last filled in grave, wondering whether the occupants were having a good laugh. What a send-off!

Daisy drove the mini-digger to the new grave site. The rain had stopped. She climbed out and checked her location map and the marked out area. She looked at the graves on either side, and stilled at the list of names on one gravestone.

Six names.

Six girls.

Their earth time clock stopped on the same day.

A shiver ran down her spine. Daisy thought of her six sisters. She thought how she would feel if she was the only one left. Suddenly she couldn't breathe. She didn't want to dig the grave here. Next to those people. But she had a job to do.

She had to distract herself, so she got on with her job.

Daisy drove her yellow Holden EH 1964 Ute home in a blur. Auto-pilot driving they called it. Her mind wandering to thoughts completely unrelated to the everyday journey home. She thought about the events of the day. Technically, she was not the grave digger, she was the cemetery carpenter. Fixing this and that. But today, she was the grave digger.

The *bloody* grave digger.

And that grave of six sisters had rattled her to the core. She suddenly had the urge to get home and hug each of her sisters and tell them how much she loved them.

Daisy dragged her feet through the door to the sight of Oliver Twist with a bone-in-his-mouth. 'Oli, Oli, Oli… Oi. Oi. Oi!' she said more slowly than usual. He rolled over and she gave him a belly rub. Daisy was exhausted and needed sleep.

After a long shower, she sat at her study desk, grabbed her yellow note paper and pen, and wrote a note to Jane.

Daisy went downstairs to the long wooden dining table and pushed her yellow note into the Jar-of-Jane-Notes, and headed upstairs to bed and turned off the light.

Before 9pm.

Chapter 16

Wednesday night
Jane

Jane Piccadilly pretended to polish the banister rail to remove the non-existent dust. Her mother would approve. She glanced over at Daisy's room, checking to see if her light had been turned off at 9pm. It had. She gave a nod of approval, then returned to her room and opened her white French doors and the scent of roses floated in. She smiled and wondered if Rose too could smell the fruity notes floating with messages of love.

Jane closed her French doors and climbed into bed and snuggled under the cover. Thoughts of Rose entered her mind. One of two sisters she was the closest to. Rose who would run around with an empty frame of wood their father had made for her. She'd put it in front of objects and her sisters, like it was a photo frame. '*Click*. Perfect,' she would say.

Jane smiled. Her beautiful Rose.

She pulled out her phone and hit speed dial. She needed a Rose story from her mother or father. Her dad answered the video call after the third ring.

'Hi Dad. Hi Mum.'

'Hello, my girl. What's up?' Frank said.

'Tell me about when Rose was born,' said Jane.

Jane's father chuckled. 'We've told you that one a million times!'

'Well... I want to here it for the millionth and oneth time.' Jane frowned. Was oneth even a word?

Jane watched as her mother lifted her "hambag" and took out a ham sandwich and started to eat it.

Jane's dad shifted in his seat. 'Nope. One million times is sufficient!'

Jane pulled a sad face hoping he would change his mind. He didn't. But still, she loved the video calls with her parents. If only they would come to visit.

'When will you be able to come to live with us, Pa?'

Frank looked over at Alice. She was only half way through her ham sandwich. 'We'll try to visit first I think, Jane,' he said.

Jane nodded. 'Probably a wise thing to do.' Jane stared at her father's face for a moment more, then said, 'Gotta get some sleep now. Chat later. Mum, Dad, love you.'

'And we love you, my dear Alice Jane Piccadilly the 4th. Take care.'

Jane disconnected from the video call and placed her phone onto her bedside table and turned off the light.

She lifted her flaxen-coloured-hair from under her head and spread it out around her, like she was floating in water, lifeless.

She was playing with repressed memories her psychologist had said. Trauma does that. Fragments of her unconscious mind poking through. Part of her grief journey.

But when does grief end, Jane wondered.

She closed her eyes, tears drawing a line of sadness, encrypted with names and hearts of love, and Jane's broken heart. Then sleep sprinkled its embrace of the void of consciousness, where no thoughts or memories or emotions existed. The only place she could find peace.

And that was a day, and a night.

Chapter 17

Thursday
Rose

Rose looked at her schedule for Thursday.

- free time this morning
- a wedding in the afternoon

She smiled. She had time to take the hound for a walk to the café for a coffee. A real coffee. She needed it after three days of the white rose loose leaf tea Jane had bought for her. She wasn't a true tea drinker. She couldn't foster the courage to tell Jane she hated the rose tea. She couldn't foster the courage to tell Jane that just because her name was Rose, it didn't mean she liked everything rose coloured and rose related.

She smoothed down her long auburn wavy hair and exited her room, closed the door and looked up at the hole in the ceiling. She couldn't wait for the carpenters to arrive to fix it. Then she would stop getting that goosebumps feeling. Like ghosts in the attic.

Rose went downstairs to the kitchen. And there was Dash, giving her the side-eye-of-judgement. 'Dash!' she said, 'let's grab coffee.' Dash wiggled his dachshund butt when he recognised her, ran off and returned with his harness and lead and off they set. Out the front door, currently taped up for painting, along the weedy path beside the house to the driveway and out on to the footpath. As they walked past the bus stop, Dash barked.

'Dash, where are your manners?' said Rose.

'Good morning,' the man in the dark blue suit with the carpet bag said. 'And good morning to Dash.'

'I do apologise. He has such a dachshund attitude at times.'

'All good. He's just telling you a story, like all dogs.'

'That's one way of looking at it, I guess.' Rose gave Dash a pet. 'I've seen you here each morning. I'm Rose by the way.' *And I have photographed you often, sitting on the seat, getting onto the bus, reaching into your carpet bag, talking on your phone, taking off your glasses your eyes closed… clicking on that pen…* she wanted to add, but didn't.

'Luciano,' he said. 'Where's Dash taking you this morning?'

'I'm taking the Hound to the coffee shop. Hopefully they have puppucinos there.'

'Oh, they do,' said Luciano. 'Here comes my bus,' he added.

Rose frowned. She could not see nor hear a bus. But then there it was, approaching in the distance. 'Have a great day,' Rose said.

'Likewise, and lovely to meet you and the hound,' he said.

Two cappuccinos and three puppucinos later, Rose arrived back home, eager for the landscaping to be started. The yard was unsightly and she must remind Jane about it. Again. But she didn't want to be too pushy. She hated confrontation.

She walked up the four steps to the small verandah and slowed before the taped front door. What colour had Jane chosen for the door?

Rose entered the house and released Dash from his harness, then went up two flights of stairs to her room. She organised her photography equipment and packed it into her photography bag and looked at the film from her older camera that she had to develop. She loved digital photography for the ease and changes you could make to photos, like lying, but loved the process of developing photos from the negatives.

Real photographs. Unaltered. Raw.

Moments frozen in time.

Truth that couldn't be changed.

Rose went downstairs and out the back door to take some photographs with the old camera. She looked down at her feet when Dash dropped a bone he had dug up. Rose photographed it, picked it up and added it to the pile-of-bones in the laundry.

She returned to her room and changed out of her jeans and white T-shirt and into her black pants and T-shirt for the wedding photography, slipped on her black boots and grabbed her black leather camera bag. Rose bounded down two flights of stairs and put Dash in the kitchen and dining area and closed the door so he couldn't go to the front door, then stepped around the painter who was preparing the front door for painting, making sure she didn't get in his way because she would be devastated if she hindered him in some way.

'Sorry,' Rose said as she moved past him, even though she had done nothing.

Rose walked up the road to her pink moped and tied back her hair, then opened the back helmet storage and pulled out her black helmet and put it on.

She started the moped.

And then she was off.

At fifty kilometres per hour.

Driving as far to the left side of the road as she could. Annoying motorists who had to go around her.

'Sorry!' she called at each one of them, giving a sorry wave to the beepers. How she wished she could flick them the bird. At least once. But she could never do it in case she hurt someone's feelings. And *good* girls don't do that, her mother had said.

People didn't know how privileged they were to be driving cars. They didn't know how privileged she was to detour down a street at the drop of a hat to get to her destination, or to drive past the traffic jams with a hidden smirk.

After fifty minutes of riding, the vineyard with large wine barrels on either side of the entrance came into view. Sirromet Winery. Rose turned into the driveway and continued her way up the long pathway to the top of the hill, passing wallabies and an arbour on the left and Lavender Hill, standing beautifully against a colour splash of purple of the lavender field.

Rose parked her pink moped, stowed her helmet and entered the reception, meeting the wedding planner. There were three photographers today, including her, plus a videographer. Her role was one of photographing friends-and-family, creating document photography of the day. Snap shots. Candid photos. The love story seen through the eyes of the guests.

The guests... their supposedly unseen reactions. Captured by her.

Photojournalism it was called. Decentring herself, becoming the quietest voice at the wedding. This was Rose's favourite form of photography, as people changed when they saw a camera. Their behaviour changed. Their reactions changed. Their poses changed. Their emotions changed, the inner, raw, persona never captured. Truth never captured.

She was the invisible photographer, capturing the uncatchable.

Rose had started photographing before the guests arrived, the moment she entered the reception. She photographed hospitality workers, places and things, living and non-living. She photographed the open style wedding chapel, white, surrounded by rolling grape vines and manicured hedges and a lavender field. She captured the moment in time as the chapel breathed in, waiting for the exchange of hearts and rings to come. The white pews, the white bows on the end and the pastel coloured flowers on each bow. The rolling country fields. The chapel set in amongst the vineyards.

Rose toggled between digital shots and camera—35mm colour negative film. The before shots were done, so Rose walked to the Cellar Door and Café, tempted to savour a red wine while she waited for the guests to arrive. She ordered a cappuccino, not wanting to break her rule about drinking alcohol while working. She sat back and enjoyed a moment of destressing while getting her coffee hit, then walked back to the chapel to make herself invisible, to take photos of the guests, much like a sniper in an online war game.

Wait and shoot.

Smiles. Grimaces. Clothing and shoe malfunctions. A man with a black dog. *Odd.* Said dog poops but he doesn't pick it up. So Rose pulled a plastic bag out of her camera case and did her good deed, sealing the dog-poop-in-the-bag, and placed it into her camera bag as there were no bins nearby. Singlehandedly, she had saved a guest from a misfortune.

More photography. Hand holding. Arms around waists.

Male wandering eyes. Laughter. Crying flower girl. Momentarily. Blowing hairstyles. Capturing the calm. Capturing nerves as the groom and groomsmen arrived. The straightening of ties and bow ties. The adjusting of suit jackets. The whirlwind of anticipation as the bride arrived. The cellist. The expressions of guests.

The man with the black dog. Lurking. Handing a-note-to-a-guest. Then leaving.

The whispers as the bride walked down the aisle. The tilted heads. The dreamy eyes. The joy and jubilation of "I do".

Invisibly moving to different locations to take photos. Capturing moments. Emotion. Positivity. Negativity. Envy. Congratulations. Capturing truth. Behind the lens.

Rose followed the guests as they transitioned from the chapel to the light refreshments under the stunning fig trees. Then from the light refreshments to the reception in the Barrel Hall, located beneath the fine dining restaurant above, showcasing an authentic wine barrel backdrop, rustic brick arches and a warm cellar ambience. She moved invisibly around the large cellar, capturing moments in time. From sober to intoxicated. From conversations to arguments. From sitting to dancing. From stories to toasts. And to the end of the love story of the day.

Rose often thought that this was what it was like to be plain Jane. Invisible Jane. And strangely, she felt more than comfortable with it.

Rose checked in with the wedding planner at the end of the wedding banquet, for the next steps and the photo deadlines, then found her pink moped, donned her helmet and rode home amongst the wallabies on the sides of the road under the midnight stars.

She was welcomed home with the porch light on, and the most ridiculous door colour she could never envision—a front door with many squares in seven colours. Like the seven sisters.

The seven gnomes. The seven dwarfs. Seven days of seven colours. Like the seven of them.

What happened to plain Jane?

Rose would love to give her opinion about the door, but she didn't want to hurt her feelings. Making Jane feel bad would make her feel bad.

Rose opened the door of Joseph's technicolour door of many colours to a seven bedroom three story Victorian terrace house in darkness. She wanted to tell Jane that it disturbed her mind when she looked at the door, but she didn't want to hurt her feelings. So she ignored it.

She ascended the two flights of steps quietly, entered her room on the top floor and closed it again. Then opened the door again.

The ceiling had been repaired.

Pleased, Rose closed the door again, sat at her desk and wrote Jane a note. On her pink coloured note paper. Then took it downstairs and added it to the crowded Jar-of-Jane-Notes, and returned promptly to her room.

Sleep was calling.

And it was well past lights out 9pm.

Chapter 18

Thursday night
Jane

J ane Piccadilly glanced out her French doors at 11:30pm. She had discovered if Rose's lights were on, she could see it in the reflection of the house across the road.

Her light was off, which was early for Rose after wedding photography.

Jane picked up a small blankie embroidered with Zinnias, and rubbed the silken material between her fingers. A comfort object, Mama called it. A transitional object her psychologist called it. Of connections to memories and emotions. An emotional support system. And it was perfectly okay for a grown-up to have one. It's within the range of normal behaviour.

Apparently.

Jane traced the line of the Zinnia and smiled. Little sister Zinnia. A sweet sister.

Jane reached over for her phone and hit speed dial. Her dad answered the video call after the third ring.

'Hi Dad. Mum.'

'Hello, my girl. It's late. Is everything okay?' Frank said.

'Yes. It's just… I can't sleep. I've been thinking about Zinnie. Can you remind me about when she was young,' said Jane.

Frank nodded. 'Your mum went into labour while looking at the colourful Zinnia flowers she had been growing. And that's how she ended up with her name, Jane.'

'Such pretty flowers, Dad. I think I'll plant some at my house.'

'I think Zinnie should have been born in the 60s—she was a wild flower child. She was dreamy with love and peace and picked flowers and gave them away to any person she deemed needed cheering up. She made flower wreaths and bouquets and bracelets and painted flowers everywhere. And the bees… oh the bees… they were her best friends.'

Jane lowered her head with a small smile. 'When she was that age, what did you think she would grow up to be?' asked Jane.

'A florist. That's all she could ever be. She was so in love with flowers and their shape and colours and shortness and tallness and the joy they bring!'

Jane watched as her mother lifted her "hambag" onto her lap and pulled out a ham sandwich and started to eat it.

Disconnecting from the present.

Disconnecting from the world.

Wishing to be anywhere but here, in this conversation.

'Gosh. She was such a ray of sunshine that girl. Always making us laugh. Remember when she was five, walking around the house with a pen that had a pink large flower on the end, using it as a microphone… and would come up to us, ask a question with her flower microphone, then put the microphone near our lips?' Frank said.

Jane giggled. How could she forget the terrible flower jokes!

What's a flower's favourite band? The Beetles! WHAT DO YOU CALL A BABY FLOWER? A BUD-DY! What did the flower say to the sun? "You brighten my day!" HOW DO FLOWERS WHISTLE? THROUGH THEIR TULIPS! What is the scariest type of a flower? A dandelion. WHAT FLOWER DID THE MOTHER GIVE TO HER SON? A SUNFLOWER. Can we have a boy in our family, Mum?

And Jane remembered the afternoon sun casting magical sunbeams, turning them into the golden children.

The golden Piccadilly girls.

Daisy chains on their heads made by Zinnia. With love. Twirling around and around and around, falling over and spinning with vertigo. The laughter. The *pure*, unadulterated joy.

'And that Father's Day where I had to lie still while she decorated my beard with flowers. She was such a giggle girt!'

Frank's chest rose as he inhaled deeply. 'And when she set up the flower shop on the footpath, sold out of her own homegrown flowers then started selling the weeds!'

Jane and her father burst out laughing together. But Alice Jane Piccadilly the 3rd remained detached, and took the last bite of her ham sandwich. Frank looked at her with a slow blink.

Jane knew that was enough for tonight, for her mother's sake. 'Thanks, Dad. Such good times. You and Mum will have to come to visit soon. Zinnia is creating something unbelievable good.'

Frank nodded. 'Soon, Jane. Soon.' He gave a small smile and disconnected the video call.

Jane placed her phone onto the bedside table and turned off the light. She grabbed the silken Zinnia comforter and brushed it against her lips and inhaled the scent of five-year-old Zinnia the wild flower child. And suddenly, the world was right.

And that was a day, and a night.

Chapter 19

Friday
Zinnia

Zinnia ran to the bus stop outside the seven bedroom, three story, Victorian terrace house, her green sneakers slapping the concrete footpath like the flippers of a diver. She sat on the bus stop seat and let out a long audible breath, then smoothed down her short blonde hair, zig zag parted in the middle, a pink flower at the side.

'It's a beautiful morning. I'm Luciano.'

Zinnia gave a smile. 'After yesterday's waterfall, it's lovely. I'm Zinnia.'

'Like the flower?'

'Exactly like the flower. I wonder if mother had given me a different name, whether I would work in the field I am in. Do you think names guide your destiny?'

Luciano adjusted his thick sunglasses. Zinnia squinted at them. They were odd. Were they loaded with technology? 'My name means light, intelligent, driven, optimistic.'

'Are you?' Zinnia asked.

'Yes and no. What about you, do you work with flowers?'

'A botanist, currently working as a research assistant at the university, and… creating my own unique flower line on the side.' Zinnia gave the smile of a thousand flowers.

'Impressive, Zinnie. Here comes the bus.'

Zinnia looked to her right. There was no bus. And then there it was, like he had summoned it. She gave him the side-eye like the silly sausage dog she lived with, then looked down at his carpet bag that he guarded like it had the answers to everything.

Everything-in-the-universe.

Luciano stood when the bus was twenty metres away. So did Zinnia. Like peer pressure. When the bus pulled up, Luciano gestured for her to get on first, and he followed.

Ten stops later, Zinnia exited the bus at the university and walked across the campus grounds to the research building. Who knew sugarcane had health benefits? Who knew sugarcane extract had powerful properties to not just improve our gut and heart health, but our mental health too. It was the natural polyphenols that had the antioxidant and anti-inflammatory properties.

Zinnia placed her backpack and coat into her locker, then grabbed the lab coat and headed to the staff room. The feeling in the room was light and happy. With success. They had just received news that the mystery of sugarcane genetics had been unravelled. The crop's genome three times the size of the human genome and more complex. It was a stunning result of work.

Zinnia checked the roster. She was at the sugarcane field today.

After the shuttle bus to the field, Zinnia joined the end of the line, and watched the other research assistants gather their tools for measuring and recording. Photographing. Collecting samples. Mimicking their actions.

Like-she-always-did.

She joined a group of women and watched as they worked, then volunteered as the recorder to streamline the process. And besides, that way, she would look like she knew what she was doing. And that way, she was working with minimal participation, unable to ruin the vital gathered research information they were collecting.

Zinnia finished work at noon and returned home to her own work. Creating her flower line. Chrysanthemums her chosen flower to manipulate. But would they work?

She opened the colourful front door to the barking and the side-eye-of-judgement of Oliver.

'Who's a Silly Sausage?' Zinnia said, and Oliver Twist wagged his tail like it was the first time she had walked in through the door. She headed to the back door and let him out into the wild back yard, watching for snakes and the pig.

Oliver Twist returned after a bit.

A bone-in-his-mouth.

'Add it to your collection, your Royal Sausage-ness?' Oliver trotted to the basket of bones and stopped. 'Drop,' said Zinnia, and Oliver Twist dropped the bone, which she promptly picked up and added it to the collection of dog-things-box. Zinnia frowned and looked back at the backyard. She wondered where Oliver Twist had been digging the bones up from.

Zinnia went to her room on the third story. She had work to do. She was glad she didn't have to step around the carpenter tools and materials used for the attic transformation anymore.

She stood with hands on hips and pivoted, looking for the location where the light entered her room the strongest. Jane, sweet Jane, had chosen her bedroom well. It was the only one with two windows. The easterly orientation was perfect. The window at the side of the house. Zinnia pulled the glass door cabinet flat pack to the centre of the room and started to unpack it. This was going to be her indoor greenhouse. After moving house so many times she had decided to create her own indoor greenhouse for continuation of growth of her flower line. She had restarted too many times and had to abort the project. This glass cabinet, turned into an indoor greenhouse, was the perfect solution. She'd found the plan, instructions and tools needed on the Internet. She set everything out on the floor and started building, setting herself a time deadline. That was the way she worked the best.

Break time was 5pm for Oliver Twist's afternoon walk and dinner, and completion of the task was assigned for 9pm. It would be a push to complete the greenhouse complete with LED strips and a tiny computer fan and a sun-blaster. But she was confident she could do it.

Zinnia straightened her aching back and stretched her arms up high. Building the greenhouse was more difficult than she thought it would be. But she was pleased with it. The next step was to acquire the Chrysanthemums that she wanted to cross pollinate and start the process of propagation. And then to cross pollinate the next flowering plant with it to create her own unique flower. The sun-blaster LED strip lights would ensure the process was quicker.

Pleased with her achievement, Zinnia tidied her room and returned the tools to the box in her cupboard. She noted the furniture in her room like doing a stocktake:

bed ✔
bedside table ✔
desk ✔
indoor greenhouse ✔
chair ✔

And that was enough. Materialistic wealth was a waste of money and a terrible form of abuse on the earth. This throw away generation had blood on their hands.

Satisfied with her achievements, Zinnia sat at her desk and wrote a note to Jane. On the green paper she had been given of course, then went to the long wooden dining table and pushed it into the Jar-of-Jane-Notes.

Zinnia returned to her room and turned off her light at 9pm to avoid the wrath of Jane, then showered under the light of twenty-five glow sticks. They did the job of light, with an added element of fun.

Chapter 20

Friday night

Jane

Jane Piccadilly went up the timber steps to the third floor with socks on her hands and feet at 10pm, sweeping from the left to the right of each step, collecting dust. Her mother would be proud of her. In reality, she was avoiding making any sound that would wake Rose or Zinnia. And... she didn't want Zinnia to know that she was spying on her to make sure her light was turned off at 9pm.

No light beamed from under Zinnia's door. Jane gave a nod of approval, then returned to her bed and snuggled under the cover. Oliver Twist was out like a light in his own bed.

Jane closed her eyes and waited for the blanket of sleep to cover her, until she heard the loud sound of a deep bellowing and grunting. The pig was gallivanting in the back yard. Again. It was a while since she last heard it and she had hoped it had left their residence.

Jane reached over and opened the top drawer of her bedside table and pulled out her ear plugs. They worked better than sticking your fingers into your ears to stop unwanted sound, like when she was nine years old. When her mother would sob and cry hysterically, for hours on end, the gut wrenching sound bouncing off the house walls and searching for ears to worm the sound inside of, knocking on eardrums and imprinting its horror into the mind. Her fingers couldn't block out that sound that terrified her. Her fingers couldn't block out that sound that pointed its finger of guilt and shame and rejection at her, and followed her around like a shadow every waking moment.

When Jane counted to one hundred, there were no more pig sounds, so she removed her ear plugs and thought about farms. And Flora.

She reached for her phone and hit speed dial. Her father answered the call after three rings.

'Hi Dad.'

'Hello, my girl. How is Alice?' Frank said.

'Jane, Dad. Call me Jane, remember.'

'Alice Piccadilly the 4th. Alice *Jane* Piccadilly. You've been calling daily. Is everything okay?'

'Yeah nah. I think a neighbour has a pet pig. It makes a terrible noise at night,' Jane lied. She couldn't remember if she had told her parents about the pig in the backyard.

'Then you'll have to call the council at once! Pigs belong on farms!'

Jane didn't want to call the council. That meant the neighbours would start to watch them. And she couldn't allow the neighbours to start to gossip about them. 'That could be a good idea, Dad,' Jane said to placate him.

Jane looked at her mum. Was she out of sorts today?

'Is Mum okay? She didn't get out her ham sandwich?'

Frank looked over at his wife. 'Yep. She's good.'

Jane frowned. She wasn't so sure. 'Gotta go now. Bye. Love you both.'

'Love you too, Jane. Now you get some sleep!'

Jane gave a slight grin and ended their video call, and placed her phone back onto her bedside table.

She lay on her back and positioned her arms and legs like she was a snow angel, but in bed.

Her angel dead-in-bed-pose.

She slowed her breathing and imagined six real angels playing around in the snow and acting like humans, moving their arms and legs and wings. Would they call the impression left behind snow people?

Jane drifted off into the nothing time in between good night and good morning. Unless you had nightmares. Then it was the-everything-in-between good night and good morning.

And that was a day, and a night.

Chapter 21

Saturday
Flora

Flora was up before dawn. The farm team huddle was at 6:15am to confirm the to-do lists for the day. She was still undecided whether it was too early to share her positive pregnancy result. Perhaps it would be better to wait twelve weeks to be sure.

She looked out her back window from her bedroom on the second floor. No other neighbours had their lights on. She was the only insane one up at this time of the morning. There weren't even any clouds where she could imagine animal shapes like she did when she was young. At least she still had her childhood encyclopedia of animals that she would read before she went to sleep each night.

Flora dashed downstairs and stopped at the back door looking for the little looooong dog. He was usually up when he heard her movements.

'Olivier?' she called.

And then he was there.

Flora opened the door for his morning ablutions and stepped outside into the chill scanning for snakes. Olivier returned quickly, a bone-in-his-mouth, which Flora promptly took from him and added to the pile-of-bones. As they were about to re-enter the house, there was a deep bellowing, grunting sound.

The pig?

Flora faced the overgrown backyard, and cupped her hands around her mouth. 'Sooooooooie!' she called in her farm hand tone, but not too loud.

No movement in the backyard. Not even a grunt.

'Here piggy-piggy!' Flora called in a singsong voice. Nothing. Not even a squeal. Flora rolled her eyes and took a deep breath, then let out a loud pig noise. A raucous, irritating grunting sound.

No pig. Only the sound of slamming windows of neighbours and a "Shut up!".

'Sorry,' Flora called, noting not to call the pig at this hour of the morning. On a Saturday. Jane would never forgive her if they had to move house again because of her pig grunting.

Flora brewed her organic Turmeric Ginger Ninja Tea and poured it into her orange tea cup. A supercharged organic wonder sip loaded with sweet, earthly notes. Chosen by Jane. Did she choose it to match her orange chair colour? The orange in her auburn hair? Her orange teapot and cup? She sipped on it while making a hearty breakfast of bacon, eggs, onion, finely cut potatoes and cheese, all in together like an omelette. It was good to keep up her energy levels for the work she had to do. As Flora swallowed the last bite, she wondered if her breakfast would be digested well enough as to not want to come up with her job today. Working on a farm had its lowlights and required a strong stomach. And today was one of those days.

Flora returned to her room and put her red and black checked farm work shirt, long khaki work pants into her back pack. She put on a black t-shirt and tied her hair into a ponytail at the back, and pushed her fringe to the side, then pulled up her pair of jeans. She did up the button on her jeans and her eyes widened. Her jeans were too tight. Had she put on weight already?

'Shhi,' she wanted to say the full swear word, but couldn't. Jane's bedroom was on the same floor as her. And walls had ears and the grapevine of gossip. Flora grimaced. The Jane-Swear-Jar.

The bloody-Jane-swear-jar!

She didn't want to owe Jane two dollars for letting a profanity slip between her lips. She undid the button on her jeans for comfort, and pulled her black t-shirt down to cover it.

After putting on runners, she alighted the steps, said goodbye to Olivier and closed the front door, opening it to the sight of four landscapers preparing to transform the yard. She stood there and applauded. Finally the landscaping had begun.

'Morning.'

Flora frowned and turned her head to a man sitting on the bus stop seat. A man in a dark blue suit with a carpet bag. Flora scrunched her face.

A man-with-a-carpet-bag?

'Oh. Morning,' she said. 'Off to work on a Saturday?'

'No rest for the wicked,' he said. 'I'm Luciano.'

'Flora, and off to work too.'

'Like the margarine?'

'Exactly like the margarine.'

'Then commiserations on both then… or is it?' Luciano said.

'Not when you love your job!' Flora said.

'Do you?'

'Do you?'

'Not today, and you?' Luciano said.

'Everyday.'

'Lovely. Enjoy,' Luciano said.

Flora walked to her classic, retro, pastel green 1991 Nissan Figaro parked under the leafy, picturesque Jacaranda tree. This was the spot for her car. Insta worthy. Her spot. She put on her rectangular retro white sunglasses and smoothed her auburn pony tail and brushed her fingers through her extra short fringe. She checked her phone to see if the baby scans had been uploaded yet. Still nothing. She hoped everything was okay.

Flora drove for forty-five minutes to the farm. The only problem living in the seven bedroom three story Victorian Terrace house near the city was she had the longest drive to work. But Jane's low room rent was too good to pass up. So Flora changed her mindset. And instead of thinking about all of the bad things that could possibly happen on her trek to work, she decided to tune in to her playlist. But then she wondered whether she should be listening to the radio in case some vital daily information or news came in that was important for her to hear. Flora drove in silence.

She parked her car far away from the danger of animals and machinery at the farm. Once, she had seen Michael's car decimated by a harvester.

She went straight to the toilet and changed into her farm work clothes and then joined the farm crew in the shed. After morning greetings they were each handed their job lists for the day.

'Poop,' Flora said, and instantly felt relieved about not swearing. Jane would be proud of her. 'I mean literally,' Flora added to the sniggers and laughing eyes around her. She was dag scoring sheep. Disgusting but necessary. Moving the fermenting sheep manure to the trucks for fertilising the fields. Then cleaning out the sheep barn. It was going to be a stinky-day-today. She felt in her pockets for her nose plugs. Her eyes widened when she realised she had left them at home. Flora changed her mindset. At least it wasn't as bad as cleaning out the chicken coop with rotten eggs.

The sheep shot her daggers when Flora's head came in to view. Her pony tail hair was messy, and the tampons stuffed up her nose to stop the stinky-sheep-smell hung out like elephant tusks with the cords, looking like long hangs of snot dribble. Nevertheless, they would do the job of stopping-the-stink.

Flora wanted to take her time with the sheep. Like she always did. She couldn't possibly hurt them in any way. She wanted to be gentle and kind and not worry about accidentally cutting them. And that made her a very good sheep dagger-er, removing the pooey-wet-wool between their legs, the tail and the rear end and preventing flystrike. Flora even had names for each of the sheep. Her sheep.

Her-flock-of-girls.

And that's why her anxiety got the better of her. She knew them by name. It made her anxious about everything. Even when she had nothing to be anxious about. That's the most ridiculous thing about anxiety, and how *irrational* it is. She became anxious about the way the sheep spoke to her. The way they looked at her with those amber coloured eyes with the horizontal, rectangular pupils, that went wide with terror when she approached them.

Flora's eye twitched and her body tremored at-the-ick.

And then she fainted.

Flora's only job left was to clean out the sheep barn. And that was enough for today.

Flora Piccadilly drove home in her classic, retro, pastel green

1991 Nissan Figaro, the windows down to blow out the sheep poo smell. There was nothing worse than a lingering smell of ewe berries in the car.

She promptly parked her car back under her Jacaranda tree and marched inside the house and up to the second floor for a long de-sheep stink in the shower.

She came out smelling like lemon myrtle oil and manuka honey. Flora sat at her study desk and pulled out the orange note paper and wrote to Jane. She went downstairs in her jimjams and pushed the note into the Jar-of-Jane-Notes in front of Jane's dining chair. Plain. And white.

Then she returned to her room and fell asleep on the bed. Well before 9pm. Exhausted.

Chapter 22

Saturday night
Jane

Jane Piccadilly peeked out the keyhole of her bedroom door. She had a direct line of sight to Flora's bedroom. Her bedroom light was off. She gave a nod of approval, then returned to her bed and snuggled under the cover. Tomorrow was Sunday. The day of rest. Her day. *Janeday* she liked to call it. When she could do whatever she liked.

And she would like to go to church. Like they used to. Mum and Dad and the seven daughters.

And then Mum and Dad stopped going to church.

Mum was angry at God, Dad had said.

Jane wondered if God was angry at her too. Because she was the reason that her mum was angry with God.

Everything was her fault.

So when Jane was fourteen and cried because she missed going to Sunday Service where she felt accepted, no matter what, and where her words were heard, when no one else ever listened, she drew a figure of God and Jesus and placed them into her Bible that was shelved with the other brown leather books on her shelf in the library sitting room.

Jane rolled on to her side, the words from Psalm 86:5 coming to her,

> *For You, Lord, are forgiving and good, abounding in love to all who call upon You.*

'Thank you, Lord, and I'm sorry,' she whispered. Her words were meant for everyone. She closed her eyes and imagined happiness bursting from within, imbued with floral notes of forgiveness of others, and herself, her tears speckled with gold and releasing her from her self-imposed prison.

And that was a day, and a night.

Chapter 23

Sunday
Jane

Jane Piccadilly sat on the white chair at the table with her white Alice in Wonderland teapot, white matching tea cup and white jasmine loose leaf white tea with milk. A lot had been achieved in a week. The painted house. The painted front door. The attic. And now, the landscaping had started. Jane patted herself on the back for a job well done. It's not an easy feat orchestrating everything to do with moving into a new house with six other occupants. But she had done it. Again.

She pulled the note jar towards her. It had six different colour notes in it. Communication was vital in a house with so many occupants.

She turned her teapot three times, clockwise, then poured

the tea into her teacup and took a sip. She put her teacup down and reached into the jar, taking out the blue note from Monday. Poppy's.

> *Dearest Jane,*
>
> *I'm looking forward to the exterior painting of the house and the red door. I can't stand the sound of the knocking on the front door each night. Right next to my bedroom.*
>
> *Can you please organise for a ramp beside the outside stairs for my bicycle. It's a bit dodgy for Twisty when I have to carry the bike down the stairs. A safety issue for Oliver.*
>
> *Kindly,*
> *Poppy*

Jane noted the request for the ramp for Poppy's bike. It was a fair ask. Besides, by riding her bicycle to work at the library, she was being kind to the environment, doing her part for climate change. A good deed should be rewarded.

She reached into the jar and pulled out the lavender note, and opened it. Violet's from Tuesday.

> *Dear Jane,*
>
> *I hope you are going to charge your parents rent for living in the attic. I think the attic would have been better as a common room for all of us to enjoy television together, considering we don't have a TV!*

*We had two visitors at the house on Tuesday night.
They tried to tell me that I had something to sell them.
But don't worry. I dealt with them. They won't return.*

*Also, I'm worried about the taping on the front door
the painter has done. I told you a mustard front door
colour was the only way to go with light grey for the
house exterior.*

Violent

Jane winced. Violet. She had done it again. She had reminded
her about her violent temper that erupted from within at times.
Violet was the reason they had moved house so many times.
Perhaps she should encourage her back to see her therapist?
Perhaps she should slip something into her tea leaves to calm her?

Jane let out a breath and reached into the jar and pulled out
the yellow note, and opened it. Daisy's.

Dear Jane,

*Crikey! I had trouble with a bloody floating coffin
today with all this rain. We managed to sink the death
box into the ground like it was drowning in the water.*

*I also marked out a grave in a pre-purchased plot. It
was next to a multi grave of six girls. Twenty-four years
ago!*

*It rattle me a bit, I have to admit. Gosh, I'm starting
to become a softy like Flora.*

From Daisy

Jane Piccadilly froze. Six girls? Twenty-four years ago. A chill ran down her spine. She wished she had never read Daisy's note. She clutched it in her hand and went to the library sitting room and found the matches, went to the fire place, lit the match and burned the note.

There. Done.

The note never existed. Just the words stuck in her mind that she had to find a way to erase.

She reached into the jar and pulled out Flora's orange note, and opened it.

Dear Jane,

I cannot call Sooooie to the pig anymore. The neighbours are getting annoyed. And you know what happens with annoyed neighbours. I haven't seen a snake yet, and I want to group the pile of bones Oliver Twist keeps finding in the back yard. Like a paleontologist. Perhaps a beloved pet was buried in the backyard at an incorrect depth. There are rules for burying pets.

And, we really must get the landscaping finished. That will sort out the snake and the pig.

Sincerely,
Flora

P.S. I hope I didn't bring the stink home from work. Let me know if you can smell sheep poop.

Jane sniffed the air. No sheep poop. Not like the time Flora had part of a cow paddy stuck to her pants. That smell permeated the entire house. Even Oliver Twist gave the side-eye-of-judgement. But to be fair, he was the one who had searched out and located the smell so it could be removed. He was a good boi!

She reached into the jar and pulled out the pink note, and opened it. Rose.

Dear Jane,

The ceiling looks great. What a find! If I hadn't looked at the photograph I wouldn't have noticed the change in the ceiling. When is Mum and Dad moving in? I am wondering about their age and the two flights of stairs they need to take?

The front door looks interesting. I've never seen a front door in seven colours. I bet it will slow passers-by down as they take in the colours. Can't wait to photograph the finished house colours and the finished landscaping!

Warm regards,
Rose

Dear Rose, Jane thought. *She's always so positive. And thoughtful. Mum and Dad would be able to use Oliver's stair climber. Problem solved.*

She reached into the jar and pulled out the green note. The last one. And opened it.

Dear Jane,

You know I don't like to complain, but the carpenter

left a handprint on my door. I have washed it off to the best of my ability. But still. I shouldn't have had to clean someone else's mess!

I have finished my greenhouse in my room and will commence cross-pollination of flowers and plants. I am excited about this. Please, please, keep Violet calm so we don't have to move again.

I have decided I do like my room because of the two windows. I am sorry for complaining about it being on the third floor.

Zinnia

Jane smiled. She knew Zinnia would eventually see why she had chosen that room for her. She pushed the coloured notes back into the jar, and took it upstairs to her room. She lowered herself to the floor and reached under her bed for the vintage white suitcase, opened it and added the jar to the suitcase of notes, where she kept every single note ever written by her sisters. They were after all so close, they felt like a part of her.

Like-they-were-one.

She closed the suitcase of notes and pushed it back under her bed. Next to the black vintage suitcase of devastating memories, and the red vintage suitcase of flagged difficult emotions, and the floral vintage suitcase of family love. None of them ever to be opened.

Not after those two days.

She left her bedroom, closed her bedroom door and made her way to the library and opened her laptop. She had a television, bed and chairs and plants to source for the attic. Then their parents could move in.

After making a list, Jane was a list maker after all, Jane

Piccadilly left the house, closing the multi-coloured front door behind her. She grimaced. Maybe Violet was right. Maybe one colour would have made the door more of a door with a positive impact. Like people who had made up their minds and knew they were right. Like people who weren't in two minds, or seven in this case.

The landscapers gave her a wave as she walked along the path closest to the house. It would be great to be able to use the path that led directly to the gate. The shortest path. The shortcut. The rightcut. The most direct and economical path, her dad would have said.

She stopped before the landscaper project manager. 'Jerry, can you please add a ramp beside the front steps to the verandah… to wheel a bicycle down.' Jane twisted her shoe on the ground, berating herself. She had forgotten to start the conversation with a greeting. It annoyed her when she forgot. She was a get to the point type of person. Had always been. She never saw the need of friendly introductions with people who weren't friends. People she would never see again, but needed to get a job done. Her mother had said she needed to start with a welcoming greeting. An opener. Like letting sunshine into the conversation. People were kinder to you then.

Jerry looked over at the steps, frowned, then said, 'Sure. Concrete? Timber?'

'I'll leave those decisions up to you with your expertise.' Jane gave a smile and left with quick footsteps. Anxiety of getting stuck in a conversation with small talk with the worker getting the better of her.

She stopped at the bus stop and sat on the seat. On a Sunday. She let out an audible sigh, wondering whether she should have just borrowed one of the cars from her sisters.

'Morning.'

Jane froze. She preferred to talk to herself. Not to strange men. Strangers. Stranger danger. Jane coughed loudly. Oscar worthy. She hoped he would give up with pleasantries.

'Wet cough? No, more of a dry cough. Tickly cough. Can't be a night cough. Nervous cough. Fake cough?'

Jane froze. She wished she didn't have to sit on this seat next to the man-with-the-carpet-bag. And glasses. Dressed-in-a-suit. Analysing her type of cough. On a Sunday. Had he called her out with his comment? 'Morning to you, too,' Jane said. 'Off to work?'

'Always but never.'

Jane frowned. Was he being pretentious? Then she raised her eyebrows as she understood what he meant. 'It must be nice have a job like that.'

'Like what?'

'When you love what you do so it doesn't feel like work.'

'Luciano must be an artist then,' he said without looking at her.

'Are you Luciano?' Jane said, confused by the conversation.

'Today. Yes.'

'Are you normally not Luciano?'

'Most of the time. Depending on how I feel. Who would I like to be today instead? And you are?'

'Jane.'

'Nice to meet you, Jane. The bus is coming,' he said.

Jane looked to her right. There was no bus. But then there it was. At the speed of Sunday.

Jane Piccadilly and Luciano the man in the suit stood. The bus brakes squeaked. The door whooshed open. And Jane boarded the bus first, taking a seat near the front of the bus. She watched as Luciano made his way to the centre, directly opposite the middle door. He sat. Placed his carpet bag beside him and kept his head still.

After seven stops, Jane left the bus and entered the home maker store. She exited two hours later with an order for a bed, sofa, large LED TV, two chairs and curtains. They would be delivered on Wednesday. Jane stopped for a cup of tea before she ventured into a plant nursery, and ordered three plants to be delivered. On Wednesday. Then caught the bus home.

Jane stepped off the bus and waited for it to move on. Then she gazed up at her seven bedroom three story Victorian Terrace house. The exterior white façade was fabulous, but the door not so. It made her think of a person who couldn't make a decision. A person who was mixed up and chaotic.

An-unpredictable-person.

Like Violet. Then and there, Jane decided that the door must be painted dark blue. Like a person who was of sound mind and a solid decision maker. Someone who could be trusted.

Jane took a step onto the road and crossed it without fuss. Unlike her cat that day at the second house, who jumped high as a car was about to hit her, then she rode the bonnet of the car for two blocks before she jumped off and decided to make a different house her home.

Jane stopped before her front garden, now organised, landscaped and presently being transplanted with plants. It was magnificent. She opened the new front white wrought iron gate, now adorned with white climbing roses on either side, where once, her perfectly white shoe was embedded in the perfectly atrocious dog poop.

The shoe-in-the-poo.

The perfume of the roses was stunning.

She walked along the once overgrown path, perfectly splitting the front garden into two. A left garden. And a right garden. Plants with spirals – *the vertigo garden* – she had called it, complete with some weird plants, including the peculiar brain on a stick plant, aka the Celosia argentea, and the Aloe polyphylla that was in the shape of a spiral, like the cochlea of the inner ear. There were some odd sculptures too. Created by Poppy over the years. The funny stone face family of seven. The Scream, Poppy style. The ugly hybrid animals. The car in the pond. The seven eyes. The Hand of Help. Seven mini bird cages, all empty, except one that had a trapped clay painted bird. Poppy had succeeded in making the sculptures to challenge onlookers to think about the hidden meaning behind them. The stories of them.

The-stories-of-us.

Jane Piccadilly took a deep cathartic breath. The front landscaping was now planted with a perfectly balanced crescendo of a garden that ended with a bang. Like *Haydn's Symphony No. 94, 2nd movement*, also known as the Surprise Symphony. Embedded with *Twinkle Twinkle Little Star*. Which came first? She gazed at the newly constructed recycled timber ramp to the left of the steps. A stark contrast to the sandstone steps. It was perfect.

As Jane reached the top step, she froze. There sat her perfect white sneaker, adhered to the atrocious dog poo. Like a trophy. The shoe-in-the-poo had returned. Like a piece of art on a white pedestal. 'Crap,' Jane said under her breath.

'Is it yours, Miss Piccadilly?' asked Jerry.

Jane narrowed her eyes and let out a low yes.

'The poop is turning white to match your shoe. There was a heap of dog shit along your front fence by the way. We cleaned it up.'

'Thank you,' Jane said in jest, annoyed by his swearing. 'And thank you for cleaning it up.' She wanted to hold out her swear jar. But that might make her look odd. And Jane Piccadilly wasn't odd. Or a nincompoop.

Jane stepped over her shoe-in-the-poo and took three steps to the front chaotic door. The moment her key touched the lock the four-legged doorbell sounded.

'Good day, Oliver Twist,' Jane said. 'Let's see how the back yard is shaping up.'

Oliver Twist did the dachshund strut in front of her as he walked to the back door. As soon as she opened the back door he flew out like an aggressive black Doberman, but then stopped and barked. Three men and three women were working on the landscaping. Shovels. Mattocks. Dingo mini loader. Brush cutter. It was a whirlwind of activity and a racket of noise like a toddler playing with pots and pans.

Jane scanned the backyard, currently a dirt backyard.

Where was the pig?

Where was the snake?

Jerry made a beeline towards her. *O-oh.* Jane took a step back, her stomach anxiety-ing. 'Jane, we have found two things you need to be aware of.'

Jane Piccadilly's eyes widened. She didn't like "things-to-be-aware-of". It sounded like another mistake. 'You found the snake and the pig?'

Jerry frowned at her. 'There seems to be a shed, not shown on your landscape planning, and an area behind that brick wall that is at the end of your driveway. It's a bit odd. But we can't access it.'

Jane frowned. How could she not see a shed in the backyard?

The-backyard-shed.

She looked to her right, and there it was. A green wooden shed with a door and windows. The vegetation that hid it had been cut. Rule number one had stung her again, exactly like an angry bee. Inspecting the house before buying it. 'And…'

'What would you like to do with the shed?' Jerry said.

'Inspect it, as I will do with the area behind the brick wall. I'll do it soon. Meanwhile, keep working on the rest of the landscaping.' Jerry nodded and Jane watched as the mini loader spread fresh soil over the backyard, leveling it up. She looked down at Oliver Twist, wagging his tail in a frenzy. 'Jerry?'

'Yes?'

'Can you please add a sand pit for Oliver, much like a sand pit you would make for a child.' Jane looked at Oliver and then back at Jerry. 'He's a digger. He like to dig until he's dug out.'

Jerry turned and looked over the back yard. He pulled out the landscaping plan from his back pocket.

'Directly in the centre and against the back fence please,' Jane said.

'Consider it done,' Jerry said, and called in the landscapers to inform them of the new plan.

Jane returned to the house and went to her room. She changed into jeans and a white t-shirt, and found her white gumboots, then returned to the backyard and walked to the newfound shed, Oliver Twist in tow. She put her hand on the doorknob and turned it. But it was locked. She stood before a dirt smudged window and rubbed a spot on the glass, clockwise of course. She didn't want to reverse time with an anti-clockwise motion. When it was clear, she peered inside the shed. It was quite tidy, with a chair and a desk, an open ledger book, and envelope with what looked like a recipe poking out. Plus some lab equipment and plastic zip lock bags. She would call for a locksmith later to open the shed.

'Jerry… leave the shed, but landscape around it,' Jane said as she walked to the brick structure that had the driveway on the other side.

Where there were once weeds and rubble were now brick size pavers, and a square in the centre made from timber. Not laid by

Jerry's landscaping, but uncovered.

Jerry squatted down and lifted it up a smidgen. 'There's a room down below.'

Jane's eyes followed the steps to the darkness. 'Did you go down and have a look?'

'No, Ma'am. I thought you might like to see what is there first.'

Jane's imagination went to a snake pit. Investigating the unknown down in a dark pit was not her cup of tea. She wished it wasn't there. She wished she didn't have to make a decision like this. 'How brave are you, Jerry?'

'Curious more than anything. This is unusual,' he said.

Jane let out a breath. Curiosity killed the cat. If Jerry went down there, would he become the curious cat? She looked at Jerry. He was like the human form of Oliver Twist, smiling, excited and wagging his tail, ready to go as soon as she said the word. Jane gestured to the curiosity. Jerry pulled out his phone and turned on the torch, and down he went, the timber stairs creaking with each step.

He ascended a mere moment later, ashen faced. 'Nothing to see, Miss.' Monotone voice.

Jane felt like she was at school. The teacher. A lone student the deterrent to the misdemeanour being perpetrated, "Nothing to see, Miss". Like a group of students huddled around one other, the snipping of scissors, and when the students run, a lone student sitting, shaking, hair cut beyond salvageable, except for a head shave. Jerry's words absolutely were that there was something to see. 'Did you take photos?'

Jerry slid his phone into his back pocket. He shook his head. He absolutely did see something. Jane would speak to Flora. She was the one to venture into the unknown. She was a brave farmhand, after all. Flora the farmhand, Jane mouthed.

'What do you suggest we do with the underground?' Jane asked.

'Fill it in.'

'What do you think it was used for?'

He thought for a moment. 'I… wouldn't like to speculate.'

'Thanks, Jerry. I'll let you know tomorrow what we'll do with it.'

Jerry tipped his head and went back to work. Jane tiptoed through the fresh dirt and back to the wooden deck of the house, removed her gumboots and headed upstairs to the third floor of the terrace. She needed some advice.

She pushed the white button on the wall, and stairs lowered from the ceiling. Jane smiled. The workers had excelled in creating the magical staircase to the attic. Jane walked up in to the attic. There was a wall opposite the stairs ready for the LED TV, and on the left and right walls were double windows. She mind mapped where the bed and sofa would go, then sat on the polished timber floor and pulled out her phone and hit speed dial.

'Hi Dad. I've got good news for you.'

'Hello, my girl. How is Alice?'

'Jane, Dad. Call me Jane, remember.'

'Alice Piccadilly the 4th. Alice *Jane* Piccadilly. You've got good news?'

'Sure do. The house I bought has an attic. It's perfect for you and Mum!' Jane said.

'Nooo! That's soooo unexpected. And it is good news! But I don't think we can move in yet.'

'Why?'

'Your mother is in the middle of leading a Sound Healing Retreat. But we will get there,' Frank said.

'Like the last time, Dad?'

'You know your mother likes to… help people—'

'Except her own daughter—' Jane's throat closed up.

'Now, now… you know you have been indignantly independent and stubborn since you were a wee tot. Jane, we will get there.'

'I know. It's just… I really miss you both. I want you back with me… Dad… the landscaper found an underground bunker. Should I keep it, or fill it in?'

'If it's… of sound structure… I would keep it,' he said.

'Why?'

'Oh, I don't know… a secret reading place, a place to hide away from the world, a little party room. Maybe you could lock Violet in there when she loses the plot.'

'I would never do that to Violet, Dad. How could you even suggest that?'

'She's always been partial to being indifferent. Bullish. Angry. It might teach her to tame her inner wild self,' he said.

'She's getting better, Dad. When you and Mum move in, you'll see.'

'Oh, I'm certain of that.'

'Gotta go now. The landscaping is nearly finished. Chat later, Dad. Love you.'

'And I love you, my dear Alice Jane Piccadilly the 4th. Take care.'

Jane turned off her phone and looked around the room once more. This house was certainly giving her more than she expected.

A shed.

A bunker.

An attic.

So many choices.

She smiled. Jane turned on her phone again. She opened up

the group chat and told the girls about the exciting finds in the backyard and asked them about what they wanted to do with the shed and the dugout.

Group Chat

Jane - *great news girls! We have discovered a shed and a dug-out… or a bunker, or something or other, in the backyard. Any ideas about what we can use them for?*

Poppy – *the shed an art/writing studio and the bunker, a library for sure!*

Violet – *how about a hairdressing room in the shed for me to work from home. I already have clients I can lure to my own business, and for the bunker, let's brew our own boutique women's beer!*

Daisy – *exciting Jane. And unexpected. Being practical, how about using the shed for the mower and other gardening tools, and the bunker for a time out room when we need to escape from the world.*

Flora – *garden tools for the shed and a snake and pig catcher for the bunker…*

Rose – *I could use the bunker as my dark room for my photography for developing negatives—it would be perfect, and the shed for garden stuff.*

Zinnia – *I need the shed for my propagation room for my flower line. It would be better than having the greenhouse in my bedroom which is also not good for the house, and I'm sure you don't want the repugnant waft of organic fertiliser travelling through the house, nor the exorbitant electricity bill from keeping my greenhouse heated in my room. The bunker I don't have an opinion on. Do with it what you please.*

Jane Piccadilly wrote a list, and added tally marks.

Shed	Votes
garden tools	III
hair studio	I
art/writer studio	I
plant propagation	I

Jane cocked an eyebrow. The obvious use for the shed was what sheds were created for—mowers and shovels and clippers and blower vacs and hammers and secateurs and hoses and screw drivers and bags of soil. But. Getting Zinnia's little botany habit out of the house would be better for everyone. Violet could use the garage for her hair dressing gig. Oh wait. They don't have a garage… and we already have a library in the house. Poppy could just continue to paint and write in her room. Problem solved.

Bunker	Votes
escape from reality	I
brewery	I
dark room for photography	I
snake and pig space	I
funky library	I

Jane wasn't particularly fond of the other ideas for the bunker. She had 'Women's Secret Business' stuck in her head. Perhaps they could all work with that idea and what it looked like.

Jane added to the group chat: *It is in the best interest of our house and our health that Zinnia relocate her greenhouse into the shed. We can all benefit from her flower line when it sells well.*

There was no response. Just a bombardment of angry and happy and shocked and crying and sad face and flower emojis.

Jane: *And the bunker. While I like all your suggestions (except the snake and pig), I am thinking of a place for 'Secret Women's Business'. I don't know what that looks like or feels like yet, but I would like you to ponder on it.*

Jane turned off her phone before the barrage of replies and arguments would come, then she went down four flights of stairs and out the front door. She wanted to absorb the glorious landscaping art as the sun went down, casting a filtered light over it, enhancing the natural hues.

She inhaled deeply, feeling a peace surround her. Everything was coming together. Like pieces of a puzzle. She about turned to enter her house, and spotted an envelope at the door.

Jane Piccadilly blinked three times, picked up the envelope and entered her house for dinner and a tidy up. Then she went to her bedroom and got ready for bed. Early.

At 9pm she leaned over to turn off the light and the envelope at the door was there. Waiting. For her. Jane picked it up, turned it over and slid her finger under the back fold of paper, and opened it.

A-messy-handwritten-note.

I'm just wondering. Have you found it yet?
The secrets of the house?

Jane's eye twitched and her body tremored at-the-ick. This house certainly had no secrets. It had been rubbed and scrubbed and renovated to within an inch of its life. He, and she assumed it was a he, was overstepping her boundary again.

The words-in-the-letter.

He… was putting words into her mind causing a domino of thoughts to write their questions onto each of her bones.

All two-hundred-and-six of them.

Her hand shook as she pushed the words-in-the-letter back into the envelope, and slipped it into the drawer of emptiness beside her bed, where it could enter the void and be consumed in a celestial black hole.

9pm. Lights out.

Jane turned off the lamp and snuggled down into her bed. She crossed her hands over her chest and held her breath. She stared. Like she did that night. Staring into the dam in the darkness.

Jane Piccadilly resumed breathing, and closed her eyes.

And that was a day, and a night.

Chapter 24

Monday
Poppy

Poppy pulled a book off the shelf. *The History of Backyard Bunkers*. And another. *How to Build a Backyard Bunker*. And another. *Uses for a Backyard Bunker*. And another. *The Secret Life of a Bunker*. Jane had told her to do it. Bossy Jane. Maybe Poppy could find a book called, *Jane Stuck in the Bloody Bunker!* Poppy stacked the books on top of each other, and placed them into her locker. Jane's work was done.

Poppy then went to the kids' area to find Oliver Twist, aka, Twisty, aka, Schnitzel Von Krumm, the library reading dog. He was dressed as Captain Vertigo with a cochlear implant today. His hearing disability had become his super-ability.

Schnitzel had his chin resting on a child's leg, listening to the story *Henry Bear*, the bear with terribly bad manners, probably wishing he had the last cupcake instead of Henry Bear. Schnitzel rolled on to his back when the boy closed the book, and waited for an amazing gentle tummy rub that only kids could give.

'Good boy, Captain Vertigo!' Poppy said, and threw him a treat. Which hit him on the nose then fell to the floor. Oliver Twist was not a good food-catching dog. Maybe he needed glasses? 'Captain Vertigo can spin, you know. Do you want to see it?'

The boy nodded.

Schnitzel Von Krumm stood.

'Spin!' Poppy said, and he spun around two times. 'Good boy!' Poppy held a treat before his nose, and he took it, gently. He was the gentlest boi. They walked around the library then, sniffing out where the kids were, and Oliver performed his spin trick for them while Poppy showed them the chapter book, *Captain Vertigo and Fart Man*. It certainly was one way to get kids interested in a book, especially when there was a Super Sausage Dog in it as well. And especially when Schnitzel Von Krumm farted, right on cue.

Schnitzel Von Krumm stilled and stared. Poppy followed his line of sight to the corner of the library. There sat a child with a cochlear implant. 'Hi five, Schnitz!'

They walked over to the boy, and his eyes lit up when he saw the little looooong dog with a cochlear implant processor on his head. They sat with him. Talked to him. Exchanged smiles full of sunshine and read parts of the book. This book, *Captain Vertigo*, was for him. Captain Vertigo who had a cochlear implant and was a superhero. A warm fuzzy feeling travelled through Poppy.

This… is when books were magic. When they connected to the reader and made them feel seen and heard and understood. Poppy's heart glowed and a tear fell from her eye.

This… is what books did.

Poppy let Schnitzel walk the floor of the library by himself, while she made her way to the computer. She typed in "most heartbreaking novels", then made her way to the fiction section and grabbed the book from the shelf. She flipped through it and found a page that would connect to the last page she had stuck to her bedroom wall, where she was creating her own novel from other authors' novels, then she stood in front of a plant with the open book to conceal what she was doing.

RRRrrrrrriiiiiiip.

Slowly but surely, and quietly, Poppy separated a page from the book. But left the ripped page partly hanging out. She walked with purpose to the main desk and placed the book on the counter in front of the library manager. 'A loose page. Repair or throw?'

The library manager picked up the book and looked at the damage. She pressed her lips into a hard line. 'See what you can do, Poppy. If it's irreparable, can you make some book page art with it?'

Poppy gave her a wide smile. 'Sure,' she said, then took the book and went into the back book room, pulled the page right out of the book and placed it into her pocket, then started to rip out other pages. She broke the spine of the book so it laid out flat, then created flowers out of the pages and glued them onto the book.

Poppy stopped to admire her book artistry. It looked like the book was a garden of stories. Her library manager loved her artistic side and the positives it gave to the library, inspiring readers. Once, she had even taken a class on making flowers from book pages. It brought in a record number of people to the library, just like Schnitzel Von Krumm did for the kids.

At 4pm, Poppy popped Twisty, aka, Captain Vertigo into the

front basket of her bike, put on her helmet, and pedalled home, the Captain Vertigo cape blowing with the breeze. Poppy was sure she could see Twisty smiling.

Twisty ran up the new front step ramp when they arrived home, and waited at the front door for Poppy. They entered the house together. And after storing her bike and removing Twisty's costume, Poppy went to her room and retrieved the ripped page from her pocket, and the bunker books from her work bag. She added the new page of her story to her story wall, then took the bunker books and placed them on the long wooden dining table in front of Jane's white chair.

Poppy opened the back door and Twisty ran out into his newly landscaped backyard. Poppy followed, looking over the backyard in awe. It was like another room of the house. The reconnection room, where the mind and body were regenerated by nature. The yard had been planned well. She reminded herself to compliment Flora on her design.

Poppy walked to the shed. The old-fashioned variety made of wood and glass, painted British green. The one mentioned by Jane. She didn't want to go to it. She wanted nothing to do with it because it wasn't hers.

A scorned child, she thought.

But still. She was a writer, and couldn't stop her mind from entering the imaginarium. She was curious as to what could have been. She imagined the door creaking open as she stepped in. But the door had a lock on it. So she peered through the glass panels instead.

A desk.

A chair.

An open ledger book.

An envelope with a letter, or is a recipe, partly poking out.

Some lab equipment and plastic bags.

Poppy wandered over to the paved area in front of the brick wall. A garden seat and party lights would look amazing here. Her shoe clunked on the wooden square on the ground. The sound was hollow like that book in Jane's library that wasn't a real book. She had opened it once. It was once a real book but the middle of the pages were cut out, leaving a rectangular hole that you could hide something in. Like a secret. And there was something in it. There were six tufts of hair bound with different coloured ribbons. Poppy's heart had startled and she had snapped the book closed and pushed it back onto the shelf promptly.

Poppy took a step back from the wooden square on the ground, leaned over and pulled on the metal ring. She lifted the wooden structure and a puff of wind blew her hair. The descending stairs were uninviting and dangerous.

Stay away came a whisper. So Poppy put the hatch down as quickly as she had opened it.

And besides, she had been denied to use it as a library. And she would never enter it based on her principles after being rejected.

She returned to the house and went to the kitchen and prepared dinner. As she cooked, she watched Twisty walk around the new backyard, exploring, and suddenly, he began to dig. He lowered his head and retrieved a bone, then trotted back to the house, his head held high in that proud dachshund way. He dropped the bone next to the other bones he had collected. Then returned and returned and returned.

Poppy frowned. The House of Bones typed itself on an old fashioned typewriter in her imagination, the sound of the click-clacking keys echoing in her mind.

Poppy sat in the blue chair at the long wooden dining table, her dinner plate on a blue placemat. Poppy snorted. What would Jane do if she sat at the green chair with a pink dinner plate and a yellow glass? She sighed then cut up her food, placed her knife down, and opened yesterday's chat with the girls and looked at what had been decided about the shed and the bunker.

She sniggered as she reread the suggestions. She should never have suggested what she wanted. Rejection hurt. And Jane had obviously forgotten the sibling pecking order. She was first born and should always get her own way.

As-simple-as-that.

And then everyone would be happy.

Poppy turned off her phone. She would have nothing to do with either the shed or the bunker. How many times did it take for her to learn that she could not depend on other people. Only she could enable good things for herself. Relying on others only ended in heartbreak.

Misery-of-the-deepest-kind.

Poppy cleaned up after dinner and went to her room. Jane would be here soon, and she most certainly did not want to have any dealings with her. Not while she was feeling this way.

Short-changed-and-disregarded.

She sat at her art desk and pulled out her sketch book. She needed to do some concept designs for the cover of her novel. She was torn between creating digital art, or using acrylic paint, or watercolour. The final choice would come to her as she worked on the design. She knew it would.

Poppy gazed out the window and into the night. A tear slid down her face. A tear that told seven stories and held a thousand technicolour memories like a family movie night.

She left no note to Jane.

And that was a day, and a night.

Chapter 25

❀

'Shhi!' Violet said with wide eyes, stopping the rest of the expletive from leaving her mouth. For Jane's sake. The eastern sun burned onto the tip of her nose. She had slept through the alarm which was set to precisely thirty minutes before the dreadful sun sneaked into her room to assault her. She sat up like she was a sit-up-ninja-warrior at the highest profile gym in the city, her perfect technique scorching her core.

Violet blinked. *Jane's bloody friggin' swear jar?* she thought. At least her word was only worth two dollar a hit, if she had said the entire word.

'Ollie Wollie, why didn't you bark at the alarm?' She rolled three times to get over to the other side of the bed. There was

172

no way she was getting out on the wrong side of the bed this morning. Violet hit the floor with a thump; the bed sheet tangled around her foot.

Violet fumed and looked up. 'FFFFFFFFFFFFF.' Violet stopped the rest of the letters from zooming from her mouth, and flying through the sound vibrations and into Jane's ear, knocking on her ear drum like a delivery had been made and landing with a clattering of letters with the loudest echo. The "F" word was a ten dollar donation to the swear jar. And Jane always heard it. *Always*. Because, you know, f@(^ was a loud word in Violet's vocabulary. She could never say it quietly. Ever.

'Violet doesn't do wrong, does she Ollie?' she said when she finally caught her breath and saved her bank balance from Jane's bulging aggressive swearing account. She stood and gave her body a shake as if she was covered in wet fur like a dog, and shook all the colours of wrong and oops and not my faults off her. She lifted her chin high, then walked to her en suite like she was on the catwalk, looked in the mirror and battered her eyes, looking this way and that. 'Shhhhi.'

Oliver Twist gave her the side-eye-of-judgement.

Violet rolled her eyes. 'Not you too, Ollie. Judging my language.' She pushed her lips into a hard line. Perhaps Ollie was right. Profanities were coarse and vulgar and desensitizing and offensive, and focused on lower bodily functions, making her appear less intelligent, less educated and less refined. They also made her feel bad about herself. Could it be that swearing was like self-harm using words.

Violet squeezed her eyes shut. She had to be kind to herself.

Including words.

Words are powerful.

Violet inhaled deeply to reset herself. 'Right. Ten minutes to get out the door. Violet can do this!' she pep talked herself.

base makeup ✔
face makeup ✔
eye makeup ✔

She pulled out the bright red lipstick, removed the cap and wound out the colour, leaned toward the mirror and applied it. Perfect. Failure was never a choice. ✔

Perfume—the liquid green Wood Infusion ✔

Violet emerged seven minutes later, her blonde, long-fringed pixie hair cut hair-sprayed into position, her makeup flawless. She rummaged through her closet for Tuesday's hairdressing black shirt and black skinny jeans, spied her forest green lace-up boots and got dressed. She grabbed her forest green suede bespoke tote, and left her room, closing the door behind her. A Jane rule. Then skipped down the steps to the ground floor.

It was Tuesday. Her favourite client, the vintage Ness, was coming in today. Her weekly visit.

Violet exited the house and made her way to her vintage blue and white Kombi Van Deluxe, and turned her head to the right. The man at the bus stop was holding his drink bottle tightly.

'Is that… Wood Infusion perfume I smell?' he called.

Violet beamed and then grimaced. *How did he know?* 'Yes. Did I put too much on… I mean… if you can smell it from all the way over there?' she said. Violet lifted her wrist to her nose, the tip reddened by this morning's sun. She was like a walking, talking Rudolf the Red-Nosed Reindeer. She inhaled, gently, like a sophisticated woman would. Sandalwood. Agarwood. Sweet orange. Musk.

'I have a perfumer's nose. A… *refined*… sense of smell. The wood notes remind me of a car that sat in the trees beside a dam. The car had been there for a while. There was a smaller tree growing inside it, and vines and flowers.'

'Oh,' said Violet. 'Were there Violet's growing in it too?' she added in jest.

Luciano laughed. 'Yes, and daisies, roses, zinnias and some other wild flowers, and gladiolus. I remember the gladiolus. They were such a riot of colour.'

'Sounds beautiful. Did you take a photograph? It would make a stunning photo. What type of car was it?'

'A… ah… Range Rover, I think. It was a dark green colour. So it blended in with the forest.'

Dark green, the colour Jane hated, Violet thought. But she quite liked it. 'Gotta get to work. Have a great day, Luciano!'

'You'd better make a dash. You're running a little late today!' he said.

Violet squished up her face. She didn't like the fact that he knew what time she left for work. But, she guessed, what else is there to do while waiting for a bus.

Violet climbed into her Kombi Van, squinted and pulled out green sunglasses from the glove box. She turned on the klak-klak engine, turned on her good-vibes music list, popped some gum in her mouth, then drove with a smile singing along to the music. At each red light she blew a bubble, and popped it.

She parked her Kombi Van at the back of the shop, turned off the klak-klak engine and waited for the splatter and the bang and the sigh, and grabbed her handbag and entered the shop via the back door.

'Haaallllooooo!' she called. It echoed back to her from her fellow artisans. Violet placed her handbag into her locker, donned her black apron, and walked through to the front desk.

'Oh—thank you,' she said as she picked up her doppio— double shot of espresso coffee, inhaling the intense aroma, then took a sip.

Heaven-in-a-cup.

Violet looked over her day map. She was on hair washing duties today. It suited her perfectly. And it didn't. She was allergic to the water and the shampoo and the conditioner and the… people.

At least she couldn't fail at hair washing. Her anxiety calmed and she bobbed her head. Once. Then skulled the remainder of her coffee. 'Woooo!' she said, smacking her lips.

The doorbell ding-dinged.

Client number one. 'Good morning. Are we washing your hair today?' Violet said.

'Yes. And give me that to die for head massage please.'

'Is there a particular type of head massage you'd like?' Violet tilted her head to the left. It reminded her of Ollie Wollie when she mentioned food or treats.

'There's different ones?'

'Yes.' Violent nodded. 'I do a short and long scalp massage.' *And if you annoy me, a really quick over and done with super short scalp massage.*

The client looked at her watch. 'The short one please. And make it maximum quality. Quality is better than quantity—as in length of time.'

Violet smiled in her sweet "Violent" way. *Oh you are so wrong, dear,* thought Violet, *when it comes to head massages, looong head massages, no matter the quality, are the bomb! There's nothing better.* This was going to be a really quick over and done with super short scalp massage. Clients should be thankful. Not bossy. Not judgy. How dare she give her the lecture about quality over quantity. She will give her both—low quality and super short.

'Lovely. Shall do.' Violet gestured to the hair washing basin. She put the towel around the client's shoulders and leaned the chair back. She ducked out the back and googled how to do a scalp massage. Violet returned to the client, started the stream of water, a little warmer than needed for this quality client. Grabbed the shampoo. And in five seconds was done. She grabbed the conditioner, poured it over the client's head and mixed it into her hair, then did the stroking technique of head massage—applying a gentle pressure and sweeping the hand from the front to the back, alternating hands—like stroking a cat. Apt. After one minute of stoking, Violet stopped and rinsed out the conditioner and wrapped the clients head up in the towel, and led her to her seat.

Violet smiled as the client sat in the chair. Her practised hairdresser smile. Customer relations were important.

Violet cleaned the wash basin area and swept the hair covered floor until client number two arrived. Lovely client number two. Just a shampoo and condition. No massage. No fuss. 'Would you like a cup of tea or coffee?' Violet asked her when she was done.

'No thank you.'

The BEST client, thought Violet.

And then came client number three. *The* number three. Things happen in threes.

The sniffing client number three.

The loud talking client number three.

The dirtiest, knottiest hair client number three.

Violet snapped her rubber gloves on and turned on the water.

She reached for a brush and tugged it through the knots.

'My partner has the weirdest zit,' she said in a harsh voice, 'high up on his thigh, near his—'.

Violet cleared her throat loudly. Drowning out her words. She didn't want to know about zits. And even more, she didn't want visualise high up on his thigh. Violet's eye twitched and her body tremored at-the-ick.

She turned on three taps of water and said loudly, 'Sorry, I can't hear well today.' Violet changed the music track to cringey dance music, turned up the volume and then hooked in to hair washing with scratching and pulling. Gently, of course. She watched on as the client pulled faces. Of irritation. Violet squirted the conditioner into her hair like she was a drunk guy relieving himself at a fence, and rubbed the conditioner in like trying to scrub blood off a white glove, and washed it out with a blast of water a firefighter would be pleased with. She wrapped up the client's hair and led her to her chair.

She gave her practised hairdresser smile.

Then left her there.

Client number four was male. Violet rolled her eyes. He was one of those males who only went to female hair dressers, basking in the attention he received. Not that he was deserving. It was customer relations. He'd been here before. And he was an unwelcome flirty type. And now all of the therapy-for-free-chatter between the women would stop, or change topics, just because of him. If Violet had her way, this hair salon would be women only. It would feel safer that way.

She sidled up to Amy, the apprentice. 'I'll pay you fifty dollars to wash his hair.'

'One hundred, and do my job of cleaning the toilets,' Amy said.

'Deal,' Violet said, and left to clean the toilets. Perhaps she could shove his head into the toilet bowl and flush the water and tell him his hair had been washed? *Now, now,* Violet thought, *not all men are violent and aggressive. He might be a good one? But why doesn't he go to a barber?*

At noon, Violet slipped Amy a one hundred note, and left the salon and headed across the road to the park. Away from the clients. Away from the hairdressing smells. Away from the cut hair that always found its way into her food or drink if she had lunch out the back. She opened up her handbag, and pulled out her salad sandwich, wrapped in her floral Beeswax Food Wrap.

Violet gave a lopsided smile. Maybe she wasn't that different to her mama, who always kept a ham sandwich in her "hambag".

As she lifted her salad sandwich to her mouth, her phone pinged. She wiped her hand, pulled out her phone and opened it up. It was a group text from Jane.

Hi everyone. Our house is now fully finished. Nothing more needs to be done. Thanks for your patience with the process of renovating. Does anyone want to change or rearrange anything? Let me know soon.

Violet rolled her eyes. Jane always asked this question. Like she was trying to make them feel part of the house with the ownership. Violet and her sisters knew that Jane was using the ownership mindset to make them feel invested in the house. A type of manipulation… oops, *strategy*… installed by organisations worldwide to make their employees feel "heard". And then Jane did what Jane always did. She chose what *she* wanted to do. Regardless. She missed the whole point of asking for input, and listening to it.

Violet texted back: *All good with me.*

What else could she do? Nobody liked to incur the wrath of Jane. Scary Jane. It wasn't worth the angst.

Fifteen minutes after Violet was back at the salon, the door dinged.

'Ness. Hello!' Violet walked over to the ninety-two-year-old and offered her elbow. Ness put her arm through Violet's and they walked side by side to the salon chair like they were best friends. Like grandmother and granddaughter.

'You look fabulous, Ness!'

'Thank you, dear.'

'What would you like today?' said Violet.

'The usual, please. And a cup of tea.' Ness gave Violet a wink. Their secret code.

'Your wish is my command.' Violet bent at her waist with a roll of her hand like a servant. She made Ness a cup of "wink tea" in her personal teacup and saucer, and returned. She placed it in front of her on the bench, the smell of bourbon drifting and smiling around them, and Violet started to brush Ness' hair.

'I'm washing your hair today. Have your cup of tea while I brush your hair first though.'

'Lovely, Violet. It sounds like a plan.' Ness closed her eyes as the brush tickled her scalp. 'I remember what happened, you know.'

'What happened when?' Violet said.

'You know… that tragic day… to the six daughters.'

Violet frowned. 'Oh'.

Ness opened her eyes and looked up at Violet in the mirror. 'The newspaper I read alleged that the girls were arguing in the back of the car, and the father turned around to tell them to settle. And that's when he veered off the road and into a dam. Only the mother, the father, and one child survived. One of the triplets.'

Violet slowed down with her hair brushing.

'Tragic. So tragic.' Ness blinked away tears.

'That is so awful, Ness. I couldn't imagine losing my sisters, living without them. Let's go over to the basin now.'

Violet walked Ness over to the wash basin and prepped

her with towels, lifted the foot rest and made sure she was comfortable. If truth be told, Violet loved Ness like she loved her mother. 'Would you like a scalp massage today?'

'Yes, please, dear Violet.'

Violet warmed the water and wet Ness' hair, then squeezed a little shampoo into her hands, warming it in her palms before placing it into Ness' hair. She worked it in, bubbles bubbling, then rinsed it out.

Violet reached back for the conditioner, Ness' favourite, fragrance free.

'You look just like her, dear,' Ness said.

Violet's head snapped back to look at Ness, her hand searching for the conditioning bottle. She knew the order of the shampoo and conditioner bottles on the shelf like the back of her hand. 'Who?' Violet said, pouring conditioner into-her-hand. 'Oh… Marilyn Munroe.'

Ness shook her head. 'You know who I'm talking about.'

Violet massaged the conditioner into Ness' scalp, gently, rhythmically, with no plan, just where she thought it would feel nice, as if she was massaging her own scalp, pulling sadness from her mind. She closed her eyes, relying on touch. 'My mother?' Violet finally said.

'The dead mother,' Ness said.

Violet sucked in a sharp breath. It was so unlike Ness to say anything like that. Maybe she was becoming senile. 'My mother is not dead!' Violet turned on the warm water to rinse Ness' hair.

The more she rinsed, the more she slowed her hand moving over her scalp.

Ness usually lost a little bit of hair in the basin. Everyone did. But not this much.

Not… *all of it!*

Violet's eyes widened and her heart raced. She was now

rinsing a bald scalp. The bald scalp of a ninety-two-year-old. Violet's eyes watered. She looked over at the conditioner bottle she had reached for without checking.

Hair remover.

Hair. Remover.

SSSSSSHHHHHH! Violet's inner voice was loud trying not to say the proper swear word. If she'd cursed properly, all the times she wanted to, that would have been eighteen dollars for Jane's swear jar. *Sssshhh——!* She may as well make it twenty dollars neat.

Sssshhh! Make that twenty-two dollars. Does intention to say a profanity count?

Violet looked left. Then right. Nobody was watching. She wrapped Ness' hairless head in the towel and pretended to dry her hair, as they always did. Then she took her over to her chair, walking slowly. 'I loooove the black leather pants you have on today. Did you ride your Harley?'

'Yes. But I'm having trouble getting the helmet over my hair lately, though. Could you give me a thinning trim today?'

Violet's eyes widened. She would have absolutely no trouble putting on the helmet now! 'How about something really radical for a ninety-two-year-old Harley woman?'

Ness' eyes lit up. 'How radical?'

'Trust me?' said Violet.

Ness narrowed her eyes at Violet. 'What the heck. YES!'

'Keep your eyes closed while I work some magic. I'll let you know when to open your eyes,' Violet said, her heart beating like drumsticks against her sternum.

Ness breathed deeply, then closed her eyes.

Violet removed the towel from her head, picked up her scissors and pretended to snip, snip, snip. *Snippety-snip.* She found the razor, turned it on and ran it over her scalp in a methodical way.

'Do you like the smell of mint and citrus and berries, dear Ness?' Violet asked.

'It sounds lovely, dear.'

Violet reached for some matte skull moisturiser, put it into her hands, rubbed them together to warm the moisturiser, then massaged it onto Ness' bald head.

'Alice, dear. You look like Annie, or was it Alice...' Ness said.

Violet frowned. She would never look like an Alice or an Annie. She was far too chic to look like one of those names! 'On the count of five, open your eyes. One, two, three, four—'

Ness opened her eyes. They reddened and filled with tears. Her lips trembled. But no sound came out.

'You'll have no trouble putting on your bike helmet now. And you'll look like one of those bad-ass bikers with a gentle heart, doing a toy run for kids. All you need is a beard!' Violet said to lighten the mood. 'And, following on from your punk hair style from last week, this is the perfect progression!' Violet fisted her hands to stop them from shaking.

Ness and Violet's eyes connected. And that's when Violet knew, that Ness knew about something that had been hidden, never to be dug up again.

And that is when Violet knew that she would not be returning to the hair salon.

Would her day have been different if the sun didn't touch the tip of her nose, and if she'd heard her alarm and got up out of bed at the right time?

Maybe getting out on the literal right side of the bed was in fact the wrong side of the bed?

Violet walked out the back of the salon and poured a glass of water, lifted the glass to her lips and drank, her hands shaking. She walked out the back door. Sunshine would help. It always did. Violet leaned against the paint washed brick wall, closed her eyes and lifted her face to the sun. Like recharging. Her mama's screams filled her head. And the image of a bearded man, not far from them. And a boy. A young boy running to the road and screaming for help.

Violet opened her eyes and returned to the salon.

Ness was gone. And so was her motorbike.

Every job has a beginning and an ending. Today, Violet's job ended. She grabbed her handbag from her locker and walked to her van. She started the klak-klak engine, turned on her moody-blues music list, popped some gum into her mouth to keep it shut, then drove without a smile. At each red light she let out a long breath, hoping the sadness would be vacuumed out of her.

She parked her Kombi Van in the driveway of the terrace. Turned off the klak-klak engine and waited for the splatter and the bang and the sigh, then grabbed her handbag and walked to the front door. The dark blue door of integrity and trust.

Violet didn't deserve to enter it. But home felt safe today. She unlocked the door to the four-legged welcoming committee giving a serious side-eye-of-judgement. 'Ollie Wollie! You wouldn't believe my day! Jane will be spewing!' She squatted down to Oliver Twist. 'Who's a good hot dog?'

Now that Oliver Twist recognised her, he gave her the happy-tail-wag-o-meter.

At 8:45pm, Violet sat at her writing desk and grabbed her lavender coloured paper and wrote a note to Jane. She descended the steps two at time and shoved the folded note into the Jar-of-Jane-Notes, then returned to her room so her lights were off by 9pm.

And that was a day, and a night.

Chapter 26

Wednesday
Daisy

'Atop of the Wednesday morning to you, Daisy!' Luciano said.

'Crikey, you scared the living daylights out of me,' said Daisy. 'The sky's so blue today it'd be a great day to chuck a sickie and head to the beach for a bludge.'

Luciano chuckled. 'That's where I'm heading today at noon.'

'Deadset!' Daisy walked over to Luciano sitting on the bus seat in his dark blue suit, his carpet bag beside him. 'It will be a ripper of a day. I hope you have your budgie smugglers in that bag of yours.'

'I do. From the Budgie Smuggler online shop.'

'Fair dinkum? What design did you get?'

'That 70's pair.'

Daisy looked it up online. 'Good onya. Ripper colours!'

'Thanks.'

'Look, mate. Gotta go. I cannot let death wait in this weather. You know… off like a bag of prawns in the hot sun, and all…'

'Death can wait, Daisy. It, or what, can't be more dead, can it?'

'No, but my boss will kill me if I'm late.'

Luciano nodded. 'Ah, another death, like 1996.'

Daisy narrowed her eyes at Luciano then raised an eyebrow. 'Who's death in 1996?'

'The entire year. It was a bad one. Best to leave it all dead and buried. Not back from the dead like nothing had ever happened and lives continued on.'

'Did… someone die in 1996. Is that what you are trying to tell me?'

'My muse, or should I say my muses. That's why it was a terrible year.'

Daisy's eye twitched and her body tremored at-the-ick. 'Bloody oath! I nearly believed your porky pie that it was a person! You dag! Gotta run. Enjoy bludging on the beach!' Daisy jogged to her Ute. She had to get away from the blue suited man with the carpet bag. Why did he choose the year 1996?

Daisy took a deep breath, then sat in her Ute in the driver's seat with her eyes closed for a minute, trying to calm her scattered mind. Then she drove to work. The dead part of town. Where the quiet people lived. She entered her work shed and checked the list of jobs for today.

Dead flower collection
Weeding
Mute x 2

It was a three type of day. Things always happen in threes. Daisy lifted her right shoulder in a shrug. She wondered when she would get to use her carpentry skills again. That's why she was employed. As a carpenter! She missed fixing things and building things and working with wood. She missed the problem solving.

Daisy did the Aussie salute to bat away a fly, said gidday to the blokes, grabbed her hat, and the keys to the cemetery limo, aka, the golf buggy. For a moment she allowed herself to enjoy the vision of golf being played at the cemetery, and landscape for the hole in one changing each day with the graves being dug.

She drove around the prime real estate plots for the dead, stopping and collecting spent flowers that could be easily buried with their recipient, nourishing-the-ground, except, the company rule was to remove them quickly as soon as they began to die. *Death wasn't a good look at the cemetery*, the director said, while people tried not to laugh.

Daisy cleared the dying flowers, and placed them into three buckets: the dead-heads for Zinnia to propagate the seeds; the still perfectly living flowers; and the ones that couldn't be salvaged.

She made her way back to the work shed and sorted her buckets. With the good flowers, she always created her own floral tributes and left them at the graves of children, or gave them to distressed mourners to place on a grave.

Today, there were only enough flowers for one floral tribute. Daisy made her way to the six sisters. She slowed as she came to the grave. When she arrived, there was already a large bouquet laid at the tombstone. Who had visited? Daisy always liked to see the people who visited the grave sites. Except at night when the disrespectful would come.

Daisy placed her floral arrangement next to the other, removed her hat, and looked at the names of the sisters:

Ophelia, aged 13
Etti, aged 11
Cordelia, aged 8
Aurelia, aged 8
Mae, aged 5
Harriet, aged 4

Together, playing in eternity in the presence and love of the Lord. 1996.

Daisy gasped. 1996. She closed her eyes and pushed the weirdness of Luciano's matching year from her mind. She would most definitely place stolen grave flowers there.

Daisy took a step back and placed her hat onto her head. As she turned to start weeding in Section B, the tombstone beside the sisters caught her attention. Not because it was outstanding by any means, but because of the last name.

In loving memory of

F. Longbottom, aged 58
A. Piccadilly, aged 56

'Hmmm... a Piccadilly. There's quite a few of them at this cemetery. I wonder if we are related?' Daisy said to herself. She knew she only noticed that last name because of the familiarity, the frequency illusion.

She continued to Section B and started weeding, reading gravestones, or *gracestones*, she liked to call them, as they brought honour to the departed. Some were ornate, some plain and many other designs in between. There was one with a photo embedded near where she was working. A lovely looking couple. She moved around to the other side of the plots where she saw some with QR codes. Life stories. As tempted as she was to get out her phone and go to the QR code link, it was against company policy.

She heard the sound of footsteps and grabbed her weeding tools. Company policy was to make yourself scarce out of respect to the visitors to allow them privacy to visit loved ones. Daisy reached for her bucket and looked up. Her eyes widened, and she fell backwards, her heart racing. In front of her were the people in the photograph.

Was this real?

Were they real?

'Sorry to give you a fright,' the man said. 'Can I help you up?'

Daisy breathed out in relief. They *were* real people. 'I'm good, thanks. It's just… I thought I saw… you were—'

'Ghosts,' added the woman. 'You saw the photo?'

Daisy nodded. 'You look awfully like your parents.'

'No. It's us. We're just not dead. Yet.'

Daisy frowned, then smiled. 'I'd have a good yarn to tell if you were dead!'

'It's just… we're organised. We are the last in the line of our families, and chose not to have kids. When we die we won't have anyone to pay for our headstone. So, you know… practicalities and all… and we are thinking of adding our life stories via the life story app, so people can see our lives like a movie.'

'Good planning, I would say,' Daisy said. She wanted to question them about the life story app. Wouldn't it be a waste of money when technology failed, and it will, or it will get changed.

'Sorry again for the scare,' the man said.

'No worries,' said Daisy. 'I needed a good heart jolt while weeding.' She gave them a smile and walked away, giving them privacy to visit their future dead selves. 'Bloody oath,' Daisy whispered out of earshot.

She returned to the work shed and changed into her black mourning clothing. It was time to be a Mute. She jumped into the cemetery golf buggy chariot and drove to the freshly dug grave, parking the buggy fifty metres away, and waited under the trees. In thirty minutes the funeral procession would be here.

Daisy was prepared as the Mute. She had done it many times before.

This burial service was going to be a small one. A man. His widow had requested a mute because only seven people would be in attendance, and she liked the number eight.

Daisy stood behind the others when they arrived, looked solemn and held her head tilted downward in respect. A couple of times she pulled out a tissue and wiped her eyes, and pretend sniffed. She hung back until the last person had left, then walked to the cemetery chariot and drove back to the work shed, changed into her work clothes and resumed weeding.

At 1:30pm she arrived for the next burial.

In her Mute attire.

She watched as the attendees arrived. A bigger group. She wondered why she was needed.

Again she stood slightly to the back with her head lowered. It was a calm and quiet service. The coffin lowered into the grave and red roses thrown on top, some mourners sobbing, and then a woman threw herself down on top of the coffin, with a thud!

Screaming.

Banging on the coffin!

Daisy's eyes widened and she looked around.

Should she step in?

Should she get a ladder?

A man laid on the ground and proffered his hand to the woman. She took it and he held on to her while two men grabbed his ankles and dragged him backwards. More hands were offered to the woman as she neared the top. The man dusted himself off, and the service returned to its scheduled words.

Daisy swallowed then cleared her throat, took out a handkerchief, dabbed at her eyes and blew her nose. She lowered her head again.

'WAYNE WAS MINE, NOT YOURS! How dare you have an affair with him, KAREN!'

Daisy lifted her head. Eyes wide. She felt like she needed a box of popcorn to watch the show.

Karen took a deep breath, pushed her somewhat large chest out and moved toward the wife. And that was when the first fist was thrown. And then came the all in brawl.

Except for Daisy. She had never seen such a scandal at a funeral before. It was outrageously preposterous.

And funny.

'Oi!' came a bellow. And everyone stopped at once, and straightened their clothing. 'And now for Scene 3, of Wayne's final act on earth.'

On the other side of the grave stood two men. They about turned, pulled down their trousers, exposing their white bottoms with the words written, "The End."

'Perfectly Wayne!' someone yelled as a roar of laughter erupted.

And with that, everyone left. Just like that.

Except for Daisy. Who stood there. Still. Who tried to work out what she had just witnessed. Daisy looked upward, and wondered how good God's sense of humour was today. Then she turned and left while her co-workers stepped in and began the task of filling the grave with dirt.

'And that was number three for today,' Daisy said to herself as she drove the cemetery chariot back to the work shed. She changed into her work clothes, and returned to Section B to finish the weeding.

At 5pm she entered the house to a bark and an Oliver Twist side-eye-of-judgement. 'Oli!' she said, and Oliver recognised her at once and rewarded her with his wagging tail.

At 8:30pm, Daisy grabbed her yellow paper and wrote Jane a note.

Dear Jane,

> *Luciano gives me the heebie-jeebies. Something he said today doesn't sit right with me. It was a year in the past he mentioned out of nowhere.*
>
> *And fair dinkum, the cemetery was full of lunatics today. It was a real rip snorter of a day. I think I'll go walkabout from that job.*
>
> *I do not wish to work at the cemetery any longer. It can bugger off!*
>
> *That is all.*

Daisy.

She descended the stairs slowly, wishing the steps could be a slide instead. She pushed her note into the Jar-of-Jane-Notes, then returned to her bedroom and turned off the lights at precisely 9pm.

And that was a day, and a night.

Chapter 27

Thursday
Rose

Rose walked briskly, returning from the coffee shop, a coffee cup in one hand and Dash's leash in the other. She spied Luciano sitting at the bus stop and slowed her pace.

'A good morning to Dash,' Luciano said without turning his head toward them, 'and to you too, Rose.'

'A good morning to you, Luciano.' Rose held a cappuccino cup in front of Luciano, the one she had bought for him.

He didn't look at it, so she moved it closer to him. 'That smells like a fine coffee,' he said.

'It's yours. Dash bought it for you. It's a flat white,' Rose said. Perhaps she shouldn't have bought him one without asking him if he would like it.

'You read me like tea leaves,' he said. 'Can you put it on my thigh for me.'

Rose frowned. *What an odd request.* But she did as he asked anyway. She watched as he moved his hand around the cup, but didn't move his head. *Odd.* 'You're quite early for the bus today, Luke,' she said.

Luciano took a sip of the coffee. 'Yes. There's beautiful bird song here, and I like to listen to it for longer some days. Today is that type of day. Do you photograph birds?'

'I'mmmm… more of an events photographer—you know, weddings, birthdays and other celebrations, oh and trees, I like to photograph trees.' Rose smiled as a memory came to her. 'Apparently, the moment I was born, according to my mother and father, I grabbed onto my father's camera and accidentally pushed the button.' Rose laughed. 'I took my first selfie!'

Luciano chuckled. 'Is that chocolate I can smell? I thought you were a latte drinker?'

'A mocha today. I needed the chocolate fix along with the caffeine hit to help me get through the morning of preparing photos for clients. Luciano… what do you think of the front door colour that we chose for the house?'

'I think it suits it,' he said.

'Yeah… the yellow certainly makes it look like it is a house full of sunshine.' Rose frowned.

'Yellow is a happy colour for a happy house,' he said.

'Absolutely,' Rose said. 'Enjoy your flat white. I thought you were more of a flat white drinker than a cappuccino drinker.' *Like your mysteriousness,* thought Rose. He knew a lot about her, but he never said a lot about himself.

'My fav coffee is iced,' he said.

'I'll remember that for next time. Gotta go. Chow,' Rose said and left.

Luciano stood.

The-bus-was-coming.

Rose hesitated before she opened the navy blue door, and looked back at Luciano. He stepped onto the bus with his carpet bag, the coffee cup left on the bus seat. She waited until the bus left, then retrieved the coffee cup. She'd hate it to spill onto someone, ruining their clothes. And besides, she could do the biometrics of his fingerprints on the cup.

She walked up the four steps to the small verandah, the hound waiting to enter his house. She released Dash from his harness once they were inside, then went up two flights of stairs to her room, poured the remainder of Luciano's flat white coffee into her en suite basin, and put the empty cup onto her desk.

Rose was nearing the end of the wedding photos from a week ago. All she had to do was a final check and some editing, if needed. She also had to scan the photos taken on the 35mm colour camera after developing them in her dark room.

She gazed out her window and saw a man with a black dog. Rose picked up her digital camera and pressed the button. *Video.* The dog rounded his back, his butt closer to the ground, and pooped near their front gate, the man looking away. When the dog finished his business, he tugged him along, not bothering to pick up the dog poo.

Captured. Idiot. Jane will be infuriated by the act.

Rose entered her dark room. The workspace was set up with the materials, ready to begin. She looked around before she turned off the light. Psychological nostalgia. A yearning for a bygone era. Her connection to the past and the present.

Rose took the film out of the cassette and cut it off with scissors and unrolled the film. She loaded the film onto another reel and wound it on, then placed the reel in the film tank and secured the lid. She turned on the lights and mixed the film developer fluid with water. She unscrewed the lid on the uppermost part of the film tank and poured the mixture directly in the funnel shaped hole, set the film tank down and set the timer.

She picked up the film tank and agitated it periodically, as per the process until the timer sounded. She poured out the stop bath liquid and replaced it with fixer, and repeated the agitation process again and left it sit for five minutes. Then she removed the film from the tank and rinsed it under cold water for a few minutes and soaked the film in a wetting agent before hanging it to dry.

Rose repeated this process for each of the 35mm films she had. While the negatives dried, she sat at her laptop computer and worked on the digital photographs, editing and colour changing to the requested style the bride and groom had asked for.

Beautiful.

Rose loved photographing weddings. And even more, she loved capturing the guests true emotions about the happy couple, and the interplay between guests. So many stories to tell in facial expressions and attitudes. Real photographs. Unaltered. Raw. Moments frozen in time. Truth that can't be changed.

Rose packed the finished digital shots into their folder, and returned to the dark room, excited to develop real photos from the negatives she had developed. There was nothing better than holding photographs in your hand, rather than looking at them digitally.

And so the process began under the red light. The enlarger for the negatives, the photo paper, the three chemical baths and a water bath and the drying line and pegs.

To Rose it felt like magic. Frozen moments of life. Of emotions. Of relationships. Of atmosphere. Just like those old photos in Jane's suitcase under her bed.

It was late at night when Rose collected the dry photos from her dark room. She shuffled through them with a smile on her face. Then stopped at one photograph.

Rose's eye twitched and her body tremored at-the-ick.

It was the guy with the dog who pooped, which Rose picked up from the grass so no one stood in it. She stood taller. The poop-in-the-bag was still in her photography bag. She reached for the bag and opened it, and pulled it out. It was still well sealed in the plastic. Thank goodness.

Evidence #1, in case she needed it.

Rose put that photograph of the collection to the side. Nobody wants to see a pooping dog at a wedding. She shuffled through the photos again. And stopped. Same man, this time handing an envelope to a guest.

Evidence #2. Rose added that photo to the other she would not give them.

Tomorrow she would wrap the photos in her unique gifting style, and add a beautiful colour print as a thank you, and deliver her work to the clients.

Before she went to bed, Rose opened the security camera feed of the house for the last 24 hours.

She .. s l o w e d . . . . t h e . . . . . r e e l . . . .

The front, sides and back of house.

Her jogging to photograph the new landscaping.

The man with the dog. The dog pooping at the gate. The man entering their yard. The man going around into the backyard and looking into the shed, and going to the bunker, about to lift the timber up. The bark of Dash, and the man leaving in haste with his dog.

The man leaving an envelope at the front door.

Rose sat at her writing desk at once, grabbed her pink paper and penned a note to Jane.

Dear Jane,

I have emailed you some photographs of situations you may be interested in.
And… there's something about Luciano…

Warm regards,
Rose

She descended the stairs with a frown. Something was brewing. She could feel it. She pushed her note into the Jar-of-Jane-Notes, then returned to her bedroom and turned off the lights, at precisely 9pm.

And that was a day, and a night.

Chapter 28

Poppy

At 10pm, after the expected lights out at 9pm, a-Jane-rule, Poppy went to her wardrobe and pulled out a Jane dress and put it on. She grabbed a Jane hat, Jane's only Jane hat, and place it onto her head, covering her hair. Poppy crept up two flights of stairs, and then the attic ladder. And into the attic of Mum and Dad.

She sat on the sofa bed and turned on the television, took Jane's phone out of her pocket and hit facetime. After one ring, mother and father appeared on the screen.

Poppy took off the Jane hat. 'Hi Dad. It's me. Poppy!'

Frank and Alice sat still. No response.

'Dad. Mum. It's me.'

Frank blinked three times, looked at Alice, then back at the screen. He cleared his throat. 'But no! It can't be… the accident—'

'They were wrong. I survived. Remember? Or are you starting to lose your memories? It's quite expected after a traumatic accident like that…'

Alice Jane Piccadilly the 3rd lifted her "hambag" to her lap, and took out a ham sandwich…

<h1 style="text-align:center">Chapter 29</h1>

Friday
Zinnia

Zinnia sat on the bus stop seat. She smoothed down her short blonde hair, zig zag parted in the middle, and adjusted the pastel pink flower positioned just above her left ear.

'Good morning,' Zinnia and Luciano said at exactly the same time.

'Jinx,' said Zinnia and laughed. 'It feels like we're in high school!'

'It does. In that navy blue and white uniform. Hair in the college cut style for the boys. Girls with single or double French braids created at morning and lunch breaks while sitting in the quadrangle sunshine.'

Zinnia reached up and ran her hand through her hair, lost

in that memory. She was sure that all girls did the same things at their high schools. 'Or pretending to be a senior and sitting in their library area, reading the books for seniors only.'

'Or skipping class by hiding under one of the tables in the library.'

Zinnia laughed again. 'I did that too!' She moved her sports shoe along the concrete, remembering the flowers she used to draw on the sole of her school shoes.

'Flowers on the soles of shoes,' Luciano said, and stood for the bus, yet to materialize from up the road.

Zinnia froze as a coldness travelled down her spine. The bus stopped and the doors opened, and Zinnia waited for Luciano to board the bus before she did. She needed to avoid him. His words sat heavily in her stomach, churning and nauseating. She needed to find an alternative way to get to work at the university.

Ten stops later, Zinnia exited the bus at the uni and walked across the campus grounds to the research building with quick steps, anxiety poisoning her circulatory system. How many times had she looked over her shoulder like she was being followed?

She-had-lost-count.

It had felt like that just before the second tragedy.

Thoughts flitted through her mind, writing words encoded with electrifying signals.

Why do we run?

Why don't we stand our ground?

Why don't we ask more questions?

Why don't good men step up when one of their kind needs help, needs correcting?

Zinnia wanted to swallow the sea of memories that had been given to her by another.

Zinnia placed her backpack into her locker, grabbed her lab coat and headed to the staff room. She checked the roster. She was collecting data on sugarcane again today. Research data. This time in the mature plants. Good. Perhaps her hands would stop shaking then, hidden in the green fields of tall sugar cane stalks and the green long leaves blowing in the wind, dancing their cares away.

Zinnia joined the end of the line, and watched the members of her research crew gather their tools for measuring and recording. For photographing. For collecting samples. And Zinnia mimicked their actions.

Like-she-always-did.

She joined a group of women and watched as they worked so she knew what she was to do, then broke away from them to be alone while she pretended to look like a botanist, perfecting the imposter syndrome persona. And besides, that way, nobody would pick up the fact that she was not in fact a real botanist.

She had been making more and more mistakes at work. And today was not a good day. Her mind was distracted by the words of Luciano.

Did-he-know-something-about-her?

After four hours of inspecting and writing data she was not entirely sure was correct, Zinnia sat on the ground in the sugar cane field, tears forming in her eyes. How could she submit her work? She had no idea whether it was accurate. She should have volunteered to be the recorder again, ensuring that her scientific non-method would not ruin their years and years of research.

She ripped the paper from the clip board and crumpled it up in her hands. She wanted to rip it into a zillion pieces to help get the anger out of her. Instead, Zinnia opened it back up, smoothed it out and wrote Luciano's name on the back over and over, trying to find him in her memories, and whether he had gone to the same secondary school as her.

And then an echo of him rippled through her.

He was one of five who had asked her to be his date at the school formal. She had declined. His eyes watered as he stepped back from her, and then he acted weirdly whenever he was around her.

Zinnia icked, found the cigarette lighter in her toolkit, flicked on the flame and held it to the corner of the paper. She would let it burn then stomp on it to put it out.

A noise to her right startled her.

A snake. An eastern Taipan. Deadly. In thirty minutes.

Zinnia dropped the burning paper, grabbed her tool kit, and yelled SNAKE to warn the others as she ran out of sugarcane field 11B, to the safe, open space. She stopped, leaning over to catch her breath, and when she straightened up, she saw what she knew would be the biggest disaster in the history of sugarcane research at the university.

At first, the plume of smoke was small, hardly recognisable, until it filled the sky with terribly bad news.

And sugarcane field 11B was gone. With the research.

Just. Like. That.

All. Her. Fault.

Zinnia did a quick head count to ensure all the team had made it out. They had. As well as the snakes that had been flushed from 11B.

Everybody stood still. Frozen. Like the ice age. It was their survival tactic in the field of sugarcane, which could also be the field of snakes. Adding to a snake's agitation was the quickest way to ensure a bite, the poison entering your blood stream until ...

Fire truck sirens screamed, bouncing off the embers and smoke and collecting in Zinnia's ears with blame. Water flooded Field 11B, separated far enough from the other sugarcane fields as a fire break, as planned for any unexpected emergencies, like this.

An-emergency-created-by-Zinnia.

And Zinnia finished working at noon, after an investigation about the fire, admitting fault, but blaming a snake sighting while she had out the lighter, and that's how it started. Right?

She returned home in a state of dismay. She had some big decisions to make. High on her list was that she could no longer catch the bus to work. She had to avoid Luciano at all costs. She no longer had the long blonde hair with braids that he would remember from school. She was mature now, and not awkward like she once was in high school. Surely, he didn't recognise her.

Zinnia paced her room, trying not to be distraught by what ifs. She needed a distraction, and it resided in moving her flower study and greenhouse into the new garden shed. It would be a long and arduous process that would keep her mind from wandering back to the past. Removing the plants and taking them down two flights of steps and out the back to the garden shed, returning numerous times, then disassembling her greenhouse, and taking it to the shed, piece by piece, before reassembling it again. It would keep her focussed on the present. She couldn't wait to successfully create her own flower line. Chrysanthemums her chosen flower to manipulate.

Zinnia placed her hands on her hips and stood in front of her new botany lab aka the garden shed. She pulled on the door but it was locked. And the previous owner had not left a key for it. Disappointed, Zinnia entered the house, Oliver behind her, a bone-in-his-mouth.

'Add it to your collection, your Royal Sausage-ness!' Zinnia said, downcast. Oliver trotted to the collection of dog things box. 'Drop,' said Zinnia, and Oliver Twist dropped the bone, which she promptly picked up and added to the bones he had collected.

Zinnia frowned and looked over at the backyard. She wondered where Oliver Twist had been digging up the bones from, even after the landscaping had been finished.

Zinnia walked up two flights of steps to her room on the third floor. The steps to the attic were lowered. Jane must have been up there.

Zinnia scowled. She hadn't invited her up there yet!

Zinnia flipped open her laptop and entered her password, she logged into the university staff site, and into plant genetics. There was a new program they had been asked to try, and she was pretty keen to put it into action using the genetics of her own flower creation.

The AI program was being used to help with research and in the creation of better crops for future sustainability.

Zinnia opened her folder with her data for her flower line, and entered it into the program, ticking the box that said, include AI created simulated image.

Fifteen seconds later, Zinnia screamed.

While she had envisioned a beautiful bloom of seven-shades-of-pink-petals in the one flower, soft pastel green leaves and stem, the image from AI that gathered her data, and her "recipe" for her flower line, threw up an image of the ugliest flower in the world. Black petals with oozing green goo, dripping from the petals, and an ugly face like creature in the middle that looked like it had risen from the dead.

Her genetic code for the flower scent created a Sulfur like odour, nothing like the perfumer's palette she had tried to integrate into the genetics of the flower.

This flower, will have people running for the hills. On the other hand, it could send a powerful message to someone who you wanted to stop annoying you, or stalking you… or gaslighting you… or violating your rights as a human being.

Zinnia ran to the bathroom and vomited. How could such an idea that was meant for beauty be something so vile.

It was then that Zinnia made up her mind about her unique flower line. She would use AI to help create it. This program would give her the image and the scent, guaranteed—saving a bucket load of time and trouble and experiments and failures in getting it right. Her product would be here in no time.

Zinnia closed eyes and listened to the music swirling around in her mind. The earworm. A musical itch. Playing on repeat. Usually a song she hated. Today, this earworm was different. It was mesmerising and catching and calming. She envisioned herself passing through a healing light and into her field of flowers. *Her* flower farm.

She opened her eyes with a new resolve and wrote a note to Jane. On the green paper she had been given, of course.

Dear Jane,

Have you met Luciano? Does he seem familiar? Have you met him in the past? I will no longer catch the bus to the university at that same time because of him.

I am waiting to move my greenhouse and propagating kits to the garden shed. It is perfect. Thank you. We just need the key to open that unusual lock.

Zinnia

P.S. I must declare that I accidentally set a sugar cane research field on fire today. I didn't mean to. I will find out the fate of my work status soon.
P.P.S. I'm so sorry, Jane. I didn't mean to let you down.
P.P.P.S. It will make me even less liked at work... if anyone liked me at all.

She descended the stairs, two flights of them, and went to the long wooden dining table. She pushed her note into the Jar-of-Jane-Notes, then returned to her bedroom and turned her light off at precisely 9pm.

And that was a day, and a night.

Chapter 30

Saturday
Flora

Flora sat in her classic, retro, pastel green 1991 Nissan Figaro and warmed her hands. She reached over to the glovebox and pulled out the long white satin gloves, and tried to erase the red lipstick on the pointer finger from her memory. No matter how many times she tried to wash it off, it was still there.

A reminder.

She wondered why she just didn't throw those gloves away and buy a new pair. Untainted. Unblemished. With new memories to be made.

She glanced in the rear view mirror and her eyes stayed there. A man with a black dog pooping near the front gate. Flora grabbed her phone and took a snapshot. The man stood with a hand in his pocket, looking up at the house, then down the side of the house. He gave a small smile then tugged his dog along, leaving the poop there. Flora's eye twitched and her body tremored at-the-ick. She wanted to get out of her car and give him a piece of her mind, but then she shrank in fear.

Was he like those men?

Those men who disrespected women.

Those men who felt threatened by women, their only strategy to react aggressively, or passively aggressively laugh in their face and shut them down?

Flora sunk down into her seat until he walked past, then repositioned herself and started the car.

'Sh–,' she whispered, not saying the whole word but wanting to, remembering that she had left her nose plugs in her bedroom. Again. She looked up at Jane's room to see if her French doors were open. She seemed to have supersonic hearing for swearing.

And a very large swear jar.

Flora opened her car door and ran back to the house and retrieved her nose plugs from her second floor room, and left, jogging down the steps, closing the door quietly behind her, along the pathway to the front gate, jumped over-the-dog-poo and stopped on the path, panting.

'Morning!' Luciano said.

Flora wondered why he never turned his head toward her to speak. 'Morning!' she replied.

He held up a large bag of carrots. 'I have too many carrots. Can you give them to the horses at the farm?'

'Of course.' Flora walked over to him and took the carrots from him. 'Thanks. But just the horses? The cows will chase me and the donkeys will steal them. I could cut them into small pieces for the llamas—'

'Just the horses, and double for the palomino one.'

Flora's eyes glazed over.

The palomino horse. The white collar with the lipstick.

The winter lake in the spring.

The argument.

The goodbye.

She swallowed to push the memory away. 'I will. Thanks. Gotta go.'

Flora ran to her car like she was running from a tsunami. She drove at one kilometre over the speed limit to get to work on time, anxiety burning her skin about not obeying the road rules, then joined the team huddle at 6:15am to confirm the to-do lists for the day.

When the silence of a moment-in-time-between-heartbeats made time stand still, Flora pulled out the baby scans from her pocket. She took a big breath and said, 'Pregnant. Finally!'

Excitement travelled through the work shed like bells ringing. Flora closed her eyes and smiled, immersing herself in the contagious joy that was around her. Conception had taken quite a while. But there it was. And she could finally shout it from the hilltops. Or the paddocks at least.

After a quick shuffle of jobs to accommodate the pregnancy, Flora received her new list.

Llamas
Watering house vegetable gardens
Paperwork
Feeding chickens

Then Flora drove the tractor to the llama paddock. She had cut up carrots to feed them. She told them the good news and that the baby should be here in six months.

On the drive to water the house vegetable gardens, she stopped by the horses and fed them carrots from Luciano, remembering to give Pal, the palomino horse, a double helping.

On the continuing journey to water the gardens, she threw carrots to the cows, sheep and goats. It was a glorious day!

Paperwork. Easy.

Feeding the chickens. Fun.

Until it wasn't.

Unit the rooster, Rodney, decided to charge at her.

And Flora ran.

Rodney in tow.

She had forgotten how to assert her dominance over him. All she thought of was the time he had put painful holes in her legs with his spurs.

Flora ran through a gate and into the cow paddock. To the placid cows she had conversations with on a daily basis.

The placid cows she knew by name. Her girls.

She slowed her pace to a stop, and turned to look for Rodney. And that's when Bessie lowered her head below Flora's behind, and gave her an almighty toss. And time slowed as Flora's feet lifted off the ground, and she became airborne before her landing was cushioned by a lovely warm cow paddy.

'Sh–!' She wanted to say the full swear word. But she just couldn't. At least Jane couldn't demand money for her friggin' swear jar. She was literally sitting in cow excrement. Flora's shoulders lifted as she took a deep breath, feeling the warmth of the cow paddy beneath her. She *was* having such a good day.

Such. A. Good. Day.

Rodney needed to be locked up. For good!

Flora stood, cow manure dripping from her bottom. Her eye twitched and her body tremored at-the-ick. She lifted her chin and walked the long walk back to the shed, her posterior hurting, her back spasming and her stomach cramping, leaving a smelly trail of cow-doo-doo behind her.

She peeled off her khaki work pants and tossed them straight into the bin with her red and black checked farm work shirt. Thankfully, she always had a second pair of clean work clothes in her locker.

She promptly clothed herself and spoke to the boss and left work, tears rolling down her cheeks as she drove. She didn't know what hurt more, her body or her pride.

Flora put her hand to her back as she walked through the front garden gate of poop at home, up the garden path and to the front door. The four-legged alarm sounded as she put her key into the lock. When she opened the door, Oliver Twist gave her the side-eye-of-judgement.

'Olivier!' she said as she stepped into the hallway.

Oliver recognised her then, and wagged his tail. He lifted his long nose higher, sniffing the air. 'I know. It was a lousy day. I'll shower and then let's go for a drive. We've got some thinking to do.'

Olivier sat in the front seat of the classic, retro, pastel green 1991 Nissan Figaro, with his funky flower bow tie bright against his long chocolate and tan fur, his long ears flapping with the wind. He looked debonaire next to Flora, dressed in her sunrise gingham ankle pants, her white ¾ sleeve boat-neck top, white Hepburn sunglasses and her long white Audrey Hepburn opera gloves, with the dab of red lipstick on the right index finger.

Flora looked at Olivier and smiled.

A-woman's-best-friend.

Loyal. Patient. Loving. Stealing hearts and wrapping them in beautiful light. 'Let's go to the winter lake for a picnic.'

Olivier barked. Once. He understood everything. Always.

The winter lake came into view and Flora gasped at the beauty of it, the turquoise blue hiding its secrets from yesteryear. She parked her car, grabbed the picnic basket and Olivier's harness and lead, and ventured to the picnic area to the right.

Flora and Olivier soaked up the sun and snacked on strawberries, blueberries, watermelon, banana and apple. She would have loved a wine to dull the ache in her back.

She looked to the right to the forest, where she had once spied Jane's partner, Hudson, on a palomino horse with another woman. That place where Hudson and Jane used to dream of stars by the winter lake. Where she had once charged over to Hudson to confront him. And where he had slapped her when she touched the red lipstick on his collar with her white gloves, the force pushing her to the ground.

She had walked to the lake with her hand over her smarting, bruised cheek, singing the miserable story to the lake of secrets, the whispering pines carrying the story on the wind until it was no more. Like Jane's partner.

Until he appeared once more, with death.

Flora turned her tear stained face to the lake. 'Let's walk, Olivier,' she said. She led Olivier down to the lake's white stony edge and watched the afternoon sun kiss the water with sparkles of light. 'It's time, I think,' Flora said. 'Time to let go.'

Flora pulled the fingers of her glove off her right hand, being careful not to touch the lipstick of truth, then in one swift action, tugged off the glove. She laid it in the water of the Lake of Secrets, and watched as it floated away, rocking to the lullaby of the drowning water.

The glove turned and waited as Flora removed the left glove, and set it free to join the other. They floated out further, together, where the deep liquid songs called the secrets to the below. To the bottom of the lake where stories of sadness scattered until their words were silenced.

'It is finished,' Flora said, and Olivier gave a little jump.

They returned home to the sunset of endings, the colour palette of yellow, orange and reds painting the sky until deep purple came to swallow them into the stars. And then the moon shouted hello with a pretend brightness of day.

Flora sat at her desk, pulled out her orange coloured paper and wrote a note to Jane.

Dear Jane,

> *The baby is due in 6 months. I'm sorry for swearing today, but to be fair, I did land in cow manure after Rodney the rooster charged at me. And yes, I am sore.*
>
> *Olivier and I visited the lake. You know which one. And I no longer own those long white gloves.*
>
> *And… there's something about Luciano. Did you tell him I worked at the farm?*

Sincerely,
Flora

P.S. I don't think I can work at the farm anymore after today's humiliation. But I must return after the baby is born to celebrate with them.

Flora descended the stairs slowly, wishing the house had an elevator. She pushed her note into the Jar-of-Jane-Notes, then returned to her bedroom and turned off her light at 9pm. On the dot.

And that was a day, and a night.

Chapter 31

Sunday
Jane

Jane Piccadilly sat on the white chair at the table with her white Alice in Wonderland teapot, white matching tea cup and white jasmine loose leaf white tea and white jug of milk. She turned her teapot three times, clockwise, then poured the tea into her teacup, added milk and took a sip.

She pulled the jar-of-notes towards her. It had five different colour notes in it from the last week. Not six. She gathered the five notes in her hand, opened and read each note, placed them back into the empty note jar, and slid it back to the middle of the table.

Then she gulped the entire contents of her teacup. A lot had happened this week.

Poppy hadn't responded to her.

Violet had an incident at the salon and that woman Ness, keeps saying Violet looks like "her", the mother.

Daisy spent more time with death at the cemetery and is asking questions about the sisters who died.

Rose had some interesting footage from around the house.

Zinnia burned down a sugarcane field used in research.

Flora's baby is due in six months! Plus, she had an accident at the farm, AND she released the gloves into *that* lake.

Jane shuddered. The glove releasing wasn't a good sign. It meant everything was about to unravel. Everything that she had been holding together for twenty years, more intensely for the last six. She hoped this wasn't the beginning of the undoing.

She turned her teapot three times, clockwise, then poured another tea into her teacup, added milk and took a sip.

She hoped that Poppy would be back to herself again soon. Communication was vital in a house with so many occupants.

'Come on, Oliver. We need to get some advice.' Jane placed her teacup and milk jug into the dishwasher and washed out her teapot, grabbed the jar of notes, then walked up the first eighteen steps to the second floor. She entered her room and pulled out the vintage white suitcase from under her bed, opened it up and added the new note jar between the other jars-of-notes. She frowned and looked at her trembling hands. Her tremour was back. The unravelling *had* started. She let out loud sigh, closed the suitcase and pushed it back under the bed next to the black suitcase of devastating memories.

She walked up the next eighteen steps to the third floor. Jane pushed the button on the wall to release the attic ladder. 'Sorry Oliver, you'll have to wait here.'

Jane climbed up the thirteen rungs on the timber ladder and stood in the attic. She looked about the timber floor, the white walls, the green plants, the floral sofa bed, and the large wall-mounted television. She walked over to a window and looked out, noting the white clouds moving past at a fast pace. Like they were rushing to witness something extraordinary.

She turned on the television, pulled out her phone and mirrored it onto the television, then dialled her mother and father's phone number. Facetime.

Her father answered the phone after three rings.

'Hi, Dad.' Jane's shoulders relaxed.

'Hello, my girl. How is Alice?'

'Jane, Dad. Call me Jane, remember.'

'Of course, Jane. I just love saying your first name! How are you?'

Jane took a deep breath. She wished her mother and father were here in person. She wished they could hug her, kiss her on the forehead. Make her laugh. Share tea and cake. 'It's just…' A tear rolled down her cheek. 'It's just been a difficult week. My sisters… they all had incidents happen at work, all in the same week, you know… it reminded me of when our periods would all correlate and we would all be moody and messy.'

'Toooo much information, Jane!' her father bellowed, putting his hands over his ears.

Jane's mum appeared on the screen. Jane smiled and watched as she whacked Jane's father on the arm. 'You remember exactly how it was, Frank! You would make yourself scarce for that entire week, you coward!' Jane's mother and father both laughed.

Another tear slid down Jane's face. 'It's good to see you, Mum! How is work going?'

'Tiring is an understatement? Are you on your period?'

Jane rolled her eyes. 'Noooo, Mum, geez!' Jane looked out the window at the flying clouds. 'It's just… I wish you were both here. I have your room set up. It's got all the things you love, including photographs of us all.'

'Oh, Jane. There's nothing more than we would like to do. It's just an… impossibility at the moment. I'll tell you what, I'll send you a letter! And maybe your father will write to you too instead of sitting and watching the bloody cricket all day!'

Jane laughed. Dad and his cricket. As soon as he turned it on the television, everyone would disappear from the family room, lest it be death by cricket. 'It's okay, Dad. I want you to be doing things that make you happy. Life is too short, you know.'

'Thank you, Jane. At least one person in the family understands,' her father said.

Jane sighed. 'Mum, Dad, what type of car did you have back in the 1990's?'

'The family car!' her mother said. 'It was a beaut people mover. We were so thankful to have it, especially after you triplets were born!'

'The forest green five door Range Rover. With the Lucas electronic fuel injection! Great fuel economy, especially with driving you girls around to school and sport and dancing and music lessons.' Jane's father laugher loudly.

'What's so funny, Dad?'

'The Popemobiles were custom made Range Rovers! If a Range Rover was good enough for the Pope, then it was good enough for us.'

Jane burst out laughing. Her dad was always full of random information. Like a Google search. Jane exhaled a long breath. *And then the Range Rover wasn't good enough for us,* she thought. Jane glanced out the window. If only her parents were here with her now, they could help her with her sisters.

'Jane,' her father's voice was softer. 'Get out of the house and do something fun. Change up your routine. I promise you it will make you feel a bit better, and you might even come up with some solutions.'

Jane nodded her head. Good advice as usual from her dad. 'Dad,' Jane said, 'do you remember anyone called Luciano, who we might have known?'

'L-u-c-i-a-n-o,' he said slowly, his eyes narrowed. 'Hmmm… Luciano… Luciano… Luciano—'

'Yes, Luciano,' Jane said, like pulling her father out of a-repetitive-glitch.

Her father pressed his lips into a hard line. 'It doesn't ring any bells.'

'Oh, okay. If we or any of my sisters knew someone by the name of Luciano, I'm sure you or mum would have remembered him.'

'Absolutely,' said Jane's mum. 'You know your father has a memory on him like an encyclopedia. That's why he is such a good partner in Trivial Pursuit!'

Jane raised her eyebrows and nodded. 'Now that is true. The King of Trivial Pursuit, he was called!' Jane kept her eyes focussed on her parents on the screen. Longer than she normally would. She so wished they could be here with her. In this room. Physically. Instead of technologically. 'Right,' she said. 'I'm going to get out into the sunshine and catch the bus to the art gallery… or maybe a movie? So, I'd better get going. Bye Mum. Bye Dad. It's so lovely to chat with you both. Love you.'

'Love you too, dear,' her father and mother said.

Alice Jane Piccadilly the 4th ended facetime.

Jane Piccadilly turned off the extra-large television.

And Jane cried.

Jane's footfall faulted with indecision before she sat on the bus seat. Next to Luciano. On a Sunday. *There's something about Luciano. The heebie-jeebies Luciano. The white pen in his pocket.*

'Morning, Jane,' he said without looking at her.

'Good morning, Luciano,' she replied.

'Is it?'

'Is it what?' Jane said.

'Good? You don't sound good!' he said.

Jane sat up a little taller. She thought she sounded good, even after a waterfall of tears after talking to her parents. Maybe she was a little sniffly because you know, the nose has tears too. 'Tough week,' Jane eventually said.

'Sorry you've had a tough week,' Luciano said.

Jane and Luciano sat in silence, the white clouds stopping above them.

'I—' they both said at once.

'You first,' Jane said.

'Ladies first,' Luciano said.

Jane let out an audible breath, undecided whether she should be talking to the heebie-jeebies what-do-you-know Luciano. 'I'm changing my day up. Going to the movies, or… just… undecided.' There. She'd said it.

'Like change is as good as a holiday change?' he asked.

'Something like that,' Jane said.

'Then why don't you come to bingo with me!'

Jane's eyebrows pulled together in shock. 'Bingo! You look too young to play bingo!'

'I don't,' he said. 'I call the numbers for the bingo players.'

Jane burst out laughing. Luciano, the man-in-the-blue-suit with the carpet bag who looked like he should be a high-flying businessman, calling the bingo numbers. It was so absurd that she had to try it. She hadn't played bingo since she was at school in Year 3 with spelling bingo.

'Sounds like a plan,' she said, her voice painted with sunshine.

'Great,' Luciano said. The corner of his lips lifted in a smile.

Jane wondered why Luciano never looked at her when she spoke. *Probably shyness, or a sore neck, maybe fused vertebra in his neck,* she thought, *or perhaps he's on the autism spectrum. And all of those are okay.*

They travelled on the bus to the local RSL and went inside.

'Wait here. I'll send Nicky to you for a place to sit, and all that jazz.'

Jane waited, and then followed Nicky to a spare seat at a long table of bingo players. Young and old. A bingo card was placed in front of her.

She squinted. The numbers were in braille, raised like a dome.

'Let's get the game started,' Luciano's voice boomed in the bingo room. 'Ready?' He reached into a box and pulled out a ping-pong ball without looking at the ball. 'Eleven. Legs eleven.' The sounds of pops echoed around the room as players pushed their legs eleven on their bingo cards, created on a reverse dome on the card.

Jane looked at her bingo card with no visual numbers, just braille numbers. Then she looked at the people around her. Vision impaired. Mostly. She caught the smile of a middle aged woman looking at her from further up the table. And Jane laughed. This was the best thing that could have happened today.

Nicky tapped Jane on the shoulder. 'Here's the braille number decoder for sighted people. Push the braille number when it is called. It will pop and create a crater in the card. A line of indented numbers or an entire dented card wins bingo.'

'Thanks,' Jane said. *This is genius,* she thought, *plus the addictive sound of the "pop".* ASMR. She smiled and sat back. She wanted to be an observer.

The-one-who-watched.

It was joy that she saw. Joy radiating from these people who were blind or vision impaired.

After an entire sheet of bingo cards, Luciano followed Nicky and sat beside Jane.

'This is the best day! Thank you, Luciano!'

'You're welcome,' he said, and placed a bingo ball on the table. There was no number, just braille.

Jane fingered the bingo ball. 'I guess you can read braille numbers, huh?'

Luciano chuckled. 'Yes.'

'When did you learn?'

'About six months after I had eye flash burns from an explosion. My eyes didn't heal completely.'

Jane stilled and her mind flashed. The heat of the flames. The blowing of her hair. The night sky turning orange. And screams.

Until there was none.

Her breath hiccupped. She cleared the emotion stuck in her throat. 'I'm sorry for your loss,' she said.

'Thank you. I was at the right place at the wrong time… trying to warn someone… but I was too late. Five minutes earlier and I would still have my sight.' Luciano's Adam's apple moved up and down as he swallowed hard.

'How long ago?' Jane asked. She wanted to turn off her ears so she could not hear his answer. But she knew what his answer would be. She had a memory of an explosion stuffed into her memory suitcase.

'Six years ago. I was twenty-two.'

Jane shuddered and anxiety started to leave a trail of destruction across her skin, burning like embers, like the fallout of an explosion, her breathing laboured. She wanted to run, leaving the tarnish of the pain of the memory behind her.

Run, Jane, run!

'Let's grab a white tea at the café across the road at the park,' Luciano said.

Jane's brain startled. How does he know about her white tea? She narrowed her eyes at him.

'It's the only place where I can buy it. If it's on a menu, I always buy it,' he said, like answering a question she hadn't asked.

'You… like white tea?' Jane asked. She also wanted to ask how he reads a menu without braille, but decided not to. The obvious answer would be he would ask the server.

'Since I tasted it at a tea shop,' he said. 'Have you tried it?'

Jane lifted her right shoulder in a Jane shrug. 'Once or twice,' she said, and stood.

Jane walked next to Luciano. Out of the RSL. Out the carpark. To the footpath. Stopping at the road, then crossing it. And over into the park to the café. Luciano navigated it all without help.

How could he do that and be blind?

Shouldn't he have a cane?

Or an eye seeing dog?

'Two white teas, with full cream milk,' he ordered.

Jane grabbed the tea cups when they were ready, and followed Luciano to a table in the park.

'I'm beginning to question your blindness, Luciano—'

'It's my high tech glasses and ear input,' he said as he placed his carpet bag beside him.

'More information,' Jane said, and lifted her tea cup to her lips.

'There's a camera attached to my glasses and some tech. It transmits visual camera information as language to my ear piece, telling me what I can't see. Telling me when it is safe to go and when I have to stop… which direction to go. It gives me a sense of independence, I think.'

Jane Piccadilly pulled a face. Then she hoped he could not

see the details of her face pulling verbalised in his ear. She took a sip of her white tea and relaxed. 'Technology and humans. We're closer to becoming cyborgs. Thank you for the white tea.'

'You're welcome,' he said.

Jane Piccadilly and Luciano-with-the-translating-glasses sat in quietness while they sipped on white tea with white milk in a white tea cup.

'I know your secret,' he said.

Jane froze. Perhaps if she sat still enough, she would become invisible to his technology and he would think she had left. Or, if she pretended-to-be-dead… his glasses would make an error and it would be as if she wasn't there. Invisible. And he would stop talking.

Then she thought, *which secret does he know?*

'Only one person lives in your house,' he said as if answering her question. *Were they mind reading glasses as well?*

'You're wrong. You can't see! I live there with my six sisters—' Jane gave a nervous chuckle, hoping he didn't pick up on the iggly-ooog of her nervousness.

'But I can hear. And my hearing is heightened. I know the nuances of your voices. You and the six women, are one and the same.'

'We have different hair colour and styles. We drive different vehicles. We work at different places—you don't know because you can't see!' At once Jane felt bad for highlighting the fact that he was blind. That was mean and nasty of her.

'And you are Jane the librarian, Jane the hairdresser, Jane the carpenter, Jane the photographer, Jane the botanist, Jane the farmhand, and… Sunday Jane.'

Sunday Jane.

Jane Piccadilly let out an audible breath. 'It's true,' she said, trying to placate him and make him back down a little. 'We look similar and sound similar. But that's genetics for you.'

Luciano shook his head and turned his head slightly to the left as if he was looking into the distance.

'Come dancing with me, in keeping with my change my day up,' Jane said to redirect the topic.

Luciano drained his white tea and put down the cup. 'Okay,' he said.

'But I have to warn you… I can't dance. But the fact that you can't see is to your advantage.' Jane wanted to kick herself. She had reminded him again that he was blind. 'Sorry,' she said.

'Hmmm… well… it will be a good challenge for my vision technology,' he said.

Jane walked around the table and grabbed his hand. 'This way,' she said, and led him down the road to club and in the door.

The music was loud and the lights were flashing, and Jane froze for a moment in time. She was an introvert and she hated the dance scene. She hated people looking at her. That's why she liked to borrow the light from her sisters.

She pulled Luciano onto the dance floor at once. She had a plan. Dance a little. Like a microscopic bit, then escape back into the normal world. No harm done. Right?

Jane stood under the strobe light in the middle of the dance floor, because after all, Jane was the middle child, the middle of triplets, the middle woman in the household, and she began to dance in her Jane Piccadilly way—uncoordinated, out of time with the music, jerky movements here and there, and a bit of a wombat womble, a kangaroo jump and an emu head movement, all perfected when she was five. Laughter erupted on the dance floor, and Jane felt the eyes of the other dancers burning onto her skin.

She stopped dancing and looked at Luciano bobbing up and

down with a little sway, in time with the music. Smiling. And then he did the sprinkler move.

Once, this had happened when she was ten. When people laughed at her dancing. When she had finally mustered the courage to stand up and dance.

Once, and she vowed never to dance again. And now, she had done it twice.

And it had ended badly.

Twice.

There would be no third time.

Except, this was the third time. She had blotted out the second time from her memory.

Run, Jane, run!

Jane stopped dancing and stared at Luciano; her shoulders drooped. That was enough. She grabbed his hand and whisked him out of the dance club. She stopped outside and leaned against the brick work, panting, her heart in melt down.

She, Jane Piccadilly, had done this to herself.

This self-sabotage could have been prevented.

'That. Was. Spectacular. Thanks,' Luciano said.

'What? How?' Jane's pounding heart was louder than the music.

'The music. The lights,' he said.

'And the people laughing?'

'What people laughing?'

'You didn't hear it?' said Jane.

'Nope. I was having too much fun,' he said. 'Like at the school formal.'

Like at the school formal? Jane reversed in time. To the second time. Back to her school formal. When she was dancing and the laughter started. And Hudson had rushed her outside, to the darkness and… that next part of the memory was locked in her suitcase. Under the bed. Neatly stored and locked up.

The suitcase-of-horrible-memories.

Ones that hurt.

Right there in the heart.

Why had it jumped out now?

'Could you see me dancing in your mind with your eye technology?' Jane asked.

'Nope. There was too much input for the glasses,' he said.

Good, Jane thought. 'I need to get home. That's enough with changing my day up,' she said. 'I'm catching the bus home. Where do you need to be?'

'Nowhere and everywhere,' he said.

Jane frowned. Such a cryptic answer. 'Does that involve transport?' she said.

'I'll uber it.'

'Do you need me to stay with you until it arrives?' she asked. If only someone had asked her that after the incident at the high-school formal. She would have been protected then.

'It's more like do you need me to stay with you before the bus arrives… safety an' all. For women.'

Jane slow blinked. Trying to stop the barrage of statistics and news of violence against women, perpetrated by men, globally. She tried to stop the storm of headlines from scratching their cries for help onto her mind, swirling and twirling and colliding and exploding…

PHYSICAL VIOLENCE. 1 in 3. Psychological harm. AGGRESSION. Sexual coercion. Abuse. CONTROLLING BEHAVIOURS. One in three women. RAPE. There is no excuse whatsoever for violence against women. 30% OF WOMEN. Dead. BRUISES. Man charged. HUMAN RIGHTS

VIOLATION. Serious Global Public Health Concern. BLOOD. Domestic abuse. DATING VIOLENCE. Spouse abuse. BEHIND CLOSED DOORS. Emotional. 736 MILLION WOMEN AROUND THE WORLD ARE VICTIMS. Gender based violence is A PANDEMIC. Emotional abuse. DOMESTIC VIOLENCE. Technology-facilitated harassment. Broken bones. 60% OF WOMEN. Less than 40% of women seek help. FEWER THAN 10% REPORTED TO POLICE. Assault. Horrific abuse. Sexist remarks. Online violence. ENDING VIOLENCE AGAINST WOMEN.

Violence against women.
Violence against women.
Violence against women.
Epidemic of violence against women.

Male perpetrators of violence were rendered largely invisible in the news.

VIOLENCE BY MEN. Tell the ugly truth!

Change headlines in media so the onus is on men, instead of taking men out of the headline, diminishing their accountability!

Story angles. Story structures and lexical features.

End violence PERPETUATED BY MEN!

Jane Piccadilly's heart was racing. She pushed her palm against her forehead. *If men would listen and communicate with words,* Jane thought. *If men could have empathy. If men weren't hungry for dominance, for power. If superheroes didn't use violence to win, setting a bad example for humans. Would that end world wars? Would that end violence against women and children?*

Jane Piccadilly blinked in quick succession to clear the

unrelenting poison-dipped arrows of reminders in her mind, telling herself that there were good men.

They-were-everywhere.

And they needed to step out from the shadows to help their misguided mates. Call out their behaviour and say it's not OKAY, let's get some help. Good men, like Luciano. Like first responders.

'And the sport of boxing,' Jane whispered under her breath. *Don't get me started on that,* thought Jane. *Beating someone up IS NOT A SPORT!*

'Sorry?' said Luciano, Jane's voice whisper too hard to hear.

'Okay to about waiting with me… and, thanks for today,' she said, but she didn't know which part she was thanking him for. Certainly not the flashbacks.

Jane Piccadilly paused at her gate. She felt dishevelled. She looked dishevelled. She was dishevelled. Inside. Unravelling like a tightly strung ball of yarn trying to reveal the inner most secret hidden in the centre.

She grimaced and lifted her nose, smelled the air, then cast her eyes to the ground.

There sat a pile-of-dog-poo. Fresh.

But her shoe was safe. She needed to look at the photos and camera footage Rose had sent through. She stepped over the dog deposit and walked along the garden path, up the steps and to the front door.

And there was an envelope.

An-envelope-at-the-door.

Jane Piccadilly blinked three times, picked up the envelope and pushed it into her pocket.

Out of sight. Out of mind.

As Jane inserted the key into the door lock, the four-legged-alarm sounded, and Jane pushed open the door. 'Home at last, Oliver Twist. Did you have a busy day?'

Oliver gave a bark and a little jump, then about turned and started the dachshund strut, his head held high, throwing out his front legs ahead of him, his little back legs keeping up with his front legs, his butt doing the wibble-wobble. He was all poise and confidence leading to the back door.

The-closed-back-door.

Which Jane opened for him. And out he went, then returned all pompous and proud not long after, with a bone-in-his-mouth. He dropped it on the floor and Jane picked it up, turned it this way and that, then added it to his collection of dog-things-box.

Jane straightened her back and put her hands on her hips. There were too many bones-in-the-box. She got onto her knees and took them out one by one, counting as she went. She picked up the last bone, number two hundred and five. Jane placed her index finger under her chin. Or was it bone number two hundred and six?

Jane looked at Oliver Twist. The busy Oliver Twist. He had his harness and lead in his mouth and was wagging his tail.

'Just a quick walk. Alright,' Jane said. She went to her room and changed into her activewear, put on her runners and grabbed her pink dachshund cap, flipping her pony tail of flaxen-coloured-hair through the back, and out the front door they went.

And up cardiac hill.

'Hello, Henry,' Jane said to the bitser of this and that. He was a rescue dog. Adorable.

'Miss Trunchbull.' Jane dipped her head to the German Shepherd.

'Max, who's a good boy?' Jane said to the chocolate labrador.

'Hairy Maclary.' The moody Scottish Terrier refused to look at Jane, or Oliver Twist.

'Subwoofer.' Jane watched the playful French Bulldog interact with Oliver Twist.

'The golden boi, Morris. I love you,' Jane said to the Golder Retriever while Oliver Twist hoisted himself higher leaning on the dog to say hello.

'Miss Piggy McSnot.' Jane smirked at the most serious Pug, known for getting her feelings hurt.

'Sherlock Bones!' said Jane, the beagle who had turned the owner's yard into a dig site.

'Hello, Brutus.' The Chinese Crested dog living a life of luxury in a dog pram looked up at her.

'Claude Monet. Have you chewed any paint brushes today?' Jane asked the Tonkinese cat on a lead.

'Howdy, Stinky Cheese,' Jane said to the gentle Saint Bernard.

Jane and Oliver Twist stopped at the top of the hill, and watched the sun lower itself just a little more, before they commenced the return trip home.

'Hello, Dump Truck,' Jane said to the Rottweiler, amused by how she knew all the names of the dogs but not their owners' names.

'McBiscuit.' Jane gave a nod to the Border Collie.

'D.O.G.' Jane wondered what other words the Boxer could spell.

'Oh, Bruiser.' The friendly Maltipoo being carried by its owner.

'Tiny! It's lovely to see you!' Oliver Twist disappeared in the shadow of the Great Dane, the gentle giant.

Jane giggled at the walking floor mop coming towards them. 'Grumble!' she said in greeting as the Komondor returned her greeting with a bark.

'Hello, none other than Hercules Morse,' Jane said to the English Mastiff.

'Bottomley Potts, hello.' The Dalmatian sported a red super cape.

'Oh B.J.' Jane's heart softened with the Old English Sheepdog. She gave him a pet.

'Here comes Snoopy!' Jane said at the white and black Sheepadoodle approached.

'Ben, hello,' Jane said to the sandy coloured Labrador.

Then in the distance were two mini dachshunds. Oliver Twist stopped, and his tail started to wag. *Dachshund alert!* He gave a little jump and pulled Jane to Pablo Picasso, the long-haired, chocolate dapple tricolour dachshund, mostly white, with a heart on his back, and one blue eye and one brown, and Hattie the silver dapple. While the dogs socialised, Jane looked at the owner, and Jane thought, *if she could choose-a-daughter, she would be exactly like her. A beautiful heart and a gentle, kind spirit.*

Teddy the Groodle joined the sausage sizzle, and then Jane and Oliver Twist returned to making their journey home.

As Jane's seven bedroom three story Victorian terrace house came in to view, she smiled. The exterior fitted perfectly with the posh neighbourhood landscape.

The neighbourhood where everyone kept to themselves.

The neighbourhood where nothing ever happened.

The neighbourhood where successful, unknown people lived.

The quiet place of luxury. Of contentment. Of safety. Of peace.

Oliver Twist led Jane into the house and fetched his food bowl the moment Jane removed his lead and harness. After dinner and clean-up, Jane retired to the library and opened her laptop, clicking on Rose's email at once.

Dear Jane,

> *Here's a link to some of the photographs and videos you may find of interest.*
> *And… there's something about Luciano… here's a link to his photographs and videos, sitting on the bus seat each morning.*
> *I'd be interested in your opinion.*

Rose

Jane opened the first link.

A man-with-a-dog.

Over and over and over. The same man and the same dog.

The man, wearing the same dark hooded jumper, hand in his pocket, or phone in his hand, holding the leash of the dog pooping-on-the-grass outside the front fence, and at the front gate.

The man entering their property, looking about, dog pooping-in-the-yard, walking down the side of the house to the back. Peering inside the garden shed. Pulling on the locked door knob. Walking over to the bunker, bending to open the door of the bunker.

The sound of Oliver barking and the man quickly exiting the yard.

Rose included photographs and a video of a verbal exchange between the man and the dog, and the man who sat at the bus stop.

Luciano.

There was a close-up photograph of the man's necklace. Something red attached to it.

The man with his dog at a wedding.

The man placing an envelope at the front door.

Jane gasped. Her eye twitched and her body tremored at-the-ick. She felt violated. An uninvited person on her property!

She stood and paced the room, then sat back at the laptop and opened the other link.

The Luciano link.

Him, Luciano, talking to each of her sisters on each day of the week, lifting a pen in his pocket and clicking it, before placing it back into his pocket. He clicks it again when their conversation ends. Luciano looking up at the house each morning before he sits on the bus seat. Luciano speaking to the man with the dog at one time. Luciano adjusting his glasses and his ear piece.

Jane stood and paced the room and thought, then sat back at the writing desk.

Jane found her note paper and six coloured pens, and began writing at once.

Dearest Poppy,

I need your help.
While at the library, can you please find information about pens that look like pens but aren't pens.

With a thankful heart,
Jane

Jane Piccadilly reread her note written in light blue pen. Did it make sense? Surely she would be able to do that research based on her words?

She folded the note, wrote Poppy's name on the front and placed it on the dining table in front of Poppy's pastel blue chair.

She reached for another piece of paper.

Dear Violet,

> *I need your help.*
> *Can you please find the time in your busy schedule to research the necklace pendant, or half necklace pendant in the attached image.*

> *Most appreciated,*
> *Jane*

Jane Piccadilly reread her note written in light purple. If anyone could find the details of the necklace pendant, it would be fashion savvy Violet. Plus, she could ask clients about it who she knew had jewellery collections worth speaking about.

She folded the note, wrote Violet's name on the front and placed it on the dining table in front of Violet's pastel lavender chair. New note:

Dear Daisy,

> *I need your help.*
> *Can you please investigate the bunker. I'm too scared to do it.*

> *A million thanks,*
> *Jane*

Jane Piccadilly reread her note written in bold yellow. Daisy was the obvious choice to investigate the bunker, after all, the bunker was a little like a grave. Rectangular. Underground. Dark. She folded the note, wrote Daisy's name on the front and placed it on the dining table in front of Daisy's pastel yellow chair.

Dear Rose,

Thank you so much for the photographs and the videos. They are equally interesting and worrying. We need to dig deeper. I need your help.

Can you please do a face analysis of both Luciano and the intruding man.

I need to know who both of them are and why they are always in our space (which extends onto the footpath and the bus seat).

Looking forward to hearing from you.
Jane

Jane Piccadilly reread her note written in light pink. She was pretty sure that Rose had clear photographs to upload to do a reverse image search on the Internet. And perhaps, with the different angles of the face of Luciano, she could reconstruct him without his glasses.

She folded the note, wrote Rose's name on the front and placed it on the dining table in front of Rose's pastel pink chair.

Dear Zinnia,

I need your help.
Can you please do a dog poo analysis of the deposited droppings at the front gate, and the sample Rose has, and the deposit in the back yard. We need to know if it is the same dog.

Thank you in advance.
Jane

Jane Piccadilly reread her note written in light green. Her eye twitched and her body tremored at-the-ick.

She was sure Zinnia would have access to poo analysis at the university, or knew someone who could do it. She folded the note, wrote Zinnia's name on the front and placed it on the dining table in front of Zinnia's pastel green chair.

Dear Flora,

Oliver Twist now has 205 bones in his collection.

I am more than curious as to how there can be that many bones in our backyard. Are you able to put them together so we know what animal we have. Maybe it's the pig — which has around 216 bones, or a cow — 207 bones? That would solve the Soooooie problem and put it to rest.

Congratulations on the baby by the way. It's a miracle! I know you have waited so long for this. It's something wonderful to look forward to.

Love,
Jane

Jane Piccadilly reread her note written in pastel orange. Being a farmhand, Flora would have seen many animal skeletons. She was the only one who could do this job.

She traced her fingers over "love Jane" a number of times, and said the words at the same time, feeling the letters on her fingertips and in her mouth, hearing the letters string sound to her ears and tasting what that positive could be like, feel like.

She did have love once. And then it was gone, shattering her being, parts of her broken heart floating away to a place of no retrieval like helium balloons floating to the heavens. She kept parts of her heart in her emotions suitcase, locked in there, where it was safer not to feel.

Jane folded the note, wrote Flora's name on the front and placed it on the dining table in front of Flora's pastel orange chair.

Jane stood and circled the dining table with the notes in front of their respective chairs. In cursive. After all, she had won all the awards for cursive hand writing at school, after she got her cursive writing license in Year 3. Her mother said that perfect writing was a sign of intelligence. And only a truly caring person would write in perfect cursive so others could read it. Jane didn't want to talk about her doctor's messy writing to her mother. She didn't want to betray her. She was an intelligent and caring doctor after all.

Jane Piccadilly went to her room. Then to her en suite. Shock had set in. She looked at her pale face. She needed to use her distraction method. She found her roll call in the drawer and pulled it out.

'Toothbrush, are you here?' Jane lifted her white toothbrush from the white container, smiled, and ticked it off on her roll.

'Toothpaste?' Jane eyeballed the pearl white toothpaste, ticked it off on her roll, then squeezed a pea size amount onto her toothbrush.

'Glass of water?' Jane picked up the empty white glass. 'You forgot your homework I see. That's okay, Glass. You can fill yourself up here. I understand you had a hard day.' Jane filled the glass half way, put it down and then ticked it off her roll. But… was it half empty or half full? Jane squinted at the glass then blinked the thought away.

'Hand towel?' Jane ran her fingers over the white hand towel. 'You love it there don't you, swaying like you're sitting on a swing.'

Jane ticked it off on her roll.

She then proceeded to brush her teeth for two minutes exactly. Because that's what dentists recommended. Then spat the toothpaste out with a minimal rinse, allowing the toothpaste to do its job on her white teeth.

She put the roll away and cleaned the vanity top and paced around her white bedroom, Oliver Twist following her. She exited her room, walked up the flight of stairs to the third floor, pushed the button on the wall and waited for the attic steps to descend, then disappeared into the attic.

She grabbed her mum's perfume and her dad's shirt she had placed in the attic for when they came to visit, or even better, to live, and sat on the sofa, turned on the television and called them for FaceTime.

Their faces appeared.

'Dad, Mum… I need you here… to help me. Something is going to happen.' Jane flicked away a tear.

'Hello, my girl. How is Jane?' her father said.

'Jane, isn't this a bit late to call? You know you should be in bed and asleep by now. It's past 9 o'clock!' her mother said.

'I know, Mum, but—'

'You know how it affects your mind if you haven't had eight hours of sl—'

'Mum. Stop. I need to talk to you and Dad.' Jane flicked off another tear. She wanted them here. With her. She needed to feel their arms around her. She needed their glue of advice and love to hold her together.

Mrs Alice Jane Piccadilly the 3rd folded her arms across her chest and pressed her lips in a hard line.

'What is it, Jane? Tell us,' her father implored.

'Well… there's bones. Lots of them. And dog faeces. A man snooping around the house with a dog. And… and… Luciano feels familiar somehow…'

'Does Luciano have dark facial hair?' her mother asked.

'Yes,' said Jane, hopeful.

'Then that's the butcher on the bus phenomenon, Jane. Simple as that!' her mother said.

'Tell me about the bones,' he father said.

'Well… Oliver Tw—'

'Not that ridiculous height challenged dog with the attitude of a busybody and a guard dog!'

'Oliver Twist is gentle and kind, Mum! He has dug up two hundred and five bones. I don't want to have animal death in the garden!'

'Are you sure it's an animal?'

'What do you mean, Dad?'

'Could be a toy? Maybe a professor lived there and it was his medical skeleton? Or maybe there was a Halloween party there and they buried the skeleton for a prank?'

Jane Piccadilly shook her head. 'It's definitely real bones… maybe Zinnia could take one to the University and have it analysed?'

'What if…' Jane's mother said, 'it's the skeleton of a person?'

Jane's eye twitched and her body tremored at-the-ick. She made a mental note to herself to look up missing persons. She sighed. It all goes back to Rule-Number-One—research the history of the house.

'Yeah nah, Alice, it's got to be a skeleton from the Mesozoic Era. Jane's probably got a dinosaur discovery in her back yard. We could call it the Janie-o-saurus!'

All three laughed. Together.

'Mum. Dad. I miss you.'

'We miss you too, Jane. Tell your sisters to give us a call. Have you asked them to help you out with this tangle?'

Jane nodded. 'I have.'

'The man with the dog has no hope against the power of the sisters and that short guard dog of yours. It will all work out, Jane,' her father said and gave her a small smile. 'Things always do in the end.'

A tear ran down Jane's cheek and she closed her eyes. 'Love you, Dad. Love you, Mum. Hope to see you soon.' Jane lifted her hands and made a heart for them, then disconnected from the call.

She left the attic, returned to her bedroom, and got ready for bed.

'Good night, Oliver,' Jane said, as she snuggled under the duvet, then leaned over to turn off the bedside lamp. And there sat the envelope.

The envelope-at-the-door.

Unopened.

Jane Piccadilly picked it up, turned it over and slid her finger under the back fold of paper, and opened it.

A-messy-handwritten-note.

I'm watching your every move, Jane.

Jane's eye twitched and her body tremored at-the-ick.

The words-in-the-letter.

He knew her name.

Her name.

Jane's hand shook as she pushed the words-in-the-letter back into the envelope, and slipped it into the drawer of emptiness beside her bed, where it could enter the void and be consumed by a pack of ravenous rats to rip and shred and gnaw.

Jane Piccadilly turned off the white beside lamp and lay back on the bed, her eyes focussed on the ceiling. She placed her left arm out beside her in a straight angle, and positioned her right arm above her head at an acute angle, one leg straight, the other outward from the hip and bent at the knee at a right angle.

She held her breath and played dead. Staring. Like she did when she was locked in the cupboard by that deplorable husband. A despicable human being. And when he opened the door again, he thought she was dead. And he gave a million apologies and showered her with gifts and said he would never do that again.

But he did.

He always did.

Jane Piccadilly reached under her pillow. The large kitchen knife was there.

Just in case.

11pm. Lights off.

And that was a day, and a night.

Chapter 32

Monday
Poppy

Poppy finished her contraband coffee in her bedroom at her writing desk, and placed her mug on the note from Jane. On the white note with the light blue-gel ink. It left a splat of coffee like the Rorschach ink-blot test for schizophrenia. A monster. That is what she saw on the ink blot. What would they make of her, a person who did not have schizophrenia? What did it reveal about her unconscious thoughts, her motives, or her desires. The Rorschach ink-blot test. A relic of the past. An x-ray of the soul, or pseudoscience, in line with phrenology, reading the bumps on the head. It's like grasping at straws, in her opinion. Paper ones obviously. Or was Poppy just angry that coffee was banned in the house? She wasn't the only one who

244

detested tea. She knew that for a fact. And why did Jane have control of the house and what food sat in the pantry? Granted, she did provide different flavoured toppings to go with the Australian made white ice-cream, and flavoured toppings like their namesake colours—blueberry, strawberry, mango, lime, pineapple, lavender. Australian made.

Who made her boss of the house?

Who gave her permission to assume that role? There were seven sisters. Seven! They all deserved to have what they liked! Fair's fair.

Poppy narrowed her eyes. Was there any such thing as white coffee beans? If there was, would Jane drink coffee then?

Poppy opened the ink blot test note:

Dearest Poppy,

I need your help.

While at the library, can you please find some information about pens that look like pens but aren't pens.

With a thankful heart,
Jane

The note dropped from her hand as the rain started to fall. When would Jane stop? When would Jane leave her alone?

Poppy watched the rain fall harder. She couldn't take Schnitzel Von Krumm to the library today on her bicycle. She couldn't go to the library on her bicycle either. She had done that once and ran into the rubbish bin when the tires skidded on the white paint. And she sat on the toilet at the library and cried for an hour while her clothes dried.

And why did she have to do all of Jane's research? Jane could easily look it up on line herself.

Poppy focussed on her novel in progress stuck to the wall temporarily. She had to get it finished. That meant she had to go the library today. Rain, hail or shine.

Poppy dressed in her library uniform, found her black umbrella painted with books on the underside. Once, she decorated the library inside with umbrellas, hanging from the ceiling. Of every colour. Everybody saw them as colourful and happy. But she saw them as sadness-shields, stopping sadness from dripping onto people and ruining their day.

'Twisty!' Poppy called.

Oliver Twist trotted to her from the kitchen, his head held high, his tail wagging.

'No library for you today. It's too wet outside. But I'll be back before you know it,' she said.

Poppy stepped out onto the verandah, umbrella open and book gumboots on. She couldn't buy any gumboots with books on them, so she painted them herself.

She walked along the garden path, through the gate and to the bus stop.

'Morning, Luciano,' she said.

'A splattering morning,' he said, sitting in his large yellow raincoat and rain bucket hat. 'It reminds me of the night of my formal, many moons ago, and all the colourful gumboots on arrival at the venue, and the changing of shoes by the girls. The gold sparkly gumboots were my favourite, that then changed into gold sparkly court shoes.'

'How dazzling that would have been!' Poppy said, her heart beating faster. A frown crossed her face. *Jane wore gold sparkly boots to her formal.*

'Where's the hound? I mean Schnitzel Von Krumm?'

'Too dangerous for a bike ride today. It's just me and my gumboots and umbrella, collecting rain drops like the tapping of keys on a typewriter, directing the symphony of letters to turn into words for a novel.'

'Then I shall catch some too, in my rain coat pockets. I'll stir them up and send the cyclone of words to add to the climax of the novel. Here comes the bus.'

Poppy looked to the right for the bus, but there was none. 'Than—' The bus appeared down the road. '—ks.'

Poppy travelled in the crowded bus for six stops, then jumped out to walk the short distance to the library. And got to work. Including ripping out a new page for her novel, and information about pens that looked like pens but weren't pens. After two million questions about where Schnitzel Von Krumm was today, and two million creative made up answers about where he was and what he was doing, Poppy finally made it home.

She changed into her Poppy attire, fetched her ripped out page and added it to her novel in progress on the wall behind her bedhead. Like a wall of dreams. It was her dream to become an author of a real print book.

She read the last page she had placed there, then added her new page. She had one page to go, and it would finally be finished.

The end.

Poppy walked over to her study desk, her fingers brushing a note she had written herself. If drifted onto the floor and she picked it up.

> *1. Meet a kind man who makes me laugh but not so much that I pee myself.*
>
> *2. Buy a house that comes with its own cleaner and chef.*

2.5. Create something that everybody needs and makes a lot of passive income so I can progress onto number three. Use cheap components so that people have to keep buying the so-called creation so the passive income doesn't end.

3. Have a baby who is well-behaved and toilet trained from birth who knows how to order groceries online.

4. Make the said house into a home that is filled with clean toilets and floors and washing and kids who play outside from sun up to sun down so they don't mess up the house.

4.5 And I suppose, add a large sprinkle of love, acceptance, happiness and forgiveness into the home, even if you have to steal the sprinkles from the tooth fairy.

5. Repeat step 3 as required.

6. Offload the kids before they turn 20 so you can spend more time with number 1 on the list.

Her list. She hadn't even progressed to number one yet. She placed it back on her desk, then sat down and wrote a note to Jane. Plain Jane. Shouldn't she have white paper to give to plain Jane, instead of the blue paper Jane had bought. For goodness sake. Why couldn't they all buy their own preferred colour note paper!

Poppy let out a breath that twisted and twirled up to the ceiling. For a moment she felt like she was Violet, turning violent. She picked up a pencil. Artists preferred pencils.

Dear Jane,

The pens that look like pens but aren't pens are most

probably conversation recording technology. Could the person using it be recording conversations?
And just to let you know, I talked to Mum and Dad. Or maybe I didn't.

Poppy

Poppy didn't start with *Dearest Jane*, because Jane was off her Christmas card list. Poppy didn't end her note with *Kindly, Poppy*, because she wasn't feeling any bone of kindness inside of her for Jane. The middle child. How did the middle child end up with all the power in the house? All the power out of the sisters? Poppy sniggered at her comment about talking to Mum and Dad. Jane would hate that she had done it without her permission. Adding confusion to her statement would make Jane confused and not want to deal with it.

Poppy left her bedroom, went to the dining room, and pushed the note in the bloody Jar-of-Jane-Notes. Stamped her foot, then returned to her room. She had some book cover art to do.

She sat at her computer and searched for winning book covers. After all, that's what good artists do, they steal, then they change parts of the picture to make it their own. And, after all, there is nothing new under the sun.

It was then that Poppy came across some AI Art, stealing from real artists' work. She growled at the audacity of those behind AI, who thought it was okay to steal from artists, to destroy their years and years of hard work. And to attack their unique giftedness that only they could give. To take away from their livelihoods. Didn't people realise that it takes heart to portray passion in art. Art is even in the word, heART. Art, in all its forms, is meant to be created by humans. To be felt *by* humans.

Humans with *hearts*…

A tear travelled down Poppy's cheek, navigating the highs and lows of her life, written on her face with invisible ink.

It was then that Poppy decided to take REVENGE on AI Art by stealing its image that technically nobody owned because AI wasn't a person, and it wasn't physically real, just codes making a picture on technology. She, Poppy Piccadilly, decided that she would do Reverse AI Art—steal an AI art, like AI steals from real people—artists of the past and present. And recreate it in real life for her book cover.

That, would feel right. That would open conversations about humans using AI art for themselves, claiming they did it, without giving the AI credit for the work.

And that, would have people looking at her book cover. And the book would become famous. And Poppy Piccadilly would be a real author, and not the imposter syndrome type… wouldn't she?

Poppy turned off her night light in the early hours of the morning. Way past 9pm. Like all good writers and artists do, their brains high on words and colour and stories. Admittedly, there was an easier way to get high on the smell of paint. But Poppy won't go there…

Tuesday

Violet opened her eyes and smiled. It was the thought of Jane spewing about her resignation that triggered the smile. She raised an eyebrow. Maybe she needed to visit her therapist again. Yeah nah. She could sleep in for as looooong as she liked.

'Sh–!' Violet said with wide eyes after another two hours. She wanted to swear properly, she really did, but she didn't want to incur the wrath of Jane. Plus, Jane had set her a task. She hated the Jane tasks. Being told to do something like a two-year-old. Who did she think she was? The boss of the house? No. No. No. They owned it equally. EQUALLY! The matron at a hospital? Definitely not. She didn't even have a Bachelor of Nursing degree. The bossy teacher who scared every student in the class? Well, that was a possibility. She did have a teaching degree. It's just that… the students scared her. Even when she fed them lollies to make them like her.

Violet sat up like she was a sit up ninja-warrior. *Sh–sh–sh–!* she thought, *Jane's bloody friggin' swear jar!* She had to stop swearing. She was running out of two dollar coins. And she didn't want to be a part of the cashless society. Violet put her finger to her chin. Since she's not working anymore, maybe she could invent her own swear words, and then she wouldn't be making plain Jane plain rich.

Violet reached for her laptop and plonked it on her lap. Actually, it was the only laptop in the house. She opened it up and placed her thumb on the fingerprint reader. It purred to life. On the desktop, she had saved the image of the half necklace pendant Rose had taken a photograph of. Violet enlarged the image, wondering why Jane had given her this task. Working with digital technology wasn't her finest attribute. Except for Instagram. Images of herself for people to admire and like, even though she had done nothing to gain or earn respect. Just photographs of her beautiful face.

Pouted lips.

Click.

Post.

Done.

But medical researchers, Violet thought. *Those were the people she truly admired. They should have like a billion likes.*

The pendant was broken in half, either the back half or front half was missing, but it was easy to see it was part of a red apple, or cherry? Violet decided to do a reverse image of it, feeling like she was smarter than she actually was, like Poppy, or Zinnia perhaps, and not just an extroverted hairdresser who was in fact, a psychologist with therapy sessions with scissors, and who made people feel amazing with a new hairstyle.

She uploaded the image and BINGO, it was a miniature cherry shaped pendant watch, created in Switzerland in 1910-1920. It was made of two parts, and when you pushed on the lock, it opened with a miniature watch in the inside.

Violet reached for her lavender coloured notepaper and started to write.

Dear Jane,

> *I, the squeaky hairdresser, have succeeded in solving your necklace pendant problem. The pendant of exhibit A is in fact, half of an enamelled pendant bezel wind watch in the shape of a cherry, an antique, made in Switzerland in 1915. 18 Kt gold, valued at around $7000. I have also sent you a link in an email.*
>
> *As a reward for my find, I do request all my money back from the swear jar.*

Love UnViolent

Violet smiled. She had nailed it. And she had asked for her swear jar money back, AND had signed off with LOVE. Surely that would be enough persuasion for Jane to be kind to her. She wished that their mum and dad were here. They would be proud of her too.

Jane's phone pinged. An email. She opened it up and read it. Her eyes widened. She knew where the other half of the red cherry pendant was. In the miscellaneous drawer. She had a piece of jewellery that belonged to the man with the dog-and-the-poo. What did he want with the shed and with the bunker on that night he came snooping?

Jane texted Daisy.

> *I nee d you to be ho me and investigated the bunnker. NOW! It is a matter of URgeNcY@*

No reply.

Jane Piccadilly paced the kitchen holding her phone so tight her hand muscles ached. What if she sent her text to the wrong person? She opened her texts. It definitely went to Daisy. Maybe she was being too bossy? What if Daisy is angry at her?

Jane Piccadilly paced some more, Oliver Twist pacing behind her, then after a while he sat in his bed, rested his chin and gave her the side-eye.

> Daisy: *What if I was bloody busy being a Mute. YOU have to wait! You know Janie, we all can't suddenly run to you whenever you command us. Fair suck of the sav! We have lives too! Calm your farm! Work is for work times, not gallivanting around doing other things at a whim. Chillax. Don't be a fruitcake.*

Jane stopped her pacing. Her shoulders dropped. Her heart dropped. She *had* upset Daisy. She didn't like upsetting people. She had to escape. To tea. A cup of tea will fix everything.

Jane slowed herself down, like she had read somewhere one day, to stop the panic. She turned on the jug, found her white tea pot, cup and saucer, then poured the hot water through the strainer in the teapot—white jasmine loose leaf scented white tea. On a tray, she placed her Alice in Wonderland teapot, teacup and milk, and carried her teapot and cup to the library.

She turned the teapot three times, clockwise, then poured the tea into her teacup, grabbed a white book off the white book shelf section, and sat in the white wing chair and began to read. Falling into the setting of a book was the only way to escape the new situation. Why did this house have so many situations? It all came down to Rule-Number-One—research the history of the house and the owners.

Jane closed her eyes for a moment. She thought of Rule-Number-Four, the one she would never admit to for her mother's sake, and of course the mistake to end all mistakes. Jane's eye twitched and her body tremored at-the-ick. That had almost happened four times already, and they had to start afresh at a new residence. She didn't even want to think about the mistake that would end all mistakes. She wasn't ready for it yet.

She couldn't possibly let them… Jane Piccadilly sucked in a deep breath and held it. It helped her to bottle up the emotion inside her that wanted to explode in seven different colours. She let out her breath through pursed lips, then focused on her book and her tea therapy. Daisy was now labelled as a waiting game. And Jane was good at waiting games. The middle, invisible child had perfected the waiting game. The timing game even more so.

Jane's phone pinged. A text message.

Daisy: *Because of you, I have rushed through my jobs like a mongrel. FOR YOU! What's pissed you off, Jane? Even your text is bloody messy. I'm ditching work to suss out the bunker to prove to you that there is no dramas about it!*

Jane Piccadilly shrunk in her chair. She hated upsetting anyone. And Daisy was not just upset, she was angry. Because of her. And where was her Aussie slang? This was absolutely not the Daisy she knew. Jane reread Daisy's angry text, and there was her slang. Jane squeezed her eyes shut and opened them. Were her eyes failing her, or was it that she could read Aussie slang and it made perfect sense to her?

Jane: *I'm so sorry for doing this to you Daisy. But thank you for interrupting your day. Text me with what you find.*

Jane drained her cup of tea. Placed her white book back onto the shelf. Took her tray of teapot and cup and saucer to the kitchen and cleaned up, then fled to her room. She couldn't bear to be there when Daisy arrived, and to see the disappointment on her face.

Wednesday

Daisy stood before the timber planks above the bunker, hands on hips. Just because she was a carpenter and graveyard worker didn't mean she was the right choice to enter the unknown. The fact that Jerry the landscaper emerged emotionless and pale faced unsettled her. And the fact the he advised Jane to fill it in raised suspicion.

Daisy thought that approaching the problem with a plan would lessen her anxiety. She would never admit to having anxiety, nor to being prone to workaholism to douse it. If only she felt she was good enough, she wouldn't have anxiety that she didn't want to acknowledge.

Daisy went to the bunker's wooden platform roof and pulled on the heavy metal ring and opened the timber hatch, and left it to air, like letting out the monsters. Sometimes she did that at the cemetery, if she had to enter a mausoleum—a family crypt.

She went and sat on a garden seat and kept an eye on the hole-in-the-ground. If some type of creature needed to escape, this was its chance. Maybe it was where the snake lived? Or the pig? Or rats? Or possums? Or mice? Or a gazillion toads that were going to jump out and cover the entire backyard creating a carpet of brown warts like a biblical plague?

Daisy put a stop to her imagination, where sometimes the monsters lived. Like the monster that stole the breath of swimmers in the dam.

Daisy's eye twitched and her body tremored at-the-ick.

After half an hour of nothingness, Daisy stood and walked to the hole-in-the-ground. She didn't want to call it a bunker, because she wasn't at war, or in a war… was she? She didn't want to call it an underground shelter, or a doomsday room because doom was about death and destruction or some other terrible fate. What if it was her terrible fate? No, it was simply a hole-in-the-ground. A wine cellar perhaps? A place to play cards and board games? Maybe it was once a pool, drained and re-purposed? She imagined fairy lights and comfy sofas and a bar, TV screen and bean bags and the smell of happiness.

But the moment she walked down two squeaky timber steps a chill ran down her spine.

Everything has memories, thought Daisy. *Maybe not her memories, but those of others.*

3, 4, 5, 6, 7, 8, 9, 10 steps.

Torch light on.

Bunker lit up.

Daisy's breath held.

This perhaps once living space was dead but filled with living secrets.

This was a room of pleasure for one person, and hell for another.

Suppression.

Oppression.

Dominance.

Belittling.

Abuse.

Violence.

Terror.

A blood stained bed.

Leather straps. Chains and locks.

This bunker was a complicated map of the secret life of someone, a part of them they could never expose to another because of guilt or shame or Stockholm syndrome. Where they went at what time. What they did. A wall of photographs. Some letters and drawings, and jewellery. Expensive jewellery. Like bribes, or apology jewellery. As if the gifts would erase all the violence.

And hate.

This bunker took away a part of a person they could never get back, and left a trail of self-hate and darkness and depression and fear.

Nausea rose, and Daisy pivoted on her heel, ready to flee.

Handprints on walls.

Handprints of blood.

Broken cups and plates.

And… a blood covered knife.

Terrified, Daisy took a step back. Heart pounding. Almost forgetting who she was. Was she standing in the middle of a crime scene?

She turned around to exit the space, her torch lighting up the trail of smudged blood, like a body had been dragged along.

'A dungeon,' Daisy whispered. 'This was a dungeon—cruel and dehumanising!'

Daisy ran up the creaky steps, stumbling near the top and fell onto the ground above. She pushed herself up, tremoring, found the platform door, lifted it and closed the hatch, her mind in a whirl, her thoughts in a state of shock.

How could she tell Jane? Plain Jane. Innocent Jane. Naïve Jane. Jane who only saw unicorns and rainbows and pure love, about what she had found in the bunker? Quiet, introverted Jane who hated things going wrong.

Daisy cleared her throat, straightened her shirt, and lifted her chin. 'Oi, Oi, Oi!' she called, and they went inside.

She ran to her room and had a shower. She had to wash the stories of the hole-in-the-ground from her skin and her hair. She returned to the dining table and sat with a cup of green tea with peppermint notes. Situations like this required a cup of tea.

She blinked, and texted Jane:

> *Going into the bloody hole-in-the-ground scared the shite out of me. I agree with Jerry. There's nothing to see. We should fill it in, as soon as possible. And yeah – I don't owe you $2 for swearing. I used 'shite' instead!*

Jane texted back after twenty minutes:

Thank you Daisy. You are the best! I accept your evaluation and will organise for it to be filled in. You still owe me $2. It was your intention to swear that is counted.

Daisy texted back after twenty minutes:

Grrr! You are correct. I owe you $2. Oh - you should ask Flora to sort out Oliver's bone collection. ASAP.

Jane texted back after twenty minutes. She used words sweetened with honey, imbued with thankfulness and good manners. It was her way to smooth things over. She was relieved that Daisy came to the same conclusion as Jerry. Now she felt silly for being in such a panicked state earlier. She reminded herself that most problems are not worth worrying about.

Shall do. And thank you for your advice. What would I do without you?

Jane texted Flora:

Dear Flora.

She took a deep, calming breath. She didn't want her text to look like she was coming undone like the text to Daisy. Like her threads that held her together were unravelling.

Daisy has demanded that you sort out Oliver's bone collection IMMEDIATELY, or else... just passing on

her message. And, please text me when you have finished.
I know that you will succeed.

Jane gave a side smile. She felt like a middle child again. The instigator, where blame would rest with others. Like that day in the car.

Flora texted back, twenty minutes later:

Is there a problem? Daisy isn't usually demanding like that. But yes, I will sort out the bone collection and text you when I am finished.

Thursday

Flora placed the last of Olivier's collection of bones on the lawn and stood back. 'Bones-on-the-lawn, Poppy would call this as an artist. There were hundreds of bones. Over two hundred at least. Small, large, skinny, thick, short, long. Absolutely some sort of animal.

Flora started to group alike bones. She hated that Jane had given her this task, just because she worked at a farm. She wanted to tell Jane that she wasn't a paleontologist. But somehow, in plain Jane's brain, bones and farms had a connection.

Flora started with the vertebrae, and piece by piece, connected bones together, as they were grouped in animals. They all followed the same shape.

Flora added the last bone and stood. All it needed was a skull.

And then she slow blinked. Before her was not an animal. It was human. And right on cue, Olivier trotted around the corner, as happy as Larry, tail up in the air, with a skull-in-his-mouth. He stopped before her and dropped the skull, and sat, looking up at her with one paw raised off the ground.

Flora nodded her head up and down with wide eyes. 'A BIG treat, Olivier. You deserve the BIGGEST doggo treat!' Olivier tilted his head to one side. Flora raced inside and grabbed Olivier five treats and returned to Olivier and the bones-on-the-lawn art. As Olivier settled in for a feast, Flora added the skull to the skeleton.

She stood back from the bones-on-the-lawn art and considered the human skeleton. She frowned. Male or female?

She pulled out her phone and Googled male and female skeletons. The difference resided in the skull, the ribcage and the pelvis. Flora compared the skeleton to the images on her phone. The bones-on-the-lawn art was male.

Flora placed her hands over her stomach. Like protecting it. She had a dilemma. Should she leave the bones-on-the-lawn art here on the lawn, or bundle it up again?

And… the police would have to be informed.

Flora thought about what Jane would want. No doubt it would be to bundle them up and put them into a box and bury it.

Out of sight, out of mind.

Like-nothing-had-ever-been-found.

But Flora knew that the bones should be left on the grass as they are. She didn't want to be implicated in interfering with evidence. But of evidence of what? Didn't people bury their deceased in their yards once? A very long time ago?

Flora looked at the bones again. And yes, Jane was right. Because she worked on a farm, the bones didn't freak her out as much as it would with a regular person. But still, Flora's eye twitched and her body tremored at-the-ick.

Flora decided to leave the bones in position on the grass. But the problem was that, by the time the police finished their investigation, the brand new grass beneath the skeleton would be yellow, then brown, leaving skeleton art on the grass. A reminder. The new green grass blemished by a skeleton memory.

Flora went to the laundry, and returned with a white sheet, and covered the skeleton. What would the neighbours think if they clearly saw a skeleton-on-the-lawn, at the house of Jane Piccadilly, who would hate to have the neighbours talking about them. Again. Just like in the other houses they once lived in.

Flora texted Jane:

We have a situation. And this situation requires a solution. AT ONCE. I have left a white sheet over the bones in the backyard for you to have a look at when you are ready, and decide on the solution to the situation.

Jane texted back twenty minutes later:

Thank you Flora.

Jane Piccadilly left her bedroom and went downstairs and outside to the backyard. And there was the white sheet, draped over the bones, making it look like a ghost, or a body underneath.

'Great prank, Flora,' Jane scoffed, then lifted off the sheet. Jane stumbled and fell onto the bones, misplacing them. She scrambled to her feet, realigned the bones and threw the sheet back over the bones. 'Flora, we most definitely have a situation!'

Jane looked about at her neighbours, hoping none had been peering outside their windows. How would the man next door who hosed footprints off his lawn cope with seeing bones laid out on grass?

What would her neighbours think?

Jane Piccadilly took a quick photograph on her phone, then raced inside, Oliver Twist following, carrying a humerus bone-in-his-mouth. Jane removed it from him and returned it to the skeleton-on-the-grass, completing the jigsaw puzzle. She lifted up the little loooong dog and carried him inside the house, and locked his doggy door so he couldn't get out into the backyard again.

Oliver Twist watched Jane pace the library sitting room floor, stopping before each bookcase, about turning and walking to the other bookcase. If she had followed rule number one and done her house research of the history of the house, this would never have happened.

And right before her parents were about to visit!

The police would be asking questions, looking in every nook and cranny. They would do a background check on her, and the occupants of the house.

Jane Piccadilly sat on the wing chair and group texted her sisters, her hands quaking:

We have a situation. A BIG SITUATION! You need to stay somewhere else while I sort the situation out. This needs to be done asap. I'll put your clothes and bathroom stuff into your vehicles. And then you must LEAVE! I'll let you know, one at a time, when to come to your vehicle.

Then she phoned her dad. If she face-timed him, he would know something was terribly wrong. He picked up after the third ring.

'Hi Dad,' Jane said, keeping her voice even.

'Hello, my girl. How is Alice?'

'Jane, Dad. Call me Jane, remember.'

'Yes, dear. How is Jane?'

'I'm good. But… you and mum will have to postpone coming to stay for a week. Poppy is unwell.'

'What a shame, Jane. Your mother and I were so looking forward to coming to see your new residence. You're obviously worried about Poppy. You have a waver in your voice. I hope you're not coming down with whatever Poppy has.'

'I'm good, Dad. Gotta go though. Send my love to Mum.'

'Shall do. Love you,' her father said.

'Love you too,' Jane said.

Jane wiped a tear from her eye, then raced to each of her sister's bedrooms, gathered their possessions, and placed them in their cars. Except for Poppy, her clothes and toiletries when into Violet's Kombi Van. Rose's possessions went into the Kombi Van too. And Zinnia's were loaded into Flora's Figaro.

And then she told her sisters to go. One at a time so not to arouse suspicion amongst the neighbours.

After they left, Jane Piccadilly slowed herself down. She went to the kitchen and turned on the jug, found her white tea pot, cup and saucer, then poured the hot water through the strainer in the teapot—white jasmine loose leaf scented white tea. On a tray, she placed her Alice in Wonderland teapot, teacup and milk, and carried her teapot and cup to the library.

She turned the teapot three times, clockwise, then poured the tea into her teacup. A cup of tea would help her to think.

But the cup of tea didn't help.

Jane Piccadilly stood and paced the sitting room floor. She didn't want her sisters dragged into the investigation. She needed to have an alias for all the rooms with beds. Rented rooms? A boarding house perhaps? She researched boarding houses. She needed a license for that. It was out of the question. But a house for students to reside in was a different matter. She would tell the police that the rooms were for students for the nearby university, and that she was just setting it up. Jane typed up an ad for the local paper and the University notice board, and saved the paper ad notice board applications on her computer.

Problem solved.

Jane Piccadilly worked into the night setting up the rooms so they looked ready to be rented, fully furnished. She arranged Poppy's downstairs room as an art studio, including lining up six wigs on their stands like a piece of artwork.

Friday

Then she dialled 000.

'You have dialled Emergency Triple Zero. Your call is being connected.'

'Hello. Do you need Police, Fire or Ambulance?'

'Police,' Jane said.

'Please hold the line while I put you through.'

'Thank you.'

'Police. How can I help you?'

'There's a person...'

'Is the person threatening you?'

'No.'

'Is the person trying to break in?'

'No. They are not br-bre—'

'Is the person conscious or breathing?'

'No.'

'Have you commenced CPR?'

'No.'

'Start that now and continue until an ambulance arrives.'

'I can't. The body is in no condition for CPR.'

Phone silence.

'Please remain at the scene until police arrive.'

'You mean, right next to the body?'

'Yes.'

'Can I... can I... keep watch of the body from my window?'

'Please send an unmarked police car. I'm new in the house and I don't want the neighbours talking about me.'

'Request noted. Is your address the same as your phone location?'

'Yes,' Jane said and disconnected the call.

Jane Piccadilly turned on the front lights and peered out Poppy's bedroom window while she waited for the police to arrive. After fifteen minutes a dark car pulled up, and two men left the car. They pushed open the front gate and wandered along the pathway, looking to the left and right, and suddenly, the garden sprinklers turned on, hosing the plants and the police.

Jane froze in horror. She had forgotten about the timing on the garden watering system. At the sound of the knock on the front door, Jane meekly opened it. There, the two plain clothed officers stood, water dripping from their faces.

'I'm so sorry about the sprinklers, officers. I'll grab a couple of towels for you.' Jane scurried off and returned and handed them each a towel. She led them to the kitchen dining area and offered them a seat.

'Alice, you have a body here?'

'Call me Jane. Alice is my mum's first name, whom I am named after, and yes... well technically, there's no body. My dog dug up the bones. They're in the backyard.'

The officers stood, and Jane followed suit. She led them out the back door, Oliver following along, and led the officers to the white sheet on the grass where the bones-on-the-grass art was.

The officers took photographs, then removed the sheet. And there were the bones. Assembled perfectly by Flora.

More photographs. A call to the police station. A notebook and pen pulled out of the tallest officer's pocket.

'You'll understand that we've called the Homicide Investigation Unit. It's illegal to bury a body in a backyard. This is now a crime scene and an official investigation has been launched.'

Jane Piccadilly tremored. She knew this would happen with the skeleton. She had to have courage.

'When did you purchase the house?'

'Six weeks ago.'

'And you moved in?'

'Two weeks ago.'

'How did the bones get here?'

Jane Piccadilly gestured to Oliver Twist. 'He kept bringing them in… from the backyard… we thought… I mean… *I* thought it was someone's pet.'

'Which part of the yard did your dog dig them up from?'

'I'm unsure, Officer. The backyard was full of long grass and hard to see anything. I've only just had it landscaped.'

The officer was taking notes. 'Who was the landscaper?'

'Jerry. I'll get his contact details.' Jane opened her phone and shared the landscaper's business details.

The sound of footsteps came from the side of the house.

Flashlights.

Police.

A carried gazebo.

Photographic equipment.

Flood lights.

Forensic equipment.

In a flurry of activity, the gazebo was erected above the skeleton and floodlights lit up the backyard like it was daytime. Jane nervously looked about at her neighbours.

Curtains pushed aside.

Eyes peering.

Lips moving as phones held to ears.

Flashes of light as photos taken.

Jane Piccadilly melted inside. She would most definitely become the centre of gossip in the street. She would no longer be invisible Jane. Plain Jane. But Jane-with-the-human-skeleton-in-the-backyard.

That Jane.

The police officer led her inside to the dining table and sat her at the orange seat—THE ORANGE SEAT—while he sat on the white seat. Jane wanted to tell him he couldn't sit there. It was her seat—

'Jane. We need to thoroughly check each room of the house for evidence. Was your house like this—' he looked about the room, 'renovated—when you moved in?'

'No. I renovated it before I moved in. I have the before photos on my laptop if that will help.'

'Indeed. Please bring your laptop here so I can have a look.'

Jane inhaled a calming breath. She left the table and went to her library sitting room and grabbed her laptop and returned to the dining table. The office was standing and talking to a colleague, so she sat in her white chair, opened her laptop with her fingerprint, and went to the folder marked "house renovations", and pulled up the photos.

The officer sat in the orange chair and inspected each of the photos of the rooms. He pulled a USB out of his pocket. 'May I?'

Jane nodded, then watched as he downloaded the photographs of the house before it was renovated to what it was now.

Four investigators entered the room and peered around the kitchen and dining area.

'We need to inspect each of the rooms in the house, Jane. We are trying to find the story of the person who is now the skeleton and what happened to him. And perhaps… it didn't even happen here; he was just buried here. But we have to be thorough to find the truth.'

Jane nodded. 'I would like to accompany you as you do your search, if I may,' Jane said.

The policeman looked at the detectives, who nodded.

Jane took the lead. 'As you can see, this is the kitchen and dining room, utilities room to the left. The kitchen and utilities room has been totally renovated—'

'We'd like the name of the people who did the renovations, please.'

Jane scrolled through her phone and gave him the details. She about turned. 'This way leads to the front door. On the left is the library sitting room for the students, as a quiet room—'

'The students?'

'Yes. I am about to rent out the rooms for university students. This terrace house is much too big for one person!' Jane opened the door and they entered the library sitting room, then waited as the detectives looked about.

They moved along to the next room and Jane's stomach jittered. She didn't like to lie, but she must do it to protect her sisters. 'This is my creative room. Art. Writing.' She stood in front of the six wigs, obscuring them from view.

They ascended the steps to the second floor. 'All of these rooms are for students—three of them—complete with beds and other furnishings, except the room at the front of this floor, that one is mine.' Jane waited in the hall while the detectives meandered about, taking photographs and notes.

They ascended the steps to the third floor. 'More student accommodation, and the photographic equipment will be moved to my creative room in the coming days… and the room with the greenhouse will have the plants and stuff shifted to the shed we… *I*… didn't know I had in the backyard until the landscaper discovered it,' Jane said. She pointed to the ceiling, 'and an attic which will be the common room.'

'Tell me more about the shed in the backyard, Jane,' the police officer said.

'The property was a mess when I bought it. I couldn't see the backyard properly because of the weeds and overgrown shrubs. When the landscaping team were clearing the backyard for the new landscaping, they discovered the shed.'

'What's inside it?'

'Just a chair and a book, I think. We haven't found the key to unlock the door.'

The officer wrote notes. 'Let's return to the dining area while the detectives conduct a thorough search of each room.' He looked up at her. 'Protocol…'

Jane Piccadilly didn't want the detectives in her sister's rooms without her there, snooping and photographing and looking in places that shouldn't be looked at. Although she had done a perfect job of moving out their belongings, it still didn't feel right. It felt like an… intrusion of privacy.

Nevertheless, Jane returned to the dining room as instructed, but before she sat down, she went to the kitchen to make a cup of tea, and while waiting for the water to boil, she stood at the large window in her kitchen and looked into her backyard.

Police were everywhere, invading her beautiful landscaping,

leaving pieces of themselves embedded into the grass and the plants. Jane Piccadilly shuddered. The thought of them finding the bunker made her blood run cold. It was already bad enough that there was a man's remains in her backyard, but for them to find the hole-in-the-ground… that would become another crime scene. All Jane wanted was to move into her seven bedroom three story terrace house and live happily ever after with lovely neighbours.

But that dream had been destroyed.

She thought of her mother and father. She would not call them to tell them of this latest situation.

She could not.

She must not.

Her father would say that she deserved this, after everything she had done.

Chapter 33

Sunday
Jane

The sun rose on every house in Queensland. But not Jane Piccadilly's. A cloud remained over it, the colour of midnight.

'Miss Piccadilly,' a new voice said, startling Jane from the hour of sleep she had finally caught. She sat up and rubbed her eyes, 'Yes?'

'Are you aware of the hidden room and staircase behind your bookshelf?'

'What! I mean… no!' Jane said, bewildered. If she had known about it, it would have made her day. A bookshelf that opened to a secret room would be the cherry on the top of owning a house like this. A little piece of golden sunshine lit up inside her before a charcoal coloured cloud covered the light. The discovery of the room and a staircase behind the bookshelf could not be a good thing when a fleshless, organ less body had been found, and a dungeon sat, awaiting discovery in the backyard. It was sounding like one of Poppy's books – the plot thickens.

Run, Jane, run! She had to escape this nightmare.

'And the staircase leads to a tunnel that opens up in a room underground in the backyard. Are you aware of the room underground?'

Jane sighed. 'Yes. The landscaper discovered it and said we… *I*… should fill it in. I hadn't gotten around to that yet. I've only just moved in.'

'Do you know what is in the underground room?'

'No. The landscaper just said to fill it in.'

'Did the landscaper tell you what is down there?'

'He just said there was nothing to see.'

The detective nodded and wrote notes. 'Did you ever meet the previous owner?' he asked.

'No.'

'Do you know the name of the previous owner?'

'No.'

The detective added notes-to-his-notes.

'Can I make you a tea or coffee?' Jane said to change the direction of the questioning.

'Coffee, please.'

Jane Piccadilly headed to the kitchen to brew a pot of tea for herself, and coffee for the detective, using the coffee supplies she had found in two of her sisters' rooms. She looked outside at the backyard, awash with police everywhere, evidence held in clear bags, furniture and other items being removed from the hole-in-the-ground.

Good, she thought, *it will save another person from being exposed to that, and certainly not her, she could never enter the hole-*

in-the-ground while it held negative stories.

And the shed. Was open. Fingerprinting being done. Photographic flashes. Items removed.

Jane placed the detective's coffee on the table, as well as her teapot and teacup. She sat down and turned her Alice in Wonderland teapot three times, clockwise, then poured her tea into her white Alice in Wonderful teacup and took a sip. She smiled. The new teapot absolutely had new stories about the house!

'Is everything okay, Miss Alice Jane Piccadilly?'

'With my cup of tea, of course, with the house, no,' Jane said. 'When will all this—' she waved her hand around, 'finish?'

'Later today I expect, tomorrow midday at the latest.' The detective gulped his coffee.

Rude, thought Jane. But she understood that he had a job to do. And it was a good sign that the coffee tasted okay.

He pulled out an ink pad and a piece of paper. 'I need to get samples of your fingerprints.'

Jane Piccadilly sat up taller. She-wasn't-a-criminal. She didn't want the police to have her fingerprints on file. 'Why?'

'To eliminate you as a suspect.'

'A suspect for what?'

'Murder, amongst other things.'

'How could that be? I've only just moved in!'

'You'd be surprised by how things play out in real life, Miss Piccadilly.'

'Am I being charged with anything?'

'No. We just want to rule you out.'

'Then no to the fingerprints if I am not being charged.'

The police officer nodded.

'Do you think the man was murdered here?' said Jane.

'How do you know it was a man?'

'The pelvis of the skeleton... Google search.'

'I can't say at this stage. There's a lot to investigate, people to interview, research of past tenants... we'll let you know the results of the investigation once we are allowed to share the details.'

'I would like that... closure to the situation... thank you.'

Chapter 34

Monday
Poppy

Poppy needed a last page to her novel. And it had to be a good ending. *Life* deserved a good ending. A happy ending. A soul healing ending. She returned to the seven bedroom three story Victorian terrace house with permission from Jane once the police had left.

She entered her bedroom and turned to the wall behind her bed head. To her novel in progress. She had one last page to add. The ending. But she couldn't get it from the library. That meant there was only one other place to go. Jane's nine hundred and ninety-nine books in the home library. The library sitting room.

Poppy read the second last page of her novel, then went to Jane's home library. She ran her finger along the spines of the books, and stopped at a novel spine that was white and pink. She pulled the novel off the shelf and flipped through it to the last page and read:

I gazed into his luminous blue eyes and breathed deeply, inhaling his scent of blended spicy cedarwood and cocoa vanilla. Warmth rushed through me as his colour shone brightly: indigo-blue, swirling with healing turquoise.

Xander brushed a ringlet of hair from my face, his brows creased with barely controlled emotion, then our eyes locked. I rose up onto my tiptoes, my lips close to his, and felt a sacred energy flowing between us as he moved his mouth to mine, his lips caressing with a tenderness that splintered everything, and changed everything as our souls touched.

I closed my eyes and bathed in the ecstasy of the sensual, unconditional love that bound our hearts, our minds, and our essence, while time stood still.

And in that moment I knew that I, Yolande Lawrence-Harrison, was no longer the colour of broken…

Poppy let out a small cry and put her hand to her mouth. This… *this* page was perfect for the ending of her novel. She held the corner of the page and ripped it out at once, pushed the novel back in between the books on the shelf, returned to her room and added it to the wall behind her bed, and photographed it.

Her novel was finished!

Poppy moved her bed to the side, grabbed a stool and pen, stood on the stool and added page numbers to her novel. Some of the fonts on the pages were a *little* different. But not obviously so.

But-that-was-okay.

She was a little bit different. And different was good. After numbering the last page, she removed each page from the wall, being careful to keep them in order. All 280 pages.

Then she prepared the pages for stitching, like she had seen on YouTube, and sewed them together.

She made the hardcover board after watching a bookbinding tutorial and secured the interior pages to the spine of the hardcover board.

And finally, she found her sketches of her Reverse AI art—art stolen from AI, and measured up the final art paper that would be glued to the hardcover.

There was one problem.

She still didn't have a title for her novel. Perhaps that would come while she was deep in the motions of creating art.

And it did.

Poppy texted Jane.

'Stolen'. Do you think that title is appropriate for my novel?

Twenty minutes later, Jane texted back.

Very appropriate. Can't wait to read it!

Poppy worked on the cover for four hours. The last thing she did was write her author name on the front, *Poppy Piccadilly*, after writing the blurb at the back and including an ISBN she had bought so she always owned this book herself. She used a hairdryer to dry the paint on the artwork, then glued it to the hardcover board, used the hairdryer again and ran her hand over the finished novel and smiled.

It was finished.

Poppy rode her bicycle to the library. Without Schnitzel Von Krumm. Her heart clenched. She stood before the heritage listed building that felt like her second home and swallowed hard. She walked toward the door and entered it, and inhaled deeply. That addictive book smell that made her feel high as a kite. The high librarian. Everyone thought she was just extra happy. Maybe the library should be decorated with kites.

This… house of books was light in her days. Borrowed light as Poppy Piccadilly.

Poppy Piccadilly, the brand new author, strode toward the P author shelves, photographed her novel in front of the shelf, then pushed it between *James Phelan* and *Jodi Picoult*. The spine was a standout. *Stolen* glistened with the gold paint while a creeping green vine reached its tendrils around it like it was about to steal the title on the pink background. Poppy photographed it again and wiped a tear from her face.

She walked to the back room, where she had spent many hours of work repairing books, sorting books, and entering data into the online data base, and sat down at the computer. She opened up 'new acquisitions' and entered the information for her new novel, and pressed done.

She sat back in the chair and looked about the room. Her throat tightened to stop the wail of a cry. She wished Schnitzel Von Krumm could be here. Today. With her. But she had to get this over and done with.

Poppy Piccadilly stood and smoothed down her dress and stepped out into the public library and looked about.

She *loved* this place.

She *loved* the people.

She *loved* the palette of old book smells—the earthy, sweet and musty scent with the faint hint of vanilla, mixed with the new book smell of the paper, the ink and the adhesives.

She *loved* the rustle of book pages being turned.

She *loved* the books.

But… it was time to say goodbye. Before she was found out and fired. How many books had she ripped pages out of? 280? At least! She was an employee costing them a lot of money.

Poppy Piccadilly, proud new author, walked the bookshelves of the library, the kids' reading area, the outdoor reading area, a million stories and smiles coming to the fore in her memory, and Schnitzel Von Krumm, *beautiful* Schnitzel Von Krumm, and his amazing dress-ups for the kids.

Just. For. The. Kids.

Although the grown-ups liked it too. Thirty-six colourful, crazy costumes. Schnitzel Von Krumm had no idea how ridiculous he looked. He had no idea how he brought light into the days of people cloaked in darkness. He was a light-bearer of the purest unconditional loving heart.

Poppy stopped at the Schnitzel Von Krumm wall of fame. She looked at each of the kids selfies with the famous library reading dog. Beaming smiles never to be forgotten.

Poppy Piccadilly's eyes welled with tears, a dam wall about to burst. She inhaled deeply in the library for the last time, sucking all the scents, words and illustrations from the books so she could keep them with her forever. She about turned and strode out with the exact same step and style that she had entered with today. As a proud author.

She didn't ride her bicycle home. She walked.

And as she entered the front garden gate, she grabbed at her hair and flung strands of it into the garden, the medium length wavy grey hair landing atop a fern, like decorating a Christmas tree.

The unravelling had begun.

Chapter 35

Jane

There was no Tuesday at the seven bedroom, three story,
Victorian terrace house.
No Wednesday.
No Thursday.
No Friday.
No Saturday.
But there was a Sunday.
Jane Piccadilly sat on the bus seat. Next to Luciano.
'Morning,' he said.
This time Jane didn't freeze or flinch when Luciano spoke.
'Good morning, Luke,' she said.
Luciano turned his head towards her for the first time ever.
'When did you know?' said Jane.

'Know what?'

'About my… aah… sisters?'

'After the first week of meeting them.' He shifted slightly on the seat. 'And then you on Sunday,' he said.

'So which one is the real me?'

'The Sunday Piccadilly,' he said.

'Why do you think that?'

'Your hair smells different to the others, and you are more apprehensive when you talk, like you are guarding something close to your heart,' he said.

Jane reached up to her mid-length, curly flaxen-coloured-hair and pulled a tendril towards her nose and smelled it. Coconut. White. Like holidays at the beach. The white sand. The white foaming waves. The white sparkles dancing on top of the sea.

'When did you become so observant, Luuke?' said Jane. She was trying to tell him she knew who he was. Luciano Antonio. Luci or Luke, from school. Except in her memories of him, he could see.

'I had no choice. When you go blind, your other senses become stronger.'

'What happened?'

A bus came and stopped.

The doors opened and closed.

And the bus left.

'I tried to save you two times, Jane. I'm sorry I failed. *I'm sorry*… I failed,' Luciano said as they both sat on the bus seat.

There was silence.

'The first time I met you was when I was a little boy. I was eight. I watched my mother and father try to rescue your family from the water. I watched as your mother and father held you next to the lifeless bodies of your sisters, two who looked exactly like you. I needed to revisit that place after a while to deal with the memory.'

'And hence why you know about the flowers and the car in the trees.' Anxiety skirted over Jane's skin. That was a conversation he had with Violet.

'Yes. And at high school, you kept hanging out with that jerk. You were too good for him. You didn't hear what he said and what he did when he wasn't with you. I tried to tell you so many times, and I didn't want him to take you to the formal, because I know the plans he had for you. He'd been bragging about it to all the guys.'

'And so you asked me to the formal first.'

'Yes. But you rejected me.' Luciano let out an audible breath.

Jane recalled the disappointed look in Luciano's blue eyes. The tear forming on his bottom eyelid before he lowered his head, put his hands in his pockets and stepped back, turned, and walked away.

'And then you married him…' Luciano shook his head. 'You looked beautiful in your wedding dress, and so happy…'

'You were there?'

'Hudson invited me to the wedding, yes.'

Jane Piccadilly closed her eyes, revisiting that day, trying to find Luciano in the church. At the reception. Nothing. Could she be so blinded, so infatuated by Hudson, that she wouldn't notice anyone else that day.

'And, predictably, he was unfaithful to you.'

Jane placed her hand over her heart. Trying to stop it from shattering once again. Trying to stop that feeling of betrayal from deep in her past. The curling into a ball in the corner of a room, her heart breaking. Moving back into her parents' house. Unable to work. How could she not see Hudson's infidelity, even at school. Friends had tried to tell her, but she brushed them off as jealous, or interfering.

A bus came and stopped.
The doors opened and closed.
And the bus left.

Jane let out a quiet sob then controlled her emotional contours. 'And after the divorce he wouldn't let go. He kept calling me. He stalked me. He threatened me. He gaslighted me, and physically abused me when he cornered me, and—'

'And that night he went to your parents to threaten you again because you had spoken to the police about him. You were his, like a possession. If he couldn't have you, no one else would.'

The clouds above stilled, listening to the story.

'But it was your parents who were affected in the explosion. I'm sorry I wasn't there early enough to stop the bomb,' Luciano said.

Jane's head snapped to the right to look at Luciano. 'You were there… that night?'

Luciano lowered his head. 'One of the guys mentioned how angry he was on Facebook and said how he was going to see you. I left as soon as I read the comment.'

'And that's where you lost your sight…' Jane whispered.

'Yes. The doctors said it was a flash burn from the heat and it would heal within seventy-two hours. But I had complications, an infection.'

'I'm so sorry, Luke. It's all my fault. It's all my fault. Again.' Jane closed her eyes and lowered her head.

'What do you mean, again?'

She lifted her head and a tear rolled down her cheek and dropped to the seat, leaving a tear-print the colour of sadness; grey with muted browns and specks of black and one micro-dosing speck of red for pain. 'My sisters died because of me. I was the one who started the argument in the car when I was eight, and Dad turned around, distracted, then we skidded off the road into the—'

'Dam.'

'Mum hates me because of it. She never forgave me.' Jane's throat tightened, stopping the texture and grain of grief from being freed.

'But Jane, your version of the accident is wrong. Your dad suffered a medical episode. And your mum lunged for the steering wheel to stop a car crash. That's why the car ended up in the dam.'

A bus came and stopped.
The doors opened and closed.
And the bus left.

And the clouds departed, leaving a blue sky.

Jane turned to Luciano. 'How do you know?'
'It was in the papers. Mum and Dad read me the story to help me understand what I had witnessed.'
Jane Piccadilly did not utter a word.
She had been told a lie. An unbearably heavy lie that she believed and carried everyday of her life since she was eight.
Jane Piccadilly's eye twitched and her body tremored at-the-ick.
She had been told a lie that was beyond ugly, and had tainted her entire life with shame and guilt and an obsession with death.

Jane Piccadilly's eyes flooded with water.

She had grown up hating herself for what happened to her sisters, punishing herself by denying herself of lovely times, food, friends. Cutting her skin. Inflicted self-injury because she didn't deserve happiness, or even the air she breathed every moment of every day.

Jane's face became pale. 'Luke… I-I-I… have to go inside. I-I… don't feel well.'

'Oh… oh. I'm sorry. That must have come as a shock. I'll come with you. I'll make you a cup of tea?'

'How are you going to do that when you can't see, Einstein?' Jane berated herself for commenting on his blindness.

'Good point.'

'I'm sorry. I didn't mean it to come out like that.' Jane took Luciano's hand and guided him inside the house and to the kitchen.

'You know the man with the dog?' Luciano said as he leaned against the kitchen bench.

'Yessss…'

'He should be the one who should be dead instead of the other guy.'

'What!'

'He used to talk on his phone all the time. To people. He'd tell them bits and pieces and people would walk by who knew him and ask why he didn't live there anymore. And they'd ask about his girlfriend, who, by the way, married another guy recently.'

Jane thought of Rose and her photographs, and the video footage.

'He knew I was blind, so he assumed I also couldn't hear.' Luciano laughed. 'I recorded his conversations on my pen audio recorder, and handed the information to the police.'

'Intriguing,' said Jane.

Jane led Luciano to the long wooden dining table. 'What's your favourite colour?'

'Green,' said Luciano. 'Like your eyes.'

Jane gave a small smile. One that Luciano would never see. She grabbed his hand and escorted him to the green chair. Zinnia's chair. Jane stalled as she decided where to sit. She always sat in her white chair. She didn't want to sit in the orange of Flora's chair on the right of Luciano, and not the pink of Rose's chair on his left. She looked opposite Luciano to Daisy's yellow chair. That was the closest to white.

Jane returned to the kitchen and prepared the tea, grabbed the tray with the two teacups of white tea.

'Thank you for coming and keeping me company,' Jane said. 'I don't know how to feel about the new information you gave me about the accident.'

'It must have been a shock. I'm sorry, I should have delivered it to you in a different way.'

Jane put her hand under her chin. Then shook her head, even though Luciano couldn't see her. 'At first I thought you were… lying. After being told I was the cause of the accident all my life, I—'

'You thought it was a lie?'

Jane took a sip of her tea. 'Yes.' Her phone rang and she answered it.

Luciano leaned back in his chair and waited for the conversation to end.

Jane put down her phone. 'That was the police. They're coming around in twenty minutes to talk to me about the case. They said I should have a lawyer present.' Jane let out a short sob and covered her face with her hands. 'I know nothing about the bones and the body and what happened here. All I did was buy this house!'

'I'm a lawyer. I can stay if you want,' Luciano said.

Jane was speechless. The man-on-the-bus-seat-with-the-carpet-bag who seemed to know too much about her, including information from her past like he was there, is a lawyer? Did he have access to information to her and wasn't who he claimed to be?

Jane's mind raced. What if he was a narcissist like Hudson? What if he had been planted outside her life by Hudson, from jail? What if Hudson had given him her life information?

What if, she was on his hit list, contracted by Hudson to end it all?

And she, Alice Jane Piccadilly the 4th, had invited him in to her house. The mistake house.

Jane put her teacup down. It clanged and echoed throughout the kitchen and dining area and tea spilled onto the table. She raced to the kitchen and grabbed some paper towel, and a sharp kitchen knife.

She looked at Oliver Twist. He laid peacefully in his dog bed.

Jane thought back to her mum and dad's rules. Rule-Number-Three—observe the behaviour of animals. Oliver Twist could read a person's character perfectly, like a special dog super-sense. If he didn't like someone, or felt a threat by a human or an animal, he would growl or bark maniacally at them.

Jane relaxed. If Oliver Twist was okay with Luciano, then she should be. And besides, Oliver would attack Luciano if he hurt her. Dachshunds, the best little guard dogs around.

'You okay, Jane?' Luciano asked.

'Yeah, nah. Just nervous with what's next today—a day full of revelations,' she said, her hands shaking.

'Yeah, nah. Sounds like something Daisy would say.' His voice was gentle with a warmth to it.

'Nah, she would say, strewth, the bloody coppers are comin'' this arvo for another sticky beak. Mum and Dad would be devo. But don't worry Luciano, they'll rack off when they know Jane isn't involved. She'll be apples.'

Luciano's laughter silenced the birds. 'You are such a bogan, you dag!'

'Bloody oath, right?'

There was a knock at the door and Jane stilled.

'You've got this, Jane. And, I'm many ears for you.'

Anxiety burned Jane's skin. She had not told the police about her sisters. Had the neighbours? Surely in their detective work they would find out about her aliases. Her... *reanimation* of the dead. Her... *borrowed light*. 'Thanks, Luke... as long as it's not Ménière's.'

'What?'

Jane shook her head. 'Your head would spin if you knew what that was.' Jane walked slowly to the front door and welcomed the police into the house. Two of them. She guided them to the dining table, standing behind her white chair so neither of them would sit there. One sat in Poppy's blue seat, and the other in Violet's purple seat.

'This is Luciano. He's a lawyer,' Jane said.

After the introductions, the police told the story of the house. The story of the previous owner. The story of the skeleton-on-the-grass.

Stories. We are all stories. Poppy would love this.

'Alice Jane Piccadilly the 4th,' the officer said.

Jane flinched at the sound of her name. She was not Alice. She was Jane.

'We have closed this case. The deceased, a man, was wrongfully murdered. He was here as a good Samaritan to help a woman, the previous owner of this house, from domestic violence. She, however, did not take the man's life, it was perpetrated by the abuser of the woman. He has been arrested and is awaiting trial.'

Jane sat still in her white seat, barely breathing.

'This house was also used for multiple purposes. At times to feed the hungry. To give a bed and shower to the homeless, and at times, where drugs exchanged hands, massages. Sex. The bunker is where the woman was abused, and the hidden garden shed was where the drugs were made, the recipe book was there, as well as the ledger to keep track of the transactions.'

Rule #2. Rule #2. Rule #2, Jane kept repeating in her head. She swallowed hard to stop her stomach contents from expelling.

Rule-Number-Two—history research of the house. She would never have purchased this house if she knew the details. No wonder the house couldn't breathe when she first entered it. It was ready to explode with the hidden stories. It's secrets. And finally it had.

And now, peace could rest over it.

'I need some water,' Jane said, and walked slowly to the kitchen, grabbed a glass and filled it with filtered water. She took a sip, then returned to the table.

'The neighbours were helpful in providing details of what went on here over the last six years, plus your photographs, videos, and the pendant piece. Thank you.'

Jane nodded her head. She felt a "but" coming. A shift in direction of their conversation.

The police officer shifted on his seat. 'Jane, we need to talk to you about your residents.'

Jane's heart sank and anxiety rippled through her. What had the neighbours said? 'Is this why I need a lawyer present? Am I being charged with anything?'

'Who are the residents you are speaking of, detective?' Luciano said, jumping into the conversation.

The detective took out his notebook and flipped through the

pages. 'We don't have names, just descriptions, like of you, Jane—the girl with the curly flaxen hair.' He looked up at Luciano. 'What the neighbours saw.' The detective smiled.

'Have any of the so called residents of this house, whom you don't have names for, just descriptions, done anything against the law?'

'No.'

'Then there is no investigation needed about them,' Luciano said. 'Just as there would be no case about the man down the road who likes to dress as a woman, uses a new name, has his luscious long wigs and fancy handbags and dresses and lovely shoes and is perfectly happy and everyone accepts him.'

The detective nodded. Jane wondered if Luciano could see the detective nodding and agreeing with his words.

The detective turned to Jane. 'Jane, would you like to know any of the details about the room behind your bookshelf, or the bunker in the backyard and how it was used, or the shed, so you can have closure?'

Memories of yelling and threats and fear rose up in Jane's mind. Domestic violence. Hers. Hiding bruises. Telling lies about bruises that could be seen. PTSD. Jane inhaled deeply to stop her tears. 'No thank you. You have told me all I need to know about what happened here. I don't want the exact details. I'd rather they stay buried. And, may I thank you and your team for the way you conducted the searches with sensitivity and consideration.'

The detective nodded his head again, then stood. He handed Jane his card. 'If you find anything else that we did not find, or have any questions, please don't hesitate to get in contact with me.'

Taking the detective's cue, she led them to the front door and watched them leave, looked at the time on her watch, and right on time, the front sprinklers turned on, giving the detectives a farewell they will remember. The corners of Jane's lips turned up, and Oliver Twist gave two barks.

She returned to the dining table but Luciano was not there. He was standing in the kitchen like he was looking out the window.

'The end of two stories,' Luciano said, and turned around to her.

'What do you mean, oh, and thank you for your words about the man down the road.'

'It was my honour to help you there. Two stories…' Luciano took a deep breath. 'The solving of the buried body here at your house. End of story. And me. I got to apologize to you. So that is the end of my story.'

Jane's heart dropped. She kind of liked having him on the bus seat each morning, playing along with her sisters' stories. She kind of liked her Sundays when she had conversed with him, and gone out with him. She hadn't laughed as much as that in years. 'So you won't be at the bus stop each morning?'

'I think I'll keep coming to this bus stop. I've grown attached to it. And the thirty minute walk to get there on time each day is good for me. Besides, Oliver Twist and I have a thing going on. I think he likes it when I slip him a treat each time we meet.' Luciano smiled. 'What about you? Are you going to stay here now that you know the history of the house?'

'I need to think about it,' Jane said. 'What happened here is too close to home for me. I don't need reminders about that every time I look at the house, or enter the rooms.'

Luciano nodded his head. Once. He crossed one leg over the other, and slipped his hands into his pockets.

'Thank you for being here in the catastrophe. I think we need to go out and celebrate the end of the two stories with dinner,' Jane said.

'I agree,' Luciano said.

'And… I think my story is coming to an end. I need to close it up and shelve it. And I need to get a blank book and start a new chapter. Start afresh and make new memories,' Jane said.

'That said, let's dine at Chapter IV, or Chapter 3 is a takeaway, or Chapters Book Shop, Café and Wine Bar, or Chapter Two Expresso. And then there's Chapter & Verse… or the Fiction Bar & Restaurant.'

'How do you know about all of those places to dine?' Jane asked.

'I like to dine out with themes. A book theme was one of them a couple of years ago.' Luciano smiled. 'I can recommend all of them, but you get to choose.'

There was silence while Jane scanned through a thousand scenarios in her head of what this meant, dining with Luciano. What did he want? Was he being a friend? Or did he want more? She certainly wasn't ready for more.

'Wait…' Luciano said. 'Does Jane drive? She does catch the bus on a Sunday.'

'Jane can drive. Which transport would you like to travel in? The vintage blue and white Kombi Van Deluxe, the yellow 1964 Holden Ute, the pink moped, or the classic, retro, pastel green 1991 Nissan Figaro?'

Luciano whistled. 'Luciano on a pink moped hanging on for dear life because he can't see is a bit of a stretch. I'm tossing up between the Kombi and the Figaro. One is fun, the other sophisticated.' He ran his hand through his dark hair and then over his beard. 'The Figaro is more… rare, so let's go in that one,' he said.

'Great. I'll just talk to Flora and grab the keys. Back soon.' Luciano laughed and Jane left to go to Flora's room.

Oliver Twist booped Luciano on the leg with his nose, and

Luciano sat on the floor with the little loooong dog. Jane returned to the kitchen to find Oliver Twist having a belly rub.

Jane smiled. 'Ready to go?' Jane said. 'You choose the restaurant.'

Chapter 36

Monday

Jane

Jane descended three flights of steps and went to the backyard and sat in silence under the listening tree, crossed legged, grounding herself. In her detachment from reality, she had a floral bouquet inside her mind of imagination. A floral bouquet of her sisters.

Colourful. Beautiful. Extraordinarily them. Together.

Except one.

Her.

Jane floated back to an earlier conversation she had with her parents. 'Mum and Dad,' she had said, 'why don't I have a floral name like my sisters?'

'Alice Jane *Lily* Piccadilly. You do have a flower as a name—'

Jane's mum had butted in. For once. Without the need to pull a ham sandwich out of her "hambag". '—But I wanted you to have a different name—the continuing family name of Jane needed to be heard. It is powerful and special and an honour to carry that name, Jane—three generations before you. A name to cherish!'

Lily, thought Jane, why hadn't she been told about her floral name before? Was it because she hadn't asked? Was it on her birth certificate, unnoticed, now all incinerated in the explosion, like they had never been born.

Jane had frowned. She was confused about last names. 'Mum, how has the Piccadilly last name continued on. Doesn't the woman traditionally take on the husband's last name?'

Jane's mother had clapped her hands and laughed out loud. It was such a rare display of happiness from her. 'Normally. But us strong Piccadilly women decided to stuff the bloody tradition of taking on the husband's last name, and our husband's took our last name. None of the Piccadilly women could pop out a son to carry on the name. And somehow, Alice Jane Piccadilly became a name to be repeated. For history's sake.'

'Wow,' Jane had said, impressed by the Piccadilly fortitude. 'What was Dad's last name before *he* became a Piccadilly?'

Frank cleared his throat and shifted his weight on the seat. 'Longbottom. Frank Herbert Longbottom.'

Jane had sniggered, thankful that she was a Piccadilly and not a Longbottom. 'Mum, Dad, what did you think I would do when I grew up?'

'Anything and everything, Jane. Remember us telling you that you could choose to do anything you wanted if you worked really hard at school, and you could change careers at any time because life is too short to spend doing one thing!'

Jane had nodded. 'Are you surprised that I don't have a job at the moment?' Jane had asked.

'Not surprised at all. Your anxiety battle has been treacherous since you've been stalked after the divorce, and since the explosion… you've felt… unsafe,' Jane's dad had said.

'I think all women feel unsafe at times in their lives, or certain locations, or time of day or night. I know Hudson's in jail now, but still, I can't shake feeling unsafe.'

'Jane, you can't keep hiding at home forever. You need to get out. Desensitise yourself,' Jane's mum had said in an accusatory tone.

'I'm trying, Mum, I'm trying!' Jane had said. A tear ran down her cheek and she flicked it away. 'I have to go now. Let's facetime another day. Love you!'

'Love you, dear,' they had said.

Jane gave a wistful smile and closed her eyes. If she was a lily flower, it would be the colourful Asiatic Lily. She felt the tug of yearning for her sisters. It would never fade. Not when you love them that much.

She opened her eyes and touched the listening tree.

'What am I going to do now?'

It was true. Her life had unravelled. She had wrapped up the truth and buried it deep within her, trying to find where she fit in the world without her sisters, divorced and then scrutinised by the police. Which, happened to be a gift in disguise.

Borrowing her sisters' light had been such a complex theatrical performance. She was exhausted. Each time she put on one of the six different wigs she had to take on a different personality to convincingly be one of her sisters. The wigs transformed her into them. It was such a tangled mess, but at the same time it gave her comfort. Until it didn't. It had all unravelled. But now it was a tangled mess. It was time to undo what she had been living.

Time for Jane to be Jane.

Just Jane.

Chapter 37

Tuesday
Jane

It was the discovery of the bones-in-the-backyard that had forced everything to come to a head. A wake-up call. Jane stood and walked over to the garden shed. Zinnia's plans for her flower creation. She needed to finish it. She went to the location of the bunker, never to be opened. Perhaps she should have it filled in. But then she thought, being a 'Thought Daughter'—introspective, intellectual and a devout over-thinker, a superpower, if she sold the house, maybe the new owners would make good use of it. And so it would stay, as well as the hidden room and passageway to the bunker. She would have it renovated with a special flair so it could be a selling point for the house.

Jane returned to the house, Oliver Twist following her, and

went to Poppy's room. She had finished her novel and added it to the local library shelves, and her artwork could be hung on walls in the house, perhaps on each level. Jane Piccadilly was Poppy. Borrowing her light.

Jane squatted down and petted Oliver Twist. 'Good boy, Oliver. You did a brilliant job as Schnitzel Von Krumm. I don't know how we convinced the council to allow you to be a library support dog, but we did it. You wonder dog!' Jane looked at each of the photographs of Oliver Twist dressed in character, hung on a line of string on the wall. A tear filled her eye.

Memories. Cherished memories.

'Thank you, Poppy,' Jane said. 'Thank you for letting me borrow your light for a short while.'

Jane walked up a flight of stairs, Oliver behind her as the operator-of-the-dog-elevator. She entered Violet's bedroom. She stepped slowly and took it all in. Opened her wardrobe of fancy, beautiful Australian designed clothes, shoes and handbags. A crooked smile erupted. How on earth did she get away with pretending to be a hairdresser without a Certificate in Professional Hair Styling, or any training at all? It was fun for a bit.

'Thank you, Violet,' Jane said. 'Thank you for letting me borrow your light for a short while.'

Jane entered Daisy's room, Flora's room, Rose's room and Zinnia's room, walking slowly in each of them, sealing her memories as being them in her mind. Borrowing their light. Living so many different lives had been fun, even if she didn't have any degrees or had studied for her jobs. She had simply looked up the job descriptions and educated herself enough to answer the interview questions. None of the employers ever asked to see a copy of her degree.

In Zinnia's room, she opened her laptop to the flower research. She knew it thoroughly. It had been her doing the research. Jane decided to continue with the flower line creation. It was almost done. She didn't want to waste all that time and hard work.

She returned to Flora's room. The pregnancy. She had to return to the farm after the birth. Six months. She patted her stomach the same way Flora did. The time it took to renovate the hidden room in the library, the tunnel and the bunker and getting the flower line started would take about the same time. And then she would leave the house.

The untangling had begun.

Jane Piccadilly's throat tightened. She hated goodbyes. She wondered if she had committed fraud by pretending to live the lives of her sisters. But it wasn't illegal to use a pseudonym name. If she had produced fake degrees, then it would have been fraud.

Jane returned to her bedroom, her stomach in a knot. She knew she had to retrieve the suitcases from under her bed. Four-of-them. The black vintage suitcase of devastating memories. The red vintage suitcase of flagged difficult emotions. The floral vintage suitcase of family love. And the white vintage suitcase of jars of notes.

She reached under her bed and pulled them out, sliding them along the floor before lifting them onto her bed. She paced her room trying to pluck up the courage to open them. To let out the truth. The truth she had conveniently packaged up and hidden to find some kind of solace and peace from her actions in the past, that, until recently, she thought she had caused the death of her sisters.

Jane covered her mouth as she let out a sob that wanted to turn into a gut-wrenching scream.

Poppy was just thirteen and had her first kiss. She was dreaming of her wedding day and babies.

Violet was eleven, and would do fancy hairstyles for her every school day.

Daisy, who was a roomie in their mama's belly together with her and Rose, was eight, and she had held her hand tightly in the sinking car until a man had scooped her out so she could suck in a deep breath of air, but not Daisy.

Rose, her other triplet sister was… Jane sobbed. Beautiful Rose. The bestie of her sisters. Her last memory of her was the terror on her face as she gasped for air before the water filled the car.

Zinnia was only five and already had plans for flowers.

Flora was four. The baby of the family. Sweet and cute and adorable.

Jane lowered herself to the floor and curled up into the foetal position. She rocked back and forth and cried hard, cathartically.

Raw. Draining. Heartbreaking.

Survivor guilt. Flashbacks. Feelings of helplessness. Obsessive thoughts about the event.

Why was she the one chosen to live, to then become the only child, loaded with blame and shame and a broken heart that she was sure would never mend.

Her sisters… she missed them… she loved them… with all her heart…

Jane crawled onto her bed and flipped open the latches of the floral vintage suitcase of love. And there were photographs. Perhaps a thousand of them. She had never counted them.

Her family.

Smiling.

Laughing.

Holidays.

In the backyard.

Birthdays.

The beach.

Day trips.

First days of school.

Christmases.

Her mum. Happy.

Her dad. Proud of his daughters.

Jane with her triplicates. The trilogy, her mum called them. Triple treats, her dad said. Baby A, Baby B and Baby C. Her sisters that she loved the most. She was part of them and they were part of her. The understood each other without words. They even had their own language they created that only they understood. And now she was the only keeper of that language. And she would cherish those made up words all the days of her life.

Jane Piccadilly picked up all the photographs in her arms and held them against her heart. If she pushed them hard enough against herself, would she absorb them all so they could mend her scarred broken heart with stitches of gold?

Jane wiped away her tears and carefully placed the treasured photographs back into the floral suitcase. She stood and took the suitcase to her walk-in robe and put it up on the shelf. For keeps.

She returned to her bed. She needed to open two suitcases today. That was all she could bear.

The white thick cardboard suitcase with leather reinforced corners was the other one. She flipped open the metal latches and opened the lid. The smell of pencil shavings was released, dry and woody, cedar, with pink pepper and cypress. Then Jane's eyes were drawn to all the jars-of-notes her sisters had written over the years. The jars-of-notes she had written, *pretending* to be them. All the colours. The beauty and the sadness. The sanity and the insanity. The grieving. The striving to give her sisters life again.

To-bring-them-back.

To her.

Jane's throat released an uncontrollable cacophony of emotionally ugly sounds. From her broken heart.

She calmed after a while, and closed the lid and engaged the latches. This suitcase had to wait. It had to stay with the floral suitcase of family love. She placed it in the walk-in robe for keeps, then went downstairs. She needed a cup of tea. And a book. A novella.

She really needed that breakfast black tea with notes of cake and cocoa, even though it wasn't the morning. She made her cup of tea then went to her library and found Lady Susan, by *Jane Austen*. It wouldn't take her long to read the novella, and then she could watch the film adaption.

Emotionally drained, Jane Piccadilly carefully walked up three flights of stairs to the attic with her breakfast tea and the Lady Susan novella tucked under her arm. She sat on the sofa bed and curled her legs underneath her and started to read while sipping her black tea.

Twenty minutes later she had finished her tea, and two and a half hours later she had finished her book, then switched on the television and searched for *Love & Friendship*, 2016, based on Jane Austen's novel.

And that was a day, and a night.

Chapter 38

Wednesday
Jane

Jane Piccadilly woke to the sound of the birds at dawn. The television was still going and her book, *Lady Susan,* was upside down on the timber floor. Outside, dark clouds were forming, pre-empting the contents of today—the black vintage suitcase of devastating memories, and the red vintage suitcase of flagged difficult emotions.

It would be best to get it over and done with. No use dilly dallying and putting off the inevitable. If it was going to be a heart-stopper of a day, she may as well injure herself early, pick up her pieces and try to find some semblance to keep going.

But tea first. Chamomile today. The calming tea. She needed it today for what she was to do. The opening of the suitcases was planned in her mind, but she couldn't verbalise it yet. It was too painful.

Jane ran her fingers over her tea collections. Maybe she should join *The T2 Tea Society*? Her index finger slowed at "The Quiet Mind Tea". De-stressing. She made a mental note to have this cup of tea after what she had to do. If she could do it. She didn't know if she was ready yet.

Or-strong-enough-yet.

Jane gave Oliver Twist his morning kibble before she took him for a morning walk, before opening the suitcases. That way she wouldn't appear to be falling apart for his afternoon walk, leaving pieces of herself behind in the gardens and latched onto the door handles of cars. And the neighbours wouldn't be asking questions while Jane Piccadilly, who lived in *that* house, visibly shattered in front of them. Poor plain Jane they would say. Finally something happened to plain Jane. She's not so plain anymore.

Jane Piccadilly didn't eat breakfast. She didn't have the stomach for it for the task she had to do.

But first, she decided, she would video call her mum and dad. They always had good advice, even if she didn't like their words at times. She *needed* to call them. Their voices were like a warm hug and a kiss on the forehead like that day at the funeral of her sisters, when their deaths didn't feel like her fault, and it felt like her mum and dad still loved her.

She sat on the sofa bed she had fallen asleep on last night. Her tea cup was still there, the tea bag inside it. Jane took a slow, deep breath, opened her phone and dialled the video call. Her parents picked up quickly. More quickly than usual.

Did-they-know-something?

'Jane. How lovely to talk to you this early in the, the, the morning!' Jane's mother's stutter was getting worse. The deaths of her sisters was the hardest on her. She had carried each of the babies inside of her. There was no other connection as deep as a mother and her children.

'Hi, Mum. How are you?'

Her mother nodded and pulled her eyebrows together. 'Good. Good, I think.'

'Hello, my daughter-est,' Jane's father piped in, a smile beamed across his face.

Jane lowered her head with a small smile. Only her father could make her feel so happy like that. 'Hi, Dad.'

'Is there something wrong, dear?'

Jane swallowed hard. She didn't want this moment ever to come with her parents. She knew it would break their hearts all over again. But she needed to hear their version of the story of the most dreadful, life changing, day. She needed the truth.

'I… I need to ask you about that day,' she said.

'What day? When you graduated from university and we had a little mishap?'

'No, not that day,' said Jane, recalling her mother having a moment of hysteria, screaming out the names of her sisters and flinging herself to the floor in inappropriate emotional behaviour while she, Jane Piccadilly, was walking across the stage to receive her degree, her father rushing to her mother, picking her up and carrying her outside while the sound of sirens came near. And Alice Jane Piccadilly the 4th, standing alone in the auditorium at the end of the graduation ceremony, her flowers up-side down, facing the floor losing their petals, while everyone else celebrated with family, with love and happiness floating around them.

Jane walked home that day, survivor guilt etched across her face and heart. She was ugly. Inside and out. She let her degree slip out of her hand and fly away with the wind. She didn't deserve this, after what her sisters had lost.

'I need to know about that day, Dad, the one where

everything became nothing suspended in time. The day my sisters disappeared from my life.' That day that Jane Piccadilly didn't want to revisit ever again.

Jane's mother sat still and stared straight ahead. She put her hand on her husband's knee. Jane's father's Adam's apple bobbed up and down as he swallowed hard. Jane didn't want to watch them relive this moment, and perhaps it would have been kinder for them to write it down and send it to her.

'We were going to the circus.' Jane's father cleared his throat. 'We had saved up our money for such a long time to be able to go. Mum and I were excited to be taking our beautiful girls to see the spectacular.' Jane's dad pushed his hand through his hair and closed his eyes, then opened them again. Her mother's face was frozen. She hadn't even blinked. It was like she was holding her breath as the words came. 'It was raining. Hard. The windscreen wipers were working so fast I couldn't see where I was driving on the windy road on a rainy sunset. You girls were all laughing and giggling, then changed to squabbling and to singing in the back, as usual. I turned my head to see your smiles. They were like sunshine to my heart.'

Jane's father turned his head to the side, then back to the video screen, a tear in his eye. 'I had a sudden pain in my chest and closed my eyes for a moment, taking my eyes off the road… and that's when we heard the car horn. Your mum grabbed the steering wheel to pull us back to the left side of the road, but the other car clipped us and we spun out of control. We went through the fence and into the dam.'

Jane's mother started sobbing and rocking to and fro. 'It was all my fault… it was all my fault… it was all my fault,' she kept whispering.

Jane's father held her mother's hand in his and brought it to his lips to kiss. 'Alice my love, it was no one's fault. It was just a series of unfortunate events beyond our control. You are forgiven. The girls understand and they still feel your love, as we can feel theirs.'

Jane's mother wiped her eyes and looked up.

'The car that clipped us stopped, and the occupants of that car helped to get us all out of the water filled car, the little boy valiantly flagging down passing cars to stop and help.'

Jane thought back to Luciano's memory.

'We are blessed to have you with us, completing our family of three, as tragic as it was.'

Jane put her hand over her mouth and started to cry. Her eyes were clenched tightly together as she felt the pain of that day envelope her. Her beautiful, crazy, funny, loving sisters. Gone. Their earthly light snuffed out. Like a candle. Three, thought Jane, everything that comes in threes is perfect, every set of three is complete, her mother would say over and over again as if soothing her soul. Now she knew why.

'Thank you, Dad, for telling me about that day. I know that was difficult for you,' Jane said.

'My beautiful Jane,' her mother said. She had never called Jane that before. Jane pulled her eyebrows together. Did her mother love her, after all? After all these years of thinking that she was appalled by the sight of her. That Jane was a disgusting human being who deserved nothing! After all these years of telling her it was her fault that her sisters were dead. 'Have you visited their graves? You might find some solace there. Some peace.'

'I will, Mama. Thank you,' Jane said, her heart lurching out to her mother, wanting to hug hers in a reconnecting, eternal, loving embrace.

'Go and do that soon, Jane. And cry as much as you need,' her father said. 'We're ending this call now. You, I think, have some things to do.'

'I do... I love you both,' said Jane.

'Chat soon,' her father said while her mother waved.

Jane disconnected the call. She left the attic and went to her room. She had two suitcases to open if she was to close chapters of this season of her life and start a new season, a new book of Jane Piccadilly.

Her hand trembled as she moved it between the two handles of the suitcases. The black vintage suitcase of devastating memories, and the red vintage suitcase of difficult emotions. She stopped her hand at the red suitcase, but then moved it to the black suitcase, and slid it out slowly across the floorboards. She lifted it onto her bed, sat in front of it and flipped open the latches one at a time. Oliver Twist walked up the dog ramp, laid beside her and put his chin on her leg and looked up at her.

Inside were newspaper articles of the accident. Death notices. Photographs taken at the funeral. Cards of condolences. Dried flowers. Letters written to Jane from her class. Handwritten eulogies. Hearts sewn onto a quilt with each of her sisters' names, and a pillow of tears. Her pillow.

Jane studied the contents through different eyes now as an adult. And now that she knew the accident was not her fault. Her heart felt lighter in that moment. Like light was able to shine through her heart scars.

Light of love.

Light of forgiveness.

Light of acceptance.

She placed the contents back into the suitcase, took it to her walk-in robe, and lifted it high next to the floral vintage suitcase of family love.

She paced the floor six times before she had the courage to pull out the red vintage suitcase of difficult emotions. Emotions of another part of her life she had separated from the rest.

The suitcase of Hudson.

She gripped on to the handle tightly, and ran out of her room and down the stairs. She entered her library and placed the suitcase next to the fireplace, grabbed some wood and started a fire.

She opened the suitcase. And stared into it. Then one by one, she removed the photographs of her high school sweetheart. Her wedding. Her husband. The photographs of inflicted bruises. Of cuts. Of hair he had pulled out from her head. Of letters written by him with the poison pen of gaslighting and blaming and denying. Of love letters he had written to her filled with love and apologies and promises to make it up to her.

The wine glass with the red lipstick on the rim.

The white shirt of his with the same red lipstick on the collar, that night she saw him in the forest by the Lake of Secrets with the other woman.

The newspaper articles about the explosion. The court hearing. The sentencing.

Jane picked up the wine glass, raised her hand and threw it into the fire, releasing an anguished cry, the glass smashing, and disappearing into the flames. Then one by one she threw in the photographs and letters and newspaper clippings.

And then the red suitcase was empty. Like her heart of Hudson.

She closed the red suitcase and ran out of the house with it, tucked the suitcase into the back carrier of the pink moped, swung her leg over the seat, and drove off, the wind blowing in her face. Blowing away the negative reel of memories of that part of her life.

She continued on to the Lake of Secrets next to the forest, where she and Hudson once dreamed of stars by the winter lake, and parked the pink moped. She dismounted it, grabbed the suitcase and walked to the water's edge. She laid the suitcase on the water of the Lake of Secrets, and watched as it floated away, rocking to the lullaby of the drowning water. The suitcase turned and waited as if it was saying goodbye, then sank to the bottom of the lake where stories of sadness dissipated until they were no more.

'Goodbye, Hudson,' Jane whispered. She looked up at the sky, scattered with heavy clouds trying to tell her it wasn't finished. She had one more task to do.

She returned to the moped and rode home; her mind cast in a silence that was deafening.

She entered the house, went to Violet's room and found her most expensive black clothes, shoes and handbag, collected Oliver Twist and flowers from her garden, then drove Daisy's blue Holden EH Ute to the cemetery.

She knew exactly where her sisters were buried. She had looked at the gracestone every Daisy Tuesday, blocking out the song her heart wanted to sing to them, in a melody that was love true and pure.

She popped open her black umbrella as the rain poured down when she stood in front of the tombstone. She bent low and placed her floral garden flowers in groups on each of her sisters. Her tears streaming.

Ophelia aged 13. 1996

'Your sweetheart name was Poppy, by Mum and Dad,' she said. 'I love you Poppy. I miss you. Thank you for letting me borrow your light for a little while. I had a ball as a librarian, and we wrote a book together.' Jane blew her a kiss.

Etti aged 11. 1996

'Your sweetheart name was Violet, by Mum and Dad,' she said. 'I love you Violet. I miss you. Thank you for letting me borrow your light for a little while. Hairdressing was interesting, and scary. But I loved it.' Jane blew her a kiss.

Cordelia aged 8. 1996

'My triplet. Your sweetheart name was Daisy, by Mum and Dad,' she said. 'I love you Daisy. I miss you. Thank you for letting me borrow your light for a little while. I know why I worked here as you. I was keeping an eye on you all. Your guardian.' Jane lowered her head and cried, then blew her a kiss.

Aurelia aged 8. 1996

'My other triplet. Your sweetheart name was Rose, by Mum and Dad,' she said. 'I love you Rose. I miss you. Thank you for letting me borrow your light for a little while. Being a photographer, looking at life through a different lens was a type of therapy, *and* we solved a crime.' Jane blew her a kiss.

Mae aged 5. 1996

'Your sweetheart name was Zinnia, by Mum and Dad,' she said. 'I love you Zinnie. I miss you. Thank you for letting me borrow your light for a little while. Thank you for studying flowers. Mum's love language and her way to remember you all without it breaking her heart every single time. I'm still working on your flower creation.' Jane blew her a kiss.

Harriet aged 4. 1996

'Your sweetheart name was Flora, by Mum and Dad,' she said. 'I love you Flora. I miss you. Thank you for letting me borrow your light for a little while. I honoured your love of animals. I can't wait to meet the baby conceived at the farm.' Jane smiled, patted her tummy like Flora would and blew her a kiss.

Together, playing in eternity in the love and light of the Lord, 1996. 'Dearly missed by sister, Jane… me,' Jane added with a whisper, then closed her umbrella and lifted her face to the rain, letting it fall on her like a thousand tears, like a thousand kisses from her sisters in heaven. 'Thank you, Heavenly Father, for taking care of my sisters. I know we'll meet again.'

'I get it. I do.' A voice behind Jane. Luciano. 'I understand why you became your sisters, more than you know.' Luciano looked at the bouquet of six flowers he had bought and placed them at the grave.

'Thank you. Acceptance has taken a long time for me. Complicated grief I think it's called, or prolonged grief disorder. But you, you Luciano, were the key that unlocked my internal prison, by telling me the truth.' Jane looked down and shook her head. She looked back at Luciano. 'It's true. The truth sets you free. I don't know how to thank you.'

'No need to thank me. I'm just happy to have helped you, in a weird sort of way. What a story, though!' Luciano turned and started to walk away. Half way back to his waiting taxi, he turned and lifted his hand in a wave.

And-then-he-was-gone.

Jane Piccadilly kissed the palm of her hand and blew one final kiss to her sisters. She felt at peace with them. And loved them with all of her heart, forever and a day. The rain stopped and the clouds cleared, and Jane lifted her face to the sky with a smile. It was time to go home. She had two more things to do. She placed a bouquet of flowers next to the gravestone beside her sisters. 'I love you both more than you know,' Jane said and placed her hand over her heart, gave one last look at her sisters' flowers, then left.

Jane returned home and walked up to the third floor, then took the steps to the attic with hesitation, dragging a heavy, weeping heart behind her. She needed to talk to her parents again.

She sat on the sofa bed, and hit video call. The phone rang several times but was not answered.

She tried again. And finally, on the third attempt, her father answered.

'Hi Dad.'

'Hello, my girl. How is Alice?' Jane's father smiled at her. But it filled her with sadness.

'Jane, Dad. Call me Jane, remember.'

'Alice Piccadilly the 4th. Alice Jane Piccadilly. Did you visit your sisters?'

'Hello, Jane,' her mother chipped in.

'Hello, Mum.' Jane's voice trembled. 'Yes. I visited them. Talked to them. Gave them flowers. Said goodbye to them and told them I loved them.'

'Oh, Jane,' said her mother. 'Are you okay?'

'You know what, Mum… I think I am.'

Jane's parents smiled with sympathy.

'Mum. Dad. It's time…'

'What do you mean, Jane?' said her father.

'It's time that the three of us, were one.'

'No. Not… not… not…not yet, Jane,' her mother screamed, like her words were affected by a glitch. Again.

'You know this was just temporary, Mum.'

Jane's father grabbed her mother's hand and held it. 'Jane is right, Alice. It's time, even though this was our way of never saying goodbye.'

Jane wasn't ready for her parents to leave her. They were all she had left.

'Thank you for being the spitting image of my parents.' Jane's throat became thick. She didn't want to have this talk, but she had to. She had to stop calling them Mum and Dad. They were not her mother and father. They were an AI created resurrection of her parents. Voice recordings and text messages and videos of her real parents. AI zombies. On call at any time of the day or night. They were nothing. A fake visualisation anchored to the earth in the saddest way like they were lost between the physical world and the spiritual one. They were stuck. Alive-but-not-alive. They were the eerie sensation of the uncanny valley, but she needed them. All she knew was that it wasn't right. It wasn't right trying to hold on to her parents like they were still alive. It was terribly unhealthy. Damaging. And it was stopping her from moving forward with her grief. Her life. She needed to honour her parents as they should be. And there was only one way to do that.

Jane sobbed and created a ripple in time. She was like the autumnal tree changing. No longer that tree with leaves that were falling like it was devoid of life. Like her world did. Little specks of green shoots had sprouted. A new season for Jane. A season of growth.

Jane took a deep breath to push out the words that were queued up in her throat. 'I'm sorry that you both died in that explosion. Hudson thought I was at home with you. He didn't intend to hurt either of you. He just wanted to do away with me. But...' Jane lowered her head and her tears fell. 'I arrived home later than I intended. When I pulled up in the driveway, the house exploded. And you were both inside.'

Jane squeezed her eyes shut at the heart-wrenching memory and the feeling of death in the room that was waiting to be released. Freed from the confines of the earth.

'Luciano called the police, who tracked Hudson down with a helicopter with night vision. He was arrested for murder that night,' the AI impersonator said.

Jane knew those exact words. They came from the newspaper report. AI was good at that. Looking for files online to make the resurrected loved ones interactions true, and thus, more believable.

Jane cleared her throat. 'So... it's time for me to say goodbye. I can't keep swimming in this never ending untruth that you are both still alive and here with me. It's a lie. It's deceit. It's...

unhealthy for me. I need to move forward with my life.'

Jane Piccadilly's mistake-number-four was now clear. The one she would never admit to for her mother's sake.

Rule-Number-Four—to leave the past in the past, forgive, and move on.

The television screen flashed three times.

'Goodbye Jane,' said the AI deep fake. Such a perfect likeness of her father.

'Goodbye Jane,' said the AI deep fake. Such a perfect likeness of her mother.

'Goodbye,' Jane said, then pushed the red button to terminate the program.

Jane closed her eyes and took a deep breath.

Mum and Dad. Those two words that undo you.

For-better-or-for-worse.

Those two words, that you forever hold on to. Forever crave to see them again, one day.

For another hug.

For another smile.

For another laugh.

For another I love you.

Jane's heart felt numb. Having the Parental Resurrection Program was like her security blanket after her parents died. It helped ease the pain in her heart. It helped her grief, she had thought. But all it did was prolong it. And put off the inevitable. It made it feel like they were still here with her and they would walk in the door at any moment.

Jane sniffed. It was indeed a blessing that the mistake-to-end-all-mistakes happened, which was Rule #1 and #2 combined together, not doing the house inspection, or the history search on the house like her parents had told her when she was looking for a house with Hudson. But it was the best mistake. Her charade was discovered, and now she could start again afresh—like a reset—a freeing.

Finding herself.

Accepting herself.

And perhaps, there was a little room to love again.

Jane chuckled and thought of Poppy's life list, based on Bronte's life list, left in a book at the library:

1. Meet a kind man who makes me laugh but not so much that I pee myself.

2. Buy a house that comes with its own cleaner and chef.

2.5. Create something that everybody needs and makes a lot of passive income so I can progress onto number three. Use cheap components so that people have to keep buying the so-called creation so the passive income doesn't end.

3. Have a baby who is well-behaved and toilet trained from birth who knows how to order groceries online.

4. Make the said house into a home that is filled with clean toilets and floors and washing and kids who play outside from sun up to sun down so they don't mess up the house.

4.5 And I suppose, add a large sprinkle of love, acceptance, happiness and forgiveness into the home, even if you have to steal the sprinkles from the tooth fairy.

5. Repeat step 3 as required.

6. Offload the kids before the age of 20 so you can spend more time with number 1 on the list.

The unravelling and untangling of her life was finished. She was emotionally spent. She needed to escape into a book, the pages, once living trees of stories, tattooed with the ink of letters and words and sentences and paragraphs and chapters and emotions spilling into her soul and cleansing and healing.

She needed a cup of tea.

And-a-book.

Jane's finger skimmed the titles of books in her library, and *To be Read at Dusk*, by Charles Dickens called to her. A short story. A cup of black tea with sweet apple and cinnamon, like a baked apple desert, might be just what she needed to go with it. Comfort in a cup of tea.

Jane Piccadilly went outside to the backyard and sat under the leafy, shady listening tree, at dusk with her baked apple black tea and Charles Dickens' book. She sat on the picnic blanket, Oliver Twist by her side, curled her legs underneath her and started to read, and took a sip of her black tea.

And nearly choked. Black tea sprayed out over the lawn from her mouth.

It was not the tea that she choked on, but the words. Words have power like that. This Charles Dickens' short story was in the horror genre. Jane Piccadilly had broken her own book cardinal rule. *Always read the blurb.* Death. Ghost stories. Spine tingling. Repression. Personal identity. This was not in her feel good, happily ever after genre. She closed the book and laid it on the picnic blanket. She much preferred *A Christmas Story*, by the same author.

Oliver Twist barked and looked up. Jane frowned and her eyes widened at the sound of a loud, deep, bellowing and grunting noise.

The pig is still here! she thought.

Oliver barked and looked up again, so Jane followed his sight. There, high up in the tree was a koala. And Jane laughed. It made perfect sense now. Koalas grunt and snort and bellow.

'Pig,' Jane said to Oliver. 'Let's call him Pig—you and I have a new friend, Oliver.'

Jane Piccadilly's focus shifted to the late afternoon sunlight that filtered through the leaves. She looked up to the sky.

The-palette-of-dusk.

A symphony of colours with the smooth blending of hues of ember and golden rays and crimson and tangerine skies, and the calm of the night.

Endings, ready for a new beginning the next day.

Jane smiled. Heaven. Her mum and dad and sisters were together, surrounded by love and light. And there was nothing better than that.

Jane finished her apple and cinnamon black tea while Oliver Twist curled up on her lap.

She no longer needed to borrow the light from her sisters. She had her own light. And always had but had smothered it. And it was time to step into it.

And Jane Piccadilly daydreamed as the hiding stars became brighter in the darkness of the night of the city skyline. Dreams painted with swirls of goodness, of joy, of thankfulness and… peace.

And that was a day, and a night.

Chapter 39

Lily

Six months later...

Lily Piccadilly stood outside her single story early white Georgian house in Evandale, Tasmania, a large tin bucket of colourful flower bouquets in her hand. Oliver Twist's tail wagged. The-happy-meter. Lily's smiling eyes reflected her love of the symmetry of the architecture, the silver iron roof, the white chimneys, dark blue front door, long sash windows and the stunning verandah of the homestead. Warmth ran over her skin like an endearing, comforting hug.

Home.

She was finally home. Physically and mentally. And spiritually. She had bravely joined the congregation at a local church. Welcomed with joy.

The journey to healing begins with forgiveness, of others and self, and Lily had forgiven herself for what she had done, as God graciously forgives us and remembers our transgressions no more.

Hope. Joy. Peace.

Jane smiled and lowered her head remembering Romans 15:13 -

> *May the God of hope fill you with all joy and peace as you trust in him.*

God wasn't just a noun. God was a verb. Action. He is working for our good always, even when we don't see it.

Jane about turned and walked along the garden path, her fingertips caressing *The Seven Sisters* flowers, her own flower line inspired by Zinnia. One floral plant with seven-flower-colours. Rare. Jane had chosen the shape of a peony, but tweaked the genetic makeup to flourish with different colour flowers on the same plant. She kept the genetic code of peonies to ensure that the plants lived for at least up to one hundred years. Sweet scented, large, beautiful flowers that bloomed in late spring and early summer. Mixing Zinnia flowers with her mother's favourite Peony flower created the light bulb moment. Bud sport. AI was instrumental with the shortening of time to make *The Seven Sisters* a reality.

Lily walked along the dirt driveway of the property, her curly titian coloured hair blowing in the gentle breeze. She placed the flowers into the buckets of water on the large wooden sun-kissed table in "The Flower Shed", as it was locally known, and fussed about them. Evandale residents and tourists came from afar just to grab the famed Seven Sisters to bless their houses.

'Zinnia did it!' A man's voice.

Lily Piccadilly froze. Who was it who knew her past? The

person she had left behind as the Jacaranda trees dropped their sea of purple flowers.

'Seven colours. The seven sisters.' There was a smile in his voice.

Lily looked up. 'Luciano?' There was no business suit or carpet bag. Just camel coloured stretch chino pants and a white linen shirt, the sleeves rolled up to his elbows. But he still sported his glasses, dark hair and trendy beard.

A smile spread across his face. He took off his glasses and looked into her eyes. 'Yes. It's me.'

Lily couldn't help but stare at those blues eyes she had first seen when they were in Year 8. He was sitting under a tree reading a book at lunch time while his mates kicked around a soccer ball. Lily and her best friend Maeve had skipped over to tease him.

A-boy-reading-a-book.

Whoever thought! Weren't all boys active and running and sweaty and stinky! Not this boy. He looked directly up at Lily and her breath was stolen. She stumbled backward, grabbed Maeve's hand and they ran away from him. But she had never forgotten that stolen moment in time.

And here he was now. And here it was again. A stolen moment in time.

'You can see the seven colours?'

'Yes. I should have had the corneal transplant years earlier, instead of waiting to see if my cornea would heal itself,' Luciano said.

Lily smiled. 'You look so much more… relaxed.'

'As you do… and your hair colour looks… nice.'

Lily reached up and touched the end of a lock of her now titian-coloured-hair, and twisted it around her finger. 'What are you doing way down under in the Apple Isle?' Lily threw Luciano an apple from her bucket of apples, freshly picked this morning.

A smile spread over his face as he caught the apple, a crisp slap sounding in the palm of his hand. 'Two things.' With his other hand he pulled a letter out from his pocket and held it out to her. 'I wanted to deliver this in person, to make sure you got it.'

Lily hesitated before she allowed her fingers to touch the paper.

An-official-letter.

Luciano noticed the slight tremor in her hands. Lily glanced up at him and he gave a quick nod. She took it from him quickly and pushed it into her pocket.

'Aren't you going to open it?'

Lily shook her head. 'I can't. I'm afraid of what it will say.'

'You will like what it says, Lily. Doing what you asked me to do is what I'm good at.'

Lily's shoulders lifted as she took a deep breath. 'Will you have a cup of tea with me while I open it.'

'If that is what you need, then yes.' Luciano eyed her warily.

'What's the other thing you came for?' Lily said as she walked beside him along the driveway to her house.

'To see the baby.'

Lily smiled and lowered her head. 'Oh—you will love the baby!'

She led him into the white and blue kitchen. 'Please sit. Would you like tea, or something else?'

'I think champagne would be more suitable for this occasion,' he said.

Lily narrowed her eyes at him. She wanted his words to mean that she was given the green light for her dream of the seven bedroom three story Victorian terrace house she had left behind. But maybe he was talking about the recovery of his eyesight?

'But I would also love to share a pot of tea with you.'

Lily opened her library of T2 teas. She wanted to give him something he probably hadn't tasted before. She wanted to watch his reaction to a picnic flavour. Mulberry Ripple Loose Leaf tea would definitely bring on the ethereal reaction.

Lily boiled some fresh water and poured it into a teapot. She added two teaspoons of lush raspberry pieces, mulberries and a scattering of marigold and jasmine petals combined with subtle creamy notes. She let the tea brew for four minutes, then added the tea pot and tea cups to a wooden tray and added freshly baked apple tea cake. She took it to the table and sat it in the middle, and took the letter out of her pocket, the Australian Government logo on the front at the top left.

Luciano poured the tea with a watchful eye. This project was close to Lily's heart.

Lily opened the envelope and unfolded the paper.

Dear Alice Jane Lily Piccadilly,

> *We are pleased to accept your offer of your house to be used as a safe home for women and children impacted by domestic violence.*
> *You have satisfied each of the requirements needed…*

Lily dropped the letter and covered her face, quieting the cry from her heart. All she needed to read was that her application was successful. Her Brisbane house would now be a safe haven for victims of domestic violence. A wonder house for women and children with a secret play room for kids behind the book shelf that led to the bunker in the back yard for "Secret Women's Business", an attic of fun games and of shared laughter. And the library of a thousand books for women and children to lose themselves in the worlds of imagination of authors and illustrators, where they could forget about all the heaviness of their pasts.

'Well done,' Luciano said. 'Your family would be so proud of you, as I am. That day our eyes first met, you know, when I was reading under the tree at school, and you ran off holding onto Maeve's hand, I could see you had a heart of light, but a troubled one. And I knew that all the things that happened to you would work together for good.'

Lily stood and walked around the table to Luciano. She hugged him from behind. 'Thank you, Luke. Thank you for your hard work to make this happen. I just had the dream, but you had the know-how. I couldn't have done this without you... and I love you for it.'

Luke placed his hand over hers on his heart. 'The pleasure was all mine.'

Lily sat at the table again. This time next to Luke, her hands still trembling from the good news. She lifted her teacup and took a sip of the Mulberry Ripple tea, watching as Luke did the same, his eyes widening at the first taste. He put the teacup down and blinked, quite a few times. 'It's like wine. An acquired taste.'

Lily beamed him a smile. 'Stay for dinner tonight... and... there's been strong magnetic solar activity recently. It's due to light up the sky with the southern aurora tonight. It would be a great gift to you with your recently returned eyesight.'

Luke frowned and ran his fingers over his beard, thinking. 'Alright,' he said after a while.

Lily wondered if Poppy had the life list in the wrong order. She already had the house, be it without the cleaner and chef. Was she supposed to meet the kind man first?

But maybe, just maybe she had already met him all those years ago. So maybe, the list was in the correct order after all. It just had to reveal itself at the correct time in her life journey.

Lily and Luke sat in the blue and white striped canvas deck chairs under the clear southern night sky, overlooking Ben Lomond Mountain. Waiting.

Waiting for colour.

Or awkward conversation.

Or just a simple shared magical moment. Together.

'I feel like I keep falling on the sky, stumbling and bouncing and tripping over the stars, madly dashing and scrambling to get through to the place I am meant to be.'

'Why do you say that?' Luke asked. Two baby llamas stood close to him and he jumped in fright, then smiled.

'Oh just… my tumultuous life.' Lily reached over to the babies. A rare twin llama birth.

Luke tasted his wine and nodded in appreciation. 'I think… you have travelled your life journey exactly the way you should have… and… I think you have finally arrived in the season of your life happiness. Maybe you stumbled and bounced on the sky because you needed to pick up God gifts of glitter and fragments of the universe like jigsaw pieces to help you through the journey?'

'And the clouds were to buffer the falls.' A tear slid down Lily's face. 'I've been doing my own style therapy… just so you know… to move forward… psychologically.'

'Like proper dance lessons?' Luciano chuckled.

'Noooo!' Lily clenched her fist and bopped him on the arm. 'Fractured light art.'

Luke lifted his wine glass to his lips and sipped. 'Elaborate.'

'It's known as broken colour. You add small, distinct strokes of contrasting colours. Adding texture effects and blending of colours is amazing. It adds a sense of movement and vibrancy. So satisfying… healing.'

'Fractured light. Like the colour of broken. Like the light of the seven sisters dispersed in one single event.'

'I guess you could look at it like that if you want to interpret the art your way, or if you want to analyse my mind,' Lily said. 'I'll show you my work in progress, if I decide you are worthy of it?'

'*If*… I am worthy of it?'

'Yes.'

'You mean it's conditional?'

'Yes.'

'Come with me to the National Penny Farthing Championship tomorrow.'

Luke smiled. 'Is that it?'

'Yep,' Lily said, popping the "p" like Poppy would have.

Luke turned his head toward Lily. He raised an eyebrow. 'Consider it done.' He looked back up at the sky.

Lily leaned her head back on the canvas deck chair, waiting for the dancing night lights. The strength of the light shows at this time in history was trying to speak to us. Did they have an important message to give us?

'How long do we have to wait?' Luke said.

'Anywhere from 10pm to 2am this time.'

Luke nodded his head.

'What does it feel like being able to see again?' said Lily.

Luke shook his head as he inhaled deeply. 'I want to use a string of swear words at how profoundly incredible it is, but I won't, because you are in my presence.' He turned his head toward Lily. 'It's like… seeing everything again for the first time. Totally overwhelming. I cried. Hard. I'm so thankful for a second chance with my sight. When you understand how eyesight works… and the composition of the eye.' Luke shook his head again. 'One hundred and thirty million photoreceptor cells. And in each of those cells, there's one hundred trillion atoms. More than all the stars in the Milky Way Galaxy!'

Lily raised her eyebrows. 'Wow! That's sort of... incomprehensible.' She raised her wine glass toward him, and he touched his wine glass to hers. 'Like ears... can you even—' Lily's eyes caught the faint glow of green light arcing across the horizon on her SLR camera, perched on the tripod. The light wasn't visible with the naked eye, all Lily could see was a silvery strange hue of grey, and white even. She felt a little underwhelmed, but in the camera, well that was another story.

And then the aurora became brighter, the arc easily seen, a dancing wave in the sky. Luke stood up, holding up his phone and stared into the ethereal phenomenon. He sucked in a sharp breath then bounced from foot to foot.

'All the colours above.' Lily's voice was soft. 'Incredulous... hey!'

Lily continued to watch the explosion of colour on her camera. The wavering bright curtain of green, red, blue, purple and yellow light.

Dancing.

Ebbing and flowing.

'Hypnotizing. Breathtakingly beautiful. Enchanting.' Luke cleared the emotion from his throat.

'A reminder,' said Lily.

'Of what?'

'How small we are. Just look at the universe! Shining. Declaring. God determines the number of stars and calls them each by name. So humbling for us humans who think we are so powerful. God so spoils us. Everything He has created benefits us. Heals us! We are so loved.'

'Do you hear that, Lily?'

Lily turned her head as if to hear more clearly. 'What?'

'The light,' Luke whispered.

'You can hear the light?'

Luciano smiled. 'Yes. Will you dance with me?'

Lily smiled and stepped in front of her camera, forgetting that she had set it to record so she wouldn't miss a moment of time of the colourful, breathtaking sky.

She closed her eyes and spread her arms, turned around and listened. And then she heard the song of the Aurora Australis.

The electric hum.

Crackles.

Whistles.

Hisses.

And claps.

Lily held her hands to her heart. This song was her jam. Not a smooth beautiful melody that swings you into complete relaxation and contentment and happiness like a ballroom dancer, but the unsyncopated, staccato, out of beat, sharp, unchoreographed movements that Jane Piccadilly was known for. Like trying to fall through the sky. Uncoordinated. Out of time. Jerky movements here and there, a wombat womble, a kangaroo jump, and an emu head movement.

Oliver Twist stood beside the canvas deck chair, giving the serious side-eye-of-judgement.

Lily opened her eyes and looked at Luciano. His smile was as breathtaking as the night colours. And he started to dance, bobbing up and down with a little interrupted sway in time with the sky music. He put his hand to his stomach and bent over with laughter. He straightened up and did the sprinkler move. Then added a wonderous new move—his hands, starting low, fingers splayed, and moving upward in a wavy way, just like the dancing aurora.

'I love you!' Lily yelled, spinning around and around with her arms outstretched. This felt like pure, unadulterated joy.

'I love you, too,' said Luciano.

'Ummmm… I was talking to God, and myself,' Lily said, surprised how freeing it was to reconnect with God and no longer hate herself.

There was an awkward silence and Lily watched Luciano deflate before her eyes. 'But I do love you too, Luke-reading-a-book-under-the-tree,' she added with a shy smile.

Lily felt a boom then. Like a reset. Not outside her, but inside. An explosion of light. It was her light. She was one of eight billion people on the Earth. She wasn't meant to borrow light from others. Or be a copy of another. She was fearfully and wonderfully made to shine her own unique light, and bloom in her own time and be who she was created to be.

Once, she was broken, but now light shined through the scars of her broken heart and mind, healing.

She was free of the past. But her past was never to be forgotten, just looked back at with wonder and thankfulness for the time she had with her parents and sisters.

That was a gift.

And then she danced again. To her own heartsong. Oliver Twist jumping and wiggle butting and spinning beside her like a vertigo dog. Tears streamed down her face, as she accepted her quirks and idiosyncrasies, with love notes to herself.

The end.

Well, not the end, but a new beginning.
For after all, endings are a new beginning.
A new chapter.

ACKNOWLEDGEMENTS

I'll never forget the time I was in hospital with bronchial pneumonia when I was five, when my dear Aunty Joan visited me. She gave me a gift that made me forget about feeling sick for a while. It was a fashion doll that had different wigs to put on its bald head—the inspiration for this story—as well as the Kombi Van Aunty Joan would drive, my beautiful mum sitting in the passenger seat as they drove to houses to sell Tupperware, Aunty Joan with different hair pieces. How awesomely fashionable and groovy and fun! Thanks, *Aunty Joan,* for your inspiration and support of my writing.

Many thanks to my amazing secondary mathematics teacher friend, *Sarah Archie.* You the mathematician, and me, a secondary visual arts teacher, connected through our love of stories. Our little chats about what I hadn't worked out in my story yet, and your suggestion of the person sitting on the bus seat who sees everything, inspired the sight-challenged Luciano. It happened to work perfectly for my story. And just for you, I weaved mathematics into the narrative. I hope it makes you smile.

All my love and gratitude to my wonderful and patient husband, *Bradley,* as he journeyed through my tenth novel with me, listening to me rave about parts of it and wondering what on earth I am talking about. And to my children, adults now, *Declan, Claire* and *Riley* and their partners. You are all very kind. And patient.

Thank you to *my lovely mum,* for your forever support of my writing, always delighted when you have another of my books in your hands. I think Dad would have loved reading this book, like he did with my others. And thanks to my brother, *Paul.* Your Australian slang words that you come out with at times always make me laugh. I borrowed them for the character of Daisy. ☺ And thanks to *Aunty Al,* who is always excited about my books.

Thank you to dear little looong dog, *Harriet* (Hattie for short). It was your digging up of the bones in the back yard of a rental house that gave me the idea for the bones in the backyard of Jane's house. And the snake skin you carried in to give to Claire. Such treasures you found just for my novel. ☺

Many thanks to *Paula* at Lynx Long Dogs for your dedication to breeding smart, loyal and lovable mini dachshunds. It was your photo of the chocolate and tan puppy for sale that caught my attention of your family of sausage dogs. When you named him Oliver Twist, I was attached and started to write him into my novel. He was sold to another family before I could claim him. And then along came the mini dachshund just for me. Pablo Picasso, a tri-colour chocolate piebald with a blue eye and a greenish-brown eye, and a patch of colour the shape of a heart on his back. A gentle and very good boi!

Thank you so very much to you, *my readers*, for giving your precious time. It makes my heart overflow with joy, even if one person loves my story. That's all I need.

If you have lost someone you love and are journeying the road of grief, I feel every heartbreaking ounce of it, every heavy tear and waterfalls of sadness, every shuddering breath of it. My loving dad. 2022. Still raw. How blessed was I to have an amazing father that made saying goodbye so hard. I know I will grieve until we meet again. But I also smile because he was my dad. "Never. We never lose our loved ones. They accompany us; they don't disappear from our lives. We are merely in different rooms." *Paulo Coelho.*

If you ever find yourself in the situation of domestic violence, you have the strength to leave. Domestic violence - it's never okay. Reach out to the many organisations who can help you. If you're a survivor of domestic violence, I send my prayers for continued healing.

To my writing and author friends. Thank you for inspiring me with your books and never giving up on our craft of storytelling, especially in this time of invasion by AI. People want and need stories written with human intelligence, a human heart and human love, to feel the emotion and empathy in words for our spiritual connection and understanding. Our light.

And to my *Heavenly Father.* Thank you for being in my life story. Thank you for being the Author of my life story. I couldn't make it through without You. Thank you for Your rescue packages You give me when I am struggling, in the way of people, animals, and nature. You spoil us, even when we don't deserve it. ♡

Soli Deo gloria.

Julieann Wallace

YOU BEFORE ME
(Young Adult Fiction)
print book   eBook

Eighteen year old ARI FLORA COHEN is stuck living in a pre-technology time, until she ventures to the forbidden Beyond where she is captured. Finally released, she staggers home through elaborate underground tunnels, reeling from the lie about the non-existence of the world outside her home. What other lies has her mama told?

ELIAS WOLFE GREEN is Ari's protector. He finds her wild and unconventional and disagreeable. Nevertheless, he has a job to do, no matter how many times she tells him she hates him.

Elias follows the rules. Ari breaks them.

Ari has questions. Elias has answers, including the truth about her father who was taken before her birth, but he cannot speak of his knowledge. So Ari must find the answers herself.

She discovers she is living in a time called *The Unfolding*, where the truth of the world is being unwrapped, layer by layer, after the time of *The Boxing*, when the earth was made singular by the covering of the stars and the universe with light pollution and surveillance satellites, when the truth of everything was hidden. She discovers there are four versions of everyone, and Ari discovers, her mama of love and light, is not who she thinks she is.

Distraught, wanting answers, Ari must dress as a boy and return to *The Beyond*. But disaster strikes.

Now you, dear reader, must choose the ending...

Amelia Grace

THE COLOUR OF BROKEN
(Long-listed to be made into a movie, twice)
print book   eBook   audiobook

A dark secret... Yolande Lawrence-Harrison was hiding a dark secret. She'd returned to her hometown of Tarrin to help her ailing grandmother in Flowers for Fleur, where she had to put her engineering career aside to learn the science of flower art.

A note... As Yolande fussed with the pale pink roses in the basket of her grandmother's 1950s Schwinn Cruiser bicycle, she discovered a note. Yolande fumed at the pitiful manners and pure arrogance of the wording, and after numerous exchanges, she became irritated by the persistent, annoying, pig-headed, obstinate human being who wouldn't take no for an answer.

Beware... But when Alexander Parker walked into Flowers for Fleur, her thoughts scattered. However, she refused to inhale the alluring potion he offered. She could see through his projected façade, where his perfection was a practised deceit. She wondered, if she could see through his pretence, could he see through hers? Could he see that she was damaged, hiding a past that ate away at her core allowing the darkness to engulf what was left of her inner light. Could he see that she was the color of broken?

Run... Yolande wanted to run. Away from the flowers. Away from Alexander Parker. But she couldn't. Her grandmother's life was fading as she battled an incurable illness, and Yolande needed to choose whether to fight her past or not, ultimately exposing her inner demons, in order to save her grandmother and herself from the same fate.

(Profits donated to Meniere's Research)

Amelia Grace

ALL THE COLOURS ABOVE
(sequel to *The Colour of Broken*)
print book   eBook

INDIGO FEATHER DANUBE is a neuroscientist studying memories, how to access them, then remove them, digitally.

One day, her parents implore her to attend a reunion at the park of her youth, where TOBIAH BROOKS dares her to climb the Jacaranda tree of her childhood.

But first, she must remember who he is.

They meet before sundown, with Indigo's intention to succeed at the dare, then leave. But his intention is to win her heart. Tobiah orchestrates a secret rendezvous at the Jacaranda tree on the luminous full moon, when it's light enough to see, but dark enough to cloak their presence.
No one could possibly know they were there once a month. Together. Alone.

Every story has a beginning. At the beginning of Indigo and Tobiah's story, is a girl who meets a boy. A girl who wasn't in the habit of falling in love, until her heart bloomed like a thousand red roses with the scent of citrus, spice, and sweet fruit, surrounded by a dreamy and exhilarating melody of love.

Until... that day that can't be undone.
On that day of the wish that can't be unwished.
And that moment in time... when she learned the truth.

Mirror. Mirror. Two mirrors. Two of me. Who am I?

(Profits donated to Meniere's Research)

Amelia Grace

A DREAM OF LIGHT
print book   eBook

Courage, temperance, wisdom, justice, patience... KADEN BERKLEY repeated the words sealing them into the depths of his consciousness, finding comfort and solace. For two hundred and sixty years he had been trapped on the earth engaged as an immortal human, after being forced to take the anti-aging elixir. Now he is plagued by emotional torment, chained to the laws of gravity and craving to return to the Light. To freedom. To love.

He takes a deep breath and stares at the blue energy mass before he lifts his hand to it, then watches as the fourth state of matter arcs to his finger tips like bolts of lightning. They tingle under the warmth until the plasma retreats back into the glowing blue energy. He wishes it was the antidote to the immortal elixir.

He thinks of MISS FINNIGAN. She has what he wants. He can feel it, vibrating in perfect harmony with his being. It sings to his soul like agonized poetry, reminding him of what he doesn't have. And he wants it. Now. Mortality. Kaden wants to reach out to her but she is forbidden. Their DNA could never absorb each other, cell to every beautiful cell, harmonizing in a melody only they can hear, unless, he finds the missing piece to his immortality that will free him.

He sighs. He wonders how long he will be subjected to this living nothingness cut off from his spiritual homeland. If he doesn't find the missing piece, he will remain an earth immortal, bound to the physical torture of remaining on the earth, unable to return to his true home.

Yet, he will dream of Light. It was his only hope.

Amelia Grace

THE BOOK KEEPER
print book   eBook

COHEN DARCY leaned over and blew the dust off the top of a book that had mysteriously appeared beside his bed. The dust flowed into the air like a wave turning over on itself, leaving the worn, brown leather cover naked to the eye.

It was there he saw an embossing. The words were unknown to him—*Mutato Nomine De Te Fabula Narratur.*

Cohen stepped out into the new day. A new rainy day. A new day of unwelcome events. It had started with the arrival of the mysterious book, then came the seduction, the unlawful act of the CAI stealing his work, and the promise that his existence would never be the same.

That night, when he opened the book and found the owner, it belonged to GEORGIA HARRISON. Now his day was about to get even worse. He needed to meet her to get rid of the book!

He doesn't do books—or relationships. As simple as that.

Could he do a system restore of his life to an earlier time, and bypass the events of today?